LASSO THE MOON

BLUE RIBBON AWARD!

"LASSO THE MOON is the epitome of romantic comedy and earns a top five spot on my keeper shelf. Filled with quirky characters, brawling good fun, plus a hero and heroine that will capture your heart, LASSO THE MOON is a rare treat to the senses." — *Romance Junkies*

BY BETH CIOTTA

Jewel Imprint: Sapphire
Medallion Press, Inc.
Printed in USA

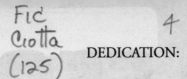
DEDICATION:

*For my mentor, Sandra Chastain. You believed in me. You
taught me. Thank you for giving me the courage to fly.*

Published 2006 by Medallion Press, Inc.
225 Seabreeze Ave.
Palm Beach, FL 33480

The MEDALLION PRESS LOGO
is a registered tradmark of Medallion Press, Inc.

Printed in the United States of America

Library of Congress Cataloging-in-Publication Data

Ciotta, Beth.
  Lasso the moon / Beth Ciotta.
    p. cm.
  ISBN 1-932815-28-7
  1. Actresses--Fiction. 2. Arizona--Fiction. I. Title.
  PS3603.I58L37 2006
  813'.6--dc22

                                2005029013

ACKNOWLEDGEMENTS:

My eternal gratitude to Cynthia Valero—my friend, critique partner, and artistic soul mate. From beginning to end, it's been a long and wild ride. Thank you for hanging in!

My heartfelt appreciation to Tammie Weaver—my friend and a spiritual inspiration. You opened arms and home to me. You opened my eyes and heart to Arizona. I am forever changed.

Also I'd like to thank Mary Stella and Julia Templeton for . . . everything. What would I do without you?

PROLOGUE

Heaven, California, 1867

Her birthday was yesterday, William."

"I know that, Elizabeth. It couldn't be helped. If we lived in San Francisco instead of Napa Valley—"

"We've been through this. I don't want our children to grow up—"

"Surrounded by culture?"

"Too fast." Elizabeth rubbed her temples and sighed. "She cried her eyes out."

"I'll make it up to her."

"With another gift? Your daughter doesn't need another music box or an autographed playbill. The boys are used to your neglect, but Paris—"

—couldn't bear to hear her parents argue. Worse, to be the cause of their row. She'd been plunking out a melody on the piano in an effort to chase a repetitive song from her mind when she heard her papa's cheerful, "I'm home!" With a whoop, she'd hopped off her cushioned stool, brushed cookie crumbs from the front of her calico dress, and raced across the parlor, pigtails flying. She'd almost made it to the foyer of the elegant Garrett home when she heard her mama's voice. Her smile drooped at the sight of Mama, hands on hips, shoulders squared for yet another battle, and Papa frowning back.

"You're home!" she shouted past the lump in her throat.

Her parents started and turned. They wouldn't fight in front of her. She wished they wouldn't fight at all, but that was like wishing one of her four brothers had been born a girl.

A striking man of substantial height, William Garrett dropped to his knees and threw his lanky arms wide. "Morning, Songbird."

Paris ran across the room and jumped into the smiling theater owner's embrace. "Morning, Papa!" She snuggled her nose against his neck. He smelled of cherry tobacco and spicy cologne. He smelled of success.

William hugged his youngest child tight, kissed her forehead, and then pushed her to arms' length. "You know how much I love you, pumpkin, don't you?"

Paris chewed her lower lip and nodded, her heart

thumping wildly, the world a zillion times brighter because *he* was home! Oh, how she wished Mama wouldn't fuss. It wasn't easy managing a theater. She should know. Before she'd been a mother, she'd been an actress. A gifted performer who'd enchanted audiences with her operatic voice and dramatic flair. "You could have been a star," Papa often said. To which Mama always replied, "I chose marriage."

Paris had always wondered if her mama had made the wrong choice. Papa seemed to think so. But then Paris and her brothers wouldn't exist. Certainly Papa wouldn't be happier if they'd never been born. Would he?

"I wanted to be here for your special day, Paris," he said, looking powerful sorry. "But Lily lost her voice. She had an understudy, of course. But the understudy was nervous. Rehearsals ran long. There was a problem with costuming." He quirked a lopsided smile. "You understand, don't you?"

Paris nodded. "It doesn't matter," she lied, willing her toothy grin strong and true. "It's just a stupid birthday."

"Eight years old," William said, "and destined for greatness. Just like your mama." He looked at Elizabeth with disappointment. The gaze he bestowed upon his daughter brimmed with pride. He tugged at one of her long, dark braids. "Always remember, Songbird. Reach for the stars."

Paris pressed her tiny hands to her chest. It felt like

one of her brothers had plopped down on her ribs. She ignored the uncomfortable ache as well as her mama's frown. Mama always frowned whenever Papa encouraged their only daughter's musical talents, saying she'd do better to concentrate on sewing and cooking. Paris didn't see the point. It's not like she ever aimed on getting hitched. Marriage equaled broken hearts and dreams.

"I'll do better than that, Papa," Paris promised, beaming up at her hero. "I'll lasso the moon."

CHAPTER 1

Territory of Arizona, 1877

He'd kill Mason Burke if he weren't already dead. Damn his will and that damned stipulation. Joshua Grant threw back a shot of rotgut, marveling at the dead man's tenacity. Six feet under, and his uncle had still managed to get in the last word.

"Can I get ya' anything else, Sheriff Grant?"

"Yeah, a wife." Josh glanced up from the bullet-nicked bar to the scrunched-up face of its owner. "Never mind. Hit me with another shot. On second thought, make it a double." His future as a wedded theater owner flashed before his eyes. "Hell. Just slide me the bottle and be done with it."

"Sure 'nuff, Sheriff."

"Stop calling me that." He snatched up the quart

bottle of whiskey Jimmy Hell slid his way. "I told you. I turned in my badge yesterday."

The proprietor of Hell's Drinkin' Hole indicated the rowdy clientele with a flick of his tattered bar rag. "So that's what this party's for?" Smirking, the hairy-knuckled wiseass braced his beefy forearms on the splintered ledge of his bar and leaned forward. "Funny, but I can't recall your reason for leaving town exactly."

Josh leaned forward as well. "That's because I never said exactly." He straightened with a smile and let the taunt settle. Maybe it was the liquor or maybe he was just plain out of his head, but he almost felt giddy when Jimmy narrowed his eyes. He'd been spoiling for a fight for days. Since Mason wasn't available, he'd settle on the nearest pair of fists. Even if those fists were the size of Christmas hams.

Only Jimmy Hell's attention had cut to the swinging doors. "What the . . . ?" His bushy brows cut into a stern V. "Here comes trouble. Good thing you're here, Sheriff. I can't afford another brawl this week. I'm down to six good tables and I'm lucky if I got ten chairs with all their legs."

"Thanks for the warning." Josh ripped the cork out of the bottle with his teeth. Spitting it clean over the barkeep's shoulder, he muttered, "I'll be mindful of where I sit. And stop calling me Sheriff. I'm not the law anymore." That said, he tipped the bottle to his lips and turned to see what form of *trouble* had stumbled into the saloon. Just for curiosity's sake. He'd figured on spying Rosco Timbers or Newt Gibbons, two of Yuma's more cantankerous yahoos, seeing that the mean-spirited Riley brothers were already in attendance. So he near about choked on his half-swallowed drink when he spotted the fresh-faced half-pint standing in the doorway, a bulging carpetbag in hand.

From a distance it was right hard to tell if the kid wearing baggy denim trousers, a faded blue, knee-length shirt, and a dirt-brown fedora was a boy or a girl. A heartbeat later the half-pint stepped forward and tripped over Moe Wiggin's king-sized boot. The hat went flying and ebony, waist-length hair spilled out.

One mystery solved.

Moe scooped up the fedora and plopped it back on the young woman's head. She smiled at the old coot as she elbowed her way through the redeye-guzzling, cheroot-smoking crowd.

Josh knew everyone in and around Yuma. He didn't recognize her. Cute as a baby coon, and his gut warned twice as bothersome.

The kid navigated her unwieldy bag through the maze of occupied tables and chairs, offering apologies as she bumped arms and legs along the way. Intrigued, Josh trained his gaze on the determined runt as she cut a deliberate path through the boodle of pokes and doves, suggesting she knew exactly where she was headed.

"If you got any four-legged chairs in the vicinity of the piano, Jimmy, I suggest you clear 'em out." Josh grabbed his quart bottle and trailed the girl. Maybe he'd get his fight after all. Unfortunately, his progress was hindered by a slew of well-wishers. Assorted doves kissed him for old-times sake. Friends and acquaintances slapped his back or pumped his arm in enthusiastic handshakes. They all wished him good luck. The law-abiding men of Yuma had insisted on throwing him this going-away party. Which was fine, dandy, and thoughtful, except he wasn't all that pleased to be going.

That had been Mason's idea.

"Damn him," he muttered again for good measure. Miserable, and not near drunk enough, he tossed back a healthy swig of whiskey before vying for a spot behind Moe Wiggins, who stood on his one good leg outside a two-man-deep crowd. "What's going on?"

Moe squinted at the kid who was in an animated discussion with the saloon's pianist. "Ain't sure. All I know is that Fingers was in the middle of *Buffalo Gals* and that gal elbowed her way in and put a stop to it."

"Why?"

Moe squinted harder, as though it might somehow improve his hearing. "Can't hear what she's sayin'."

Neither could Josh. His party had grown from loud to deafening. Jimmy Hell was right about one thing.

Trouble was brewing. He could see that even in his bleary-eyed state.

"Whatever she's up to," Moe said, "it ain't good."

"It ain't my concern." But, for the life of him, he couldn't tear his gaze from the petite girl. A cute little bunny trapped by a pack of mangy wolves, the sharpest teeth belonging to Burgess and Billy Riley.

Moe drained his beer, sleeved a dribble of brew from his pointy chin. "You've never been one to let a boilin' pot overflow."

"I'm no longer the law in these parts." He figured if he repeated it enough times, he'd get used to the idea. Still and all, he couldn't bring himself to ignore the baby-faced tomboy. The need to protect was a right hard habit to break.

Unable to resist, he moved closer to the action.

"You don't understand, sir." She dropped her bag near the rickety piano and shook a cramp out of her hand. "This is an emergency. I'm in desperate need of your instrument. If you would only accommodate me—"

"Accommodate ya'?" Fingers raised an amused eyebrow above the rim of his wired spectacles. "Ain't never heard it called that before, honey."

His drunken entourage snickered.

"You needn't worry," she hurried on. "I'm very good."

Fingers's other eyebrow shot up. "You don't say?"

She smiled and nodded. "I promise you'll enjoy it."

Josh bit back a groan. How naïve could one girl be not to realize how a passel of men were twisting her innocent words?

"Listen," Fingers said, mopping his brow as though the temperature had shot from eighty to a hundred. "I'm in the middle of a slew of requests. Give me a few minutes and then—"

"A few minutes? It's been days!"

"That long?" Fingers traded a smirk with the leering audience. "Well, now. I reckon I could take a short break." He pinned her with a smarmy look. "Just how good are ya', honey?"

"My brothers think I'm excellent."

The pianist hooted. "Your brothers?"

Owl-eyed and eager for details, the snickering mob leaned forward. Josh swayed right along with them.

The girl blinked at Fingers. A few seconds later a blush crept up her neck, making a beeline for her cheeks. "I'm sorry. I shouldn't have . . . it's just that I'm . . . " She waved off her words and glanced toward an empty table. "I'll wait over there until you've finished your requests."

Relieved, Josh reached back to massage a crick from his neck. At least the kid had sense enough to vamoose before things turned ugly.

Burgess Riley clamped his burly hand over her wrist and whirled her back around. "What's your hurry, sweet thing? If Fingers there ain't willin' to *accommodate* ya', I sure as hell am."

"Me too!" chimed his brother.

Her face lit up like a noonday sky. "You have a piano too?"

The crowd guffawed.

Josh rolled his eyes. The twinge in his neck pinched.

"No piano. But don't worry. We'll make our own music." Burgess forced her hand over the crotch of his filthy trousers. "Let's put them talented fingers to good use. What do ya' say, wildcat?"

Josh chucked his whiskey bottle and pushed forward. Here comes the fight.

The kid acted faster, kneeing Burgess square in the balls.

For the love of . . . Josh grimaced as the man's wounded howl sliced through him and every other man in the gurdy.

Wide-eyed, the raven-haired ball-buster turned to run and slammed into Billy's scrawny chest.

Flashing a gap-toothed grin, he snatched her up. "Gotcha!"

She hauled back that same deadly leg and kicked him in the shin. Billy dropped her and yowled. Hopping up and down on one foot, he spewed obscenities raunchy enough to make a hash slinger blush.

Looking only slightly embarrassed, the girl backed into a wobbly-legged Burgess.

Grabbing her by the forearms, the yahoo hauled her backside hard against his injured region and snarled. "You messed with the wrong man, sweet thing."

Josh moved faster this time. When the girl wrenched left he threw a right, ramming his knuckles into Burgess's mouth. The man flew backward, the kid with him.

Quick as lightning, Josh snatched her up and into his arms. The fedora tumbled to the floor, allowing him a full view of her heart-shaped face. The patrons' slurred heckles faded to a drone as he studied the petite minx up close and intimate like. Her smooth complexion, almighty pale in contrast to her ink-black hair, suggested she spent more time indoors than out. A surprise, given her tomboy appearance. Even more surprising was the jolt of lust he felt when he gazed into her walnut-brown eyes, eyes that sparkled with an intoxicating mix of innocence and bald appreciation. Complicating matters, a queer lump lodged in his throat when she quirked a shy smile. "What the hell?"

His gruff words snapped her out of a moony-eyed daze. Blushing now, she struggled like a roped stallion to gain her freedom. "Let me go, you big ape!"

The crowd's whoops and hollers intensified as another skirmish heated up between the Riley boys and a couple of do-gooders. Josh was too busy protecting his gingambobs from Miss Musicmaker's deadly knee and—Christ almighty—*elbows* to pay much mind.

"Watch out!"

At Moe's warning, he dipped the feisty minx just as an empty bottle whizzed past her pretty head. At the same time a chair sailed through the air, shattering the front pane. An out-and-out brawl erupted. Thanks to Mason, he had a lifetime of bar brawls ahead of him. From what he'd heard, the patrons of the Desert Moon opera house were a rowdy bunch.

At least his new life wouldn't be dull.

He glanced down at the pissed off half-pint. "Let's get you out of here, sweetheart."

"I'm not your sweetheart."

"Whose sweetheart are you?"

"No one's." Scowling, she reached behind her and tried to pry his hands from her waist. "I . . . I mean someone's. Some big fellow. An ox of a man who's going to beat you to a pulp if you don't let me go."

"You're a terrible liar." He hiked her higher in his arms and caught a whiff of her glossy hair. Lilacs. The sweet, flowery scent blindsided him, stealing him back to his childhood. A time he preferred to forget. Squashing the bittersweet memories before they reached full bloom, he focused on the swinging doors.

Three men crashed into a nearby table, fists flying. Cursing, he hastened his steps, the girl's best interests at heart. Damn if the menace didn't struggle harder as he hauled her out of harm's way.

"I'm warning you, mister!"

"Warn away."

She elbowed him in the gut.

A second later she kicked him in the shin.

"You're making it difficult for me to behave in a valiant fashion here, kid."

She slapped at his hands. "Don't make me hurt you."

He laughed for the first time in over a week.

Two feet from the doors, she twisted in his arms, reared back and socked him.

"Son of a—" He bit off the curse and worked his offended jaw. "What'd you do that for?"

"I'm sorry. But I *did* warn you."

"So you did. Now I'm warning *you*. Stop fussing. We're leaving."

"But—"

"I warned you." Grinning, he hauled her up and over his shoulder like a sack of grain and whisked her from the saloon. The rowdy mob cheered.

CHAPTER 2

Humiliated. Paris Garrett had never been so humiliated in all her born days! On second thought, yes, she had. Three or forty times at least. Athens, the most diplomatic of her four brothers, was forever pointing out her penchant for acting without thought, the consequences faithfully disastrous. Her cheeks blazed. Having her hand pressed over the privates of one man and being toted out of the saloon over the shoulder of another certainly qualified as a disaster.

Clear of flying fists and furniture, her thoughts settled back on her sole purpose for entering Hell's Drinking Hole in the first place. "I didn't get to play so much as a single note on that dratted piano."

Mumbling obscenities, the man she'd punched

ambled across the street to a moonlit corner where he eased her off of his broad shoulder. Her skin tingled as her body brushed intimately along his admirable six-foot frame.

Her rescuer or captor, whichever, was drop-dead gorgeous, in a rugged, hulking kind of way. A real heart-stopper. Bronze skin. Square jaw. Full lips. And those eyes! Soulful, cocoa-brown orbs. To her horror, she actually sighed in appreciation, unbalanced in more ways than one when her feet touched the ground.

He steadied her when she teetered then narrowed those magnificent eyes and clenched his jaw. Her eldest brother, London, had perfected that same grim expression. Out of habit, Paris braced herself for a lecture.

He cocked his head toward the rollicking saloon. "You risked your safety and reputation because you wanted to play the piano?"

Not exactly a lecture. The disapproving tone, however, was unmistakable. "You wouldn't understand."

"Try me."

His voice was husky and deep—probably a baritone, she mused—and his breath smelled of liquor. According to her youngest brother, Boston, drunks couldn't be trusted.

Brown Eyes squeezed her shoulders, prompting a response.

She glared in return. "Plan on shaking an explanation out of me?"

He uncurled his fingers and crossed his arms over his chest in a casual manner. "Better?"

"Much." She struggled to match his nonchalance. He rattled her, and not because he'd been drinking. Unlike the two baboons they'd left inside the saloon, she instinctively knew this man wouldn't harm her even though he was glowering. This man represented another kind of danger. He made her heart flutter. She shook her head, disgusted at the thought. Attracted to somebody solely based on good looks. She felt as shallow as her brother Rome.

"You're courting trouble, kid, looking at a man like that."

"Like what?" Then she realized she was staring at his mouth and thinking about *kissing*. Mortified, she retreated a step. "Listen, Mr.—"

"Grant. Joshua Grant. You can call me Josh." He closed the space between them, trying to intimidate her, no doubt, with his impressive height and brawn. "So?"

She blinked up at him. Lordy, he was handsome. Imagine if he smiled. "So, what?"

"You were going to explain your urgent need to play that piano."

She didn't know which was more mesmerizing. His seductive eyes or his to-die-for mouth. Both set her heart to pounding in triple time. "I needed to get a song out of my head."

"Pardon?"

"A new composition. It's been plaguing me for three days. I've tried singing it, humming it, writing it down. Nothing helps. The only way to get a song out of my head, once it sticks there, is to give it life. I need a piano for that."

"You're joshing."

"I told you, you wouldn't understand." Her own brothers didn't understand. Another musician would, which is why she'd been disappointed in the obtuse pianist inside. Then again, that particular person was an all-thumbed, tin-eared excuse for a musician. She'd been willing to overlook his butchered rendition of *Buffalo Gals*, but his blatant disregard for her as a fellow artist was unforgivable. All she'd wanted was to play his piano.

She wondered if it was worth a second try. Certainly it was safer than standing here with a man who prompted images of moonlight kisses. "Meeting you has been interesting, Mr. Grant." She turned on her heel and steered her thoughts toward her latest composition. "Take care."

He nabbed her shirttail and yanked her back. "Where do you think you're going?" he asked, swinging around front to block her path.

"To get my carpetbag." *And to play the piano.* She'd spent two days on a train. A train with no piano. It wasn't just a matter of getting a song out of her head. This was about reconnecting with her soul.

"Where is it?"

"In there." She jabbed an impatient finger at the saloon. "Now, please step aside so I can go in and get it."

"Stubborn as a mule and twice as contrary." Josh swept his hand toward the swinging doors, bidding her free entry. "There are two men in particular who, I'm sure, will be anxious to see you. The Riley brothers. Burgess and Billy. You remember them, don't you?" He relaxed against a wooden post and folded his arms over his impressive chest. "Feel free to give a shout if you get into another fix."

She hesitated, Athens's voice booming in her ears, *Think before you act, Squirt.* She thought about the formidable Riley brothers.

Josh arched an arrogant eyebrow and pushed off of the splintered post. "Wait here." Muttering to himself, he strode through the swinging doors.

Shaken, Paris paced the boards, wondering, for the first time in a week, what in the thunder she'd gotten herself into. Heeding her best friend, Emily McBride's, advice (Emily was ever so resourceful), she'd made it from Heaven to San Francisco and from there to Yuma without a single hitch. She'd successfully eluded four of the most overprotective brothers God had ever seen fit to place on His glorious earth. She should be dancing the jig. Instead she was fighting an indecent attraction to a man she'd just met. Not to mention pangs of guilt knowing she'd caused her brothers several restless nights' sleep—if they'd slept at all. They'd no doubt searched the better part of California by now. But dang it all, if they hadn't forbidden her to perform at the Gilded Garrett Theater, or any other San Franciscan or Napa County playhouse, she wouldn't have scanned the employment pages of a Southwestern newspaper. She wouldn't have read the advertisement—*Opera House seeking entertainers*! *Hitch your star to the Desert Moon*!

It didn't matter that the Desert Moon was smack dab in the wilds of Arizona Territory. It didn't matter that she didn't have a lick of stage experience. She had to start somewhere, and the middle of nowhere seemed like a good place since her brothers were dead set against her becoming a musical actress.

Not that she was all that excited about being a musical actress, but she figured while she was at it she could perfect her songwriting. By performing her original compositions for the patrons of an opera house she'd gain objective opinions of her work. She'd learn which of her songs were worth submitting to the persnickety music publishers. She'd acted foolishly in the past, submitting inferior songs in her haste to become a famous composer. The result: six bald rejections. Although the content of those letters stung, she refused to be beaten.

Refused to believe, as one publisher had penned, that she belonged behind a stove instead of a piano.

"This bag's nearly as big as you are, kid."

Joshua Grant's resonant voice beckoned her out of her wayward thoughts and back to her problem at hand. *Him*.

She sucked in an appreciative breath. Certainly more ladylike than cutting loose with a whistle. While she'd been pacing, he'd fixed his rumpled clothes. He'd tucked in the ends of his white shirt, buttoned his brocade vest and positioned a black Stetson atop his head at a jaunty tilt. She had the insane desire to fling that hat from his head and to tousle the dark, thick locks that curled at his collar.

Mercy! Was she insane? She'd never mussed a man's hair. She'd never even considered it. Her fingers had always been busy doing other things, namely playing the piano and scribbling down notes and words. This man had a lot of nerve being so attractive. She had plans, and those plans did not include a certain Mr. Joshua Grant!

"Thank you," she said, grabbing awkwardly at her bag. Only he didn't let go. Her hand froze on top of his, unwilling or unable to break the unexpected intimacy between them. For the second time this evening her body tingled and a strange queasiness churned in her gut. Her stomach actually flipped when she made the mistake of looking into his eyes.

"What's your name, kid?"

Paris blinked at him, wondering what in the heck was wrong with her knees. They felt all weak and jelly-like. She couldn't remember a man ever looking at her as if memorizing every freckle on her face. "Paris." Merciful heavens, her voice *cracked*. Not only that, she'd blurted out her real name. Clearing her throat, she hastily amended, "Pauline."

"Paris Pauline?"

Still pondering on how to best cover her slip, she merely nodded.

"Pauline being your middle name? Or last?"

Neither, she wanted to say. It was supposed to be her first. Getty to be the last. Emily had insisted that Paris adopt a stage name. An alias. *A precautionary measure*, she'd explained. Lord knew Emily understood the value of an alter ego. So when her friend had dubbed her Pauline Getty, explaining it would be easy to remember as it was close to her real name, Paris hadn't argued. It *had* been easy to remember. Until now. "Middle," she answered, because what kind of a name was Paris Pauline? "Getty's the last."

"Paris Pauline Getty. Interesting name for an interesting girl. What brings you to Yuma?"

"Just passing through on my way to . . . Florence," she lied. At least she had sense enough to keep her destination a secret. "Ever been there?" Blast. Her voice didn't just crack, it squeaked! She stepped back, taking her hand and senses with her.

"A few times." He glanced away for a moment, cleared his throat, and then focused back on her. "What's in Florence? Friends? Family?"

"My future. Not that it's any of your business."

His lips curved though she wouldn't exactly call it a smile. "Traveling with your ma and pa?"

"Traveling alone."

That comment earned her another frown. Honestly, the man had but two expressions—grim and grimmer. She felt her color rising under his pointed stare. "Could you please direct me to the nearest hotel?"

"The Grand Hotel is two buildings over. I'll walk you there."

"No! I mean, no, thank you. You've done quite enough already." She reached again for her carpetbag, taking special care to avoid his touch. She doubted she could withstand the intensity of it a second time. "Thank you for what you did in the saloon. For giving Mr. Riley his due. If there's anything I can ever do to repay you, well," she fluttered one hand in the air, "just let me know."

He held her gaze a breathless minute before tucking her disheveled hair behind her ears. "It's unlikely our paths will cross again, kid, seeing I'm leaving town come morning. So if you don't mind, I'll claim my thanks tonight."

He swept her up in a lover's embrace, scattering her thoughts like leaves in the autumn winds. She gasped and dropped her valise. It landed with a heavy thud, not that she noticed much since invisible angels were singing in her ears. When his lips touched down on hers, those divine voices reached an earth-shattering crescendo. She wondered fleetingly if she'd died and gone to heaven.

Shivers, hot and cold combined, tingled down her spine to the tips of her dangling toes as their mouths fused. It didn't occur to protest, nor did she encourage. She simply allowed the kiss to happen.

A wave of disappointment washed over her when her tingling feet touched the sandy streets of Yuma. Half dazed, she fought to maintain her balance when Joshua Grant, consummate kisser, released her from the strength of his enfolding arms. Even though he owed her an apology, she didn't want one. Nor was she compelled to slap his face, as well she should. Amazingly, she wanted another kiss. He'd teased her with a taste of something delicious, and suddenly she was starving. Like sugar cookies—who could have just one?

Emily's voice rang in her ears—*Life experience inspires passionate prose*—lending Paris inspiration, and an excuse to behave recklessly. Isn't that why she'd traveled this far? To experience life? To improve her lyrics? To achieve success? It's not like she did this sort of thing all the time. She'd never done this sort of thing. And it's not as if she'd ever see this man again. She swallowed hard, willing her voice not to quiver with the nervous excitement trembling just below her surface. "I want to make sure that my debt is paid in full, Mr. Grant." Decorum be hanged, she grabbed the lapels of his vest and yanked down.

"Josh," he choked out.

Relishing the shocked look in his eyes, she boldly planted her lips on his and commenced kissing him for all she was worth. She had limited experience, but she was a quick learner and more than capable of substituting enthusiasm for technique. His lips tasted of sinful liquor and blessed sweetness. She couldn't get enough. Kissing this man was a heck of a lot more satisfying than devouring a tin full of cookies.

Her addictive dessert eased back at the sound of an approaching horse. Expressionless, he held Paris steady as she blinked out of a sensual stupor.

The rider cleared his throat, tipped his hat. "Evenin', ma'am. Sheriff Grant."

"Evenin', Jenkins." Josh waited until the man rode past then clapped a hand over the back of his neck and rubbed.

Paris stared at the victim of her passionate assault, warning drums beating in her ears. A sheriff? She couldn't afford to mix with the law! What if he knew Rome and Boston? Being Wells Fargo detectives, her brothers interacted with various lawmen across several borders. If Josh figured out that she was the sister of the famous Garrett brothers, he'd turn her in. Professional courtesy and all that. Blast! Why hadn't she *experienced life* with a blacksmith? Or a gambler? Any man but a lawman!

Heart pounding, she scooped up her carpetbag and fled toward the Grand Hotel. Her gaze flicked to the quarter moon swinging high in the star-filled sky. A child's promise echoed in her ears. Determination hastened her steps as Paris fought to erase Joshua Grant and his to-die-for kisses from her seemingly lost mind.

CHAPTER 3

I f the morning was any indication, Josh decided he'd rather tangle with a bear for squatter's rights of a dark cave than continue with this day. He was operating on four hours of sleep, a pot of coffee, and a teaspoon of Dr. Klein's Miracle Bitters.

He rode through the heart of Yuma, struggling not to wince as the townsfolk shouted their fond and reluctant farewells. Men, women, and children alike made it clear that he would be missed. He tipped his hat and nodded in return, silently acknowledging their kindness. If he spoke, if he even *smiled*, he was certain his whole damn head would fall off.

He'd been a fool to drink so much. An even bigger fool because he'd known he was drunk when he'd returned to the saloon for further swilling. Poor judgment begets a mighty high price. Cursing his stupidity, he spurred Buckshot into a steady trot, trying his best to ignore the shooting pain behind his eyeballs. The sooner he got out of town, the sooner he'd have some peace and quiet. Dead sure medicine for a rotgut headache.

Fingers skidded into his path waving a Winchester and spouting some nonsense about a woman hooligan. "No tellin' what she's capable of, Sheriff Grant," he ranted at the top of his lungs. "Marshal Fedderman wants ya' over at the jailhouse lickety-split!"

Josh glowered down at the bothersome man. "What's this got to do with me? I'm not the law around here anymore."

"Marshal Fedderman says you should come right away!"

His head pounded. "Stop shouting, dammit. I'm not deaf."

"I ain't shoutin'!" Fingers shouted.

"Move the hell out of my way, piano man, or I'll shoot you where you stand."

Fingers kicked at a loose stone, sulking away like a scolded dog.

"Musicians," Josh grumbled. "Haven't met a sane one yet." A specific black-haired, brown-eyed hellion sprang to mind. He shifted in his saddle. Woman hooligan? It couldn't be. But the nagging twinge in his neck told him different.

Paris.

That girl was trouble with a capital T. His hangover was partly her fault, not to mention his restless night's sleep. He shouldn't give a gopher's ass about her state-of-being.

"*Damn*." Against his better judgment, he reined Buckshot toward the jailhouse.

"Fingers said you wanted to see me," he growled, his mood less than amiable when he dragged through the front door.

"Good morning to you, too."

"Thought we said our goodbyes yesterday, Hank."

The marshal looked up from the stack of yellowed wanted posters he'd been thumbing through and greeted him with a tobacco-stained grin. "You look like hell, son."

"Kind of you to point that out." Josh didn't take real offense. He'd worked side by side with Hank Fedderman for the last two years. He respected the aging town marshal. The man wasn't near tough enough, but he was sure as shootin' honest. Crooked officials were as common as centipedes in the Southwest and a downright hazard to upright civilians and lawmen alike. If Mason had taught Josh anything, it was to recognize and value an honest man.

Fedderman snorted. "Heard you kept the double

doors swingin' last night. Might've joined you myself, but as you can see," he gestured to the piles of ill-sorted papers littering the desktop, "I had my hands full trying to get this place in order. How did you expect me to find anything in this mess?"

"We've argued this since the day we met, Hank. You've got your filing system, and I've got mine. Don't tell me you summoned me back because you can't find a blasted pencil."

"Now that you mention it you're just about as short on supplies as you are on organizational skills. But never mind about that. I've got another problem. She stands about knee-high to a bumble bee and has the temper of an aggravated hornet."

Josh helped himself to a chair. Somehow he sensed he'd be better off sitting for this one. Settling back, he massaged his pulsing temples. "This hornet of yours got a name?"

"Paulette."

"You mean, Pauline."

"I thought she said Paulette."

"Long black hair? Big brown eyes?" Cute as the dickens, he wanted to add, but didn't.

"That's her."

Josh dropped his hands to his thighs. "Paris Pauline Getty."

Fedderman rose from his chair and took a seat on

the only clutter-free corner of the desk. "Helluva fancy name." He crossed his arms over his chest and grinned. "So Fingers is right. You're acquainted with the girl."

"We've met."

He indicated the darkening bruise on Josh's face. "So I've heard. What do you know about her?"

Josh stroked his tender jaw. Outside of the fact that she threw one hell of a right, he knew exactly two things about the wildcat. One, her future awaited in Florence. Two, her kisses jolted his brain more than an entire quart bottle of whiskey. At least that's how he remembered it, which wasn't saying much seeing that he'd been booze blind. "I know she's got a nose for trouble. What did she do now?"

Fedderman jerked a thumb toward the back room. "I've got her locked up for trespassing."

"Trespassing?"

"She broke into the saloon late last night. And get this." He leaned slightly forward. "She claims she meant no wrong. Says she just wanted to—"

"—play the piano."

"How'd you know?"

"Lucky guess."

"It would seem you know that little gal more than you let on."

Josh shrugged then stood. "Send her on her way, Hank. She's rowing with one oar in the water, but she's

31

harmless enough, near as I can tell. You've got bigger fish to fry." The Rileys came to mind.

"Yeah, well, it ain't that easy." Fedderman cleared his throat. "Fingers didn't take kindly to the intrusion. If he had his way, he'd be throwin' her a necktie party. Seems a bit severe to me. Still and all, it wouldn't surprise me if he up and shot her next time he sees her." He lowered his voice. "She called him a non-musical, all-thumbed oaf."

Josh cracked a smile. Fingers considered himself *the* finest pianist this side of the Colorado. God help the soul who challenged his self-appointed title.

Fedderman nodded. "To make matters worse, Fingers hustled over to Jimmy Hell's, roused him, and gave him an earful. You know how easily he's riled. Jimmy stalked in here just before dawn, claiming she not only broke into his saloon but started the brawl that destroyed his front pane. He's spitting mad and demanding compensation."

"You looking for me to settle her debt?"

The other man scratched his unshaven chin. "Not exactly."

"What exactly?"

"I thought you could have a talk with her. Set her straight. Get her to get going to where she's headed. Today. She's made more enemies in one night than most folks do in a year. The sooner she clears town, the better for her."

"Why me?"

Fedderman grinned. "You've got a way with women."

"Not that kind of woman." He thought back on their dust-devil encounter. He'd aimed on escorting the troublesome minx to a respectable hotel directly after retrieving her carpetbag. Sometimes good intentions aren't worth spit. Especially when that minx is downright cuter than a kitten. Spurred on by raw lust and rotgut, he'd thrown caution to the wind. He'd kissed her. In the middle of the street. Without regard to her reputation. He'd been set to apologize when she'd shocked him by initiating a second kiss, a deeper kiss, a kiss that gave him a hard-on that you could break a branding iron on.

Then, without so much as a "see ya' later," she'd hauled butt away from him faster than a lone scout from an Apache tribe. He didn't know what to make of her, but he liked her spirit, not to mention the way she'd felt in his arms. That worried him.

"So you'll talk to her?" Fedderman asked, jolting him from his thoughts.

"How about if I just kick in for the damages?"

"Not what I had in mind. Here's the deal."

Josh palmed up the brim of his Stetson. "I knew there was more to this."

"This girl, this Paulette——"

"Pauline. Paris Pauline. Try Paris. It's easier."

Fedderman frowned. "What kind of parent names his child after a foreign city?" He shook his head. "Never mind. Miss Paris. She's on her way to Florence."

"So?"

"And you're on your way to Chance."

Josh narrowed his bloodshot eyes. "So?"

"So, Florence is on the way to Chance."

"Forget it, Hank."

"She's a magnet for mayhem. She's traveling alone. Imagine what could happen to her between here and Florence."

"No."

"Where's your sense of valor?"

He pointed to his bruised jaw. "This is what she thinks of valor."

Fedderman slid off of the desk and fished a key from his vest pocket. "I'd consider it a personal favor. She kind of reminds me of Molly."

His runaway daughter. "Hell, Hank." Josh swiped his hat from his head and rammed his fingers through his freshly-washed hair. "Every dark-haired female under the age of twenty-five reminds you of Molly."

"It's more than the physical resemblance. It's the way she avoided answerin' my questions. Sidestepped 'em like a horse from a snake. I think she's runnin' from something." He paused dramatically. "Or someone. All

I ask is that you see her safely to Florence. Once there, you can ask Sheriff Wright to keep an eye on her and be on your way. Please."

Josh hadn't planned on stopping in Florence, although the thought of seeing Seth twice in two weeks did his heart good. Seth Wright was the brother he never had. Their time together with the Special Force of Rangers had cinched their friendship tighter than a fine lady's corset. Seth had wired Josh regarding Mason's death when his uncle had bit the dust on a routine supply run from Florence to the Superstition Mountains. Near as Seth could tell, something had spooked Mason's team causing the horses to bolt. The wagon had bounced over boulders and brush ultimately throwing the retired U.S. Marshal to his death. His fearless uncle had survived rustlers, bandits, and murderers only to be felled by skittish horses. Life was a damned mystery.

Fedderman coughed into his hand, reclaiming Josh's attention. "About Paris."

Hell. He couldn't argue with this man's paternal instincts. Out of respect, he wouldn't try. He stuck out his hand and accepted the key.

The marshal smiled. "You won't be sorry."

"I already am."

A queer sense of doom nagged Josh as he neared the cell. His out-of-sorts life was spinning toward the point of no return. Of course, he wasn't in the best frame of mind. Mason's death still dogged him. Mason's will still irked him. And Paris had turned out to be more of a diversion than he'd bargained.

He unlocked the door and eased it open. Stepping inside, he pushed his Stetson further onto the back of his head, stroking a day's growth of whiskers while he took in the unsettling sight.

Paris looked like a little girl, curled up, sound asleep on the jailhouse cot. Seeing her like this, all vulnerable like, no wonder Fedderman compared her to his shy and proper daughter. Thing was, judging from her behavior thus far, Paris was anything *but* shy and proper. Still and all, the old man was right. It wasn't safe for a woman to travel unescorted across the desert. Especially when that woman had more sass than sense.

Kissing his peace and quiet goodbye, he crouched down and lightly touched her shoulder. "Paris." She didn't stir, so he gave her a little shake, frowning when she didn't respond. Concerned she might be ill, he pressed his hand to her cheek. No fever. The intensity of his relief annoyed him.

He started to pull back, but she nuzzled her face deeper into his cupped palm. Dark strands of sawdust-sprinkled hair tickled her left cheek. Her lips curved into a bedeviling smile. Damn, she looked ornery even when she slept. She murmured, "Josh," and that queer lump welled up again in his throat. He swallowed hard, wondering if he was catching cold. Then he focused on the fact that he'd invaded this girl's dreams. He wasn't sure whether to feel smug or worried. Unable to help himself, he smoothed her tangled hair from her pretty face. "Morning, kid."

She shot up like a startled bobcat, smacking her head against the wall and knocking Josh on his backside.

Swearing under his breath, he righted himself then reached out to her to inspect the damage. "You all right?"

"Yes. No." She nudged away his hands, massaged the base of her skull. "That smarted."

"I'll bet." He stood and stared down at her, deciding she was not only loony but accident prone.

She blinked up at him. "What are you doing here?"

"I could ask you that question." He pointed to her bare feet. "Where in the devil are your shoes?"

"I forgot to put them on."

He plucked his hat from his head and jammed his fingers through his hair for the second time this aggravating morning. "How does a body get dressed to go out and forget to put on her shoes?" It boggled his mind, adding to the pain stabbing at his temples. "Never mind." Repositioning his hat, he got a whiff of stale beer. He leaned closer and sniffed. "Friendly tip, kid. Lay off the booze. You're short on sense as is."

She rose slowly, tilting her head up to meet his admonishing gaze. "I'm not drunk, and I'm not stupid. I knocked into a table of half-filled glasses."

"Which wouldn't have happened if you weren't in the saloon in the first place. You're lucky Fingers didn't shoot first and ask questions later."

"That hot-headed, unprofessional oaf! All I wanted was to play—"

"—the piano. I know." Had she no regard for her safety? "One of these days your reckless behavior is going to get you into serious trouble."

She rubbed the sleep out of her eyes. "You sound just like my . . ."

"Your what?"

"Never mind."

"Your husband? Fiancé?"

She wiggled the bare fingers of her left hand. "I don't have a husband or a fiancé."

He didn't want to consider why that made him so all-fired glad. "Your pa?"

She shifted her gaze toward the barred window. "Papa's dead."

Josh winced at the hitch in her voice. Once upon a time he had worshiped his own father. But that was before the man had drunk himself to death. Shoving the ancient hurt aside, he cupped her chin demanding her attention. "Your brothers then?"

"You know my brothers?"

"I know they consider you an expert. Or so you told

Fingers last night." She'd floored them all with that racy tidbit though he'd quickly surmised she'd meant her abilities as a pianist.

"Oh. Right." Looking almighty relieved, she knocked away his hand, and eyed the open door. "Can I go now?"

Maybe Fedderman was onto something. "Listen, kid, whatever you're running from—"

"I'm not running—"

"Whatever they did—"

"Who?"

"Your *brothers*."

She huffed an exasperated breath. "Am I free to go?"

"Did they mistreat you in some way?"

"No. Well . . . yes. Sort of."

For the love of . . . "Stop beating around the bush, Paris. I want to know who or what you're running from. You can trust me to—"

She snorted.

Josh dug deep, clutching the last of his patience. "What's that supposed to mean?"

"Why would I trust you? You lied to me."

The muscles in his neck bunched. Fury burned its way up from his toes to the tips of his ears. She may as well have accused him of murder. He closed the distance between them, backing her flush against the cell wall. Bracing his hands against the stones on either side of her head, he caged her between his arms and glared. "Come again?"

"Well, not outright," she explained, her voice climbing an octave. "More like by way of omission."

"Spit it out."

"Why didn't you tell me you're a sheriff?"

"I'm not. Not anymore." The fact still rankled. "I turned in my badge two days ago."

She grinned ear to ear. "Really?"

"Why does this make you happy?"

"It doesn't." Her smile slipped. "I mean, why would it? I was just curious as to why you'd failed to mention it. Your occupation, that is. Not that it matters."

He wanted to shake the living daylights out of her. "Are you among the willows?"

"What?"

"On the lam. Running from the law."

"Of all the ridiculous . . . I am *not* a criminal."

"Glad to hear it." He leaned closer. "I'd hate to have to escort you to Florence in handcuffs."

Her eyes widened like a trapped animal's. "What are you talking about? I don't need an escort."

"There are those who believe otherwise."

"I can take care of myself."

"Like hell." To prove it he kissed her. He slanted his mouth over hers again and again. Hot, hungry, calculated kisses. He wanted to send her running. Because she aggravated him. Because she'd attacked his integrity. Because she was naïve and fearless. But mostly, because she made him burn. He'd never experienced such a fast and fierce attraction. It scared the hell out of him. He needed a wife, and she was not wife material. She was a pain in his neck. Literally.

Unfortunately, his plan backfired. She countered his assault by kissing him with a clumsy enthusiasm that stirred his blood, hiking his desire to a dangerous, irrational level. If he didn't stop now, he'd end up taking her against the jailhouse wall. Next step, the altar.

Stunned, he held her at arm's length like a stick of dynamite. Surely she was just as dangerous once you lit her fuse. Never in his life had he taken liberties with a stranger. A young woman on the run, for Christ's sake. He'd kissed this one twice. And this time he was sober. What's worse, she encouraged his disgraceful behavior. "Stop doing that," he said through clenched teeth.

"Doing what?"

"Kissing me."

Her glazed eyes cleared and sparked. "You kissed me first!"

"That doesn't mean you have to like it." The thought of her kissing another man with the same sweet abandon knotted his gut. Not that he was jealous. Hell, no. Just concerned another man might take advantage of her virginal curiosity, exhibiting even less restraint than himself.

"Of all the . . . " She swung out and slapped his face with a force that rocked his head.

"That's more like it," he grumbled.

Red-faced, she swept past him and out of the cell. "I wouldn't keep company with you if you were the last man on earth, Sheriff Grant!"

"I'm not the law anymore." Ticked that he was still aroused, he ambled after her, cracking his knuckles.

She marched straight to Fedderman's desk. "I don't see why I have to put up with being harassed by that," she jerked a thumb over her shoulder, "man. Furthermore, I can't believe you seriously consider me a threat to society. I humbly beg your and *Fingers's* pardon and ask for my release. I'm leaving town now, soon, as soon as possible on the next stage out. You'll never hear from me again, except for when I send money to pay for the damage I've caused, which I promise to do as soon as I have it, which shouldn't be too long from now if all goes according to plan. May I please leave now? Thank you." She spun on her bare heel and stormed out of the jailhouse without Fedderman's permission and without a second look at Josh.

The two men crossed to the threshold. Together they marveled at her defiant barefooted march toward the Grand Hotel. Respectable citizens parted, granting the tangle-haired curmudgeon a wide berth. She appeared unaffected by the behind-the-hand whispers her tousled, boy-like appearance drew from the shopping townsfolk.

"Well, now," Fedderman said, "that was one hell of a dramatic exit."

"She's a dramatic kind of gal."

"You got her to leave town, all right." His gaze on the retreating fireball, Fedderman gave him a good-natured nudge. "Harassed her, huh? Can't say that I've ever known you to harass a woman. Especially a slip of a girl like that."

Josh rubbed the cheek she'd slapped. "She can take care of herself." He refused to believe otherwise. He had an agenda and she'd blow it sky high. As to her problem, whatever it was, plainly she didn't want his help.

"Well, well." Fedderman clucked his tongue and then chuckled softly. "If I didn't know better, I'd guess you two were sweet on each other."

"Guess again. We don't even like each other."

"Uh huh." The marshal winked. "Oughta make for an interesting trek across the desert."

"No trek." He repositioned his Stetson and set to leave. "Not together anyhow."

Fedderman turned serious. "What do you mean? You had a talk with her, didn't you? You offered to escort her to Florence, didn't you?"

"She wasn't interested."

"Why didn't you put your foot down?"

Josh shifted. "Something else came up."

"Now listen here, son. Regardless of Miss Paris's tough exterior, she's still a woman. A young one at that. It ain't fittin' nor safe for her to travel alone."

Josh stalked to the hitching post and unwound Buckshot's reins. "She won't be alone. You heard her. She's taking the stage. That particular coach is usually packed. Besides Moe Wiggins drives that rig. He'll look out for her."

"Moe Wiggins is half-deaf and long in tooth."

"He's a crack shot, and he's got Turkey Dan riding shotgun. Stop worrying."

"She'd make as good a wife as any."

Josh reached for the stirrup and missed. "Pardon?"

"Paulette . . . Paris . . . whatever her name. If you look past the dirt and muss, I bet she's right pretty. She's sure tough enough to endure a rough and rowdy place like Chance. Damned convenient if ya' ask me. Given Mason's will and all."

"No one asked you," Josh snapped, longing for a numbing shot of whiskey. Every time he thought of his uncle's accident his heart twisted into a throbbing knot. Though Mason had spent most of his time roaming the territory enforcing federal laws, he'd been the guiding force in Josh's teen years. Someone to admire, to emulate. A colorful character even by frontier standards,

Mason Burke had been his orphaned nephew's hero.

Josh rolled back his shoulders and sighed. "Sorry, Hank." Knowing his idol was dead and believing it were as different as a nun and dove. "I'm just . . . I don't know why the hell I confided in you."

Fedderman's steady gaze held a father's sympathetic gleam. "Better than letting it fester. You know you can trust me to keep your business private."

"That I do." Hank was a good friend. But Seth was an even better one, and Josh hadn't confided in him. He'd been too stunned when he'd exited the lawyer's office in Florence to say much of anything. When prodded, he had managed to tell Seth he'd inherited the Desert Moon, but had stopped short at the wife clause. Seth would have laughed himself to death, and he'd lost enough family, thank you. Between Mason's demise and Paris's appearance, the last couple of weeks had held more drama than a sensationalized novel.

"I'm just thinking since you're shopping for a wife anyway . . . "

"A body would have to be missing some marbles to take up with that Loony-Lucy," Josh said. "Last time I looked, I had a full pouch."

Fedderman grunted. "Ain't how I see it."

"Then maybe you oughta get your eyes checked." He swung into the saddle, rested his forearm on the pommel, and leaned forward. "Listen, Hank, Paris is a far cry from Molly. She's bull-headed, strong-willed, and she packs one hell of a punch. She'll be fine."

Cringing at the slump of his friend's shoulders, he racked his brain for a compromise. "Tell you what. I'll pass through Florence and ask Seth to keep an eye out for her once she gets into town."

"What about before she gets into town? What about between here and there?"

"She'll be fine," he reassured the man. Or was he trying to reassure himself? Uncomfortable with the notion, he touched the brim of his hat in farewell and spurred Buckshot toward the outskirts of town. Paris had mentioned she had a plan. Well, so did he. He aimed on fulfilling his uncle's last wishes. Aimed on settling in Chance and on running its one and only opera house: Mason's beloved Desert Moon.

He'd even resigned himself to the notion of marriage: Mason's damned stipulation. He'd approach the distasteful union in a sensible and logical manner. Marry an even-tempered woman. A woman who could cook and sew and give him a brood of babies. He could do that without risking his heart. Sensible and logical.

As he passed the Grand Hotel, his thoughts turned unwillingly to Paris. Not a sensible bone in her body or a logical thought in her head, and a damned sight far from even-tempered. Taming an impulsive girl like that would be a demanding job, if not impossible. She'd make a damned irritating wife. Not that he was actually considering Hank's suggestion.

Josh kicked Buckshot into a lope, anxious to put some distance between himself and the enigmatic girl. Whatever his irrational attraction, he'd be over it by the time he got to Chance. He smiled, suddenly looking forward to the week's ride ahead of him. Yup. He'd be over Paris Pauline Getty by then. Out of sight, out of mind.

CHAPTER 4

Paris Garrett? I believe you are next." Mrs. Bernbaum
swatted at a bothersome fly then motioned Paris to come
forward and join her and her seventeen-year-old daughter,
Mary Lee, under the sprawling shade tree.

Paris sat cross-legged on the grassy incline, panic rendering
her immobile.

Thirty-some heads turned her way.

Emily leaned into Paris, her small voice lowered to a con-
spiratorial whisper. "Did you think of a story yet?"

"No." Sweat trickled down the side of Paris's face. Why,
oh, why had Rome forced her to come to the stupid Lemonade
and Storytelling Social Club picnic? Half of the women and
men of Heaven were here. The same people she'd embarrassed
herself in front of last Sunday when she'd interrupted Preacher

McBride's sermon with an impromptu song. It's not as if she'd done it on purpose. She'd been inspired. The bouncy ditty had just...come out. Preacher McBride had been considerably more forgiving than her brothers and the rest of the congregation. "The Lord has blessed you with a mysterious talent, my child. Your melodic rhymes do tend to stick in one's mind." He sighed. "If only your song had praised God rather than Boston's blueberry pancakes."

"Paris?" Mrs. Bernbaum perched her fists on plump hips.

Mary Lee frowned.

Several of Paris's classmates pointed and giggled. Nothing like being a nine-year-old laughing stock.

Emily clasped her hand and squeezed. "Use one of mine. You know them all by heart. Just pick one."

"That would be stealing," Paris mumbled out of the side of her mouth.

"I don't mind."

"For a preacher's daughter you're mighty loose with the ten commandments, Emily McBride."

"I believe in a forgiving God." Her fair-haired friend smiled. "It's not sinful to bend the rules for the right reasons."

Paris frowned. "I know you didn't hear that from your pa."

"Course not. I heard it from Rome."

Seeing that Emily worshiped the silver-tongued Garrett, naturally she'd take his word as gospel. Paris rolled her eyes, thinking her friend was a ninny for having mushy feelings for any boy, especially one of her fickle brothers. Then again, Emily *was a full year older than Paris and given to more girly notions.*

Mrs. Bernbaum hollered for Paris to hurry up with her story. "We don't have all day, child!"

Admitting defeat, she smoothed her sweaty palms on her skirt. "Remind me to pay back Rome with a kick in the shin," she whispered to Emily. "I could've been at home practicing the piano. But, no. He thinks I need to socialize." She stood and wove her way though the maze of blankets and picnic baskets. All she had to do was tell a short story. Any story.

Nearing the shade tree, she overheard Mary Lee say, "I can't believe you invited Goofy Garrett to speak, Mother. She'll ruin everything."

Paris glared at snooty Mary Lee Bernbaum, suddenly inspired. She turned to the crowd and cleared her throat.

Her story came out in song.

"On a balmy summer day, by a babbling silver creek, sat Rome and Mary Lee. He was talking pretty talk, she was smiling—all at once, they were K-I-S-S-I-N-G! La-dee-dee! La-dee-dee! Rome was kissing Mary Lee! La-dee—"

"I hate you!" Mary Lee shrieked.

The audience burst into shocked laughter.

Rome stalked toward Paris.

Mrs. Bernbaum grabbed a stick and marched toward Rome.

Emily slapped a palm to her forehead and fell backward in the grass.

"You incorrigible little snoop!" Mary Lee flew at Paris. "You musical freak!"

"I'm not a freak! I'm not—"

"Miss Paris."

Mary Lee grabbed her by the shoulders and shook.

"Wake up, Miss."

Paris shot upright, eyes wide, and stared into the grizzly face of Moe Wiggins, her kind-hearted coach driver. A man of few words, unlike her other traveling companion, she'd grown quite fond of the weathered man over the last two days.

"You were dreaming, Miss."

Paris disagreed. "Dreams are generally pleasant." Her heart pounded. Heaven's laughter rang in her ears. More like a nightmare. She wasn't sure Rome had ever forgiven the impromptu performance that had resulted in *Mr.* Bernbaum fetching his shotgun. If it weren't for Athens's diplomatic fast-talking, their skirt-chasing brother and snooty Mary Lee Bernbaum would have found themselves good and hitched that day.

Mr. Wiggins thumbed up his sweat-stained hat, scratched his deeply creased forehead. "Want to talk about it?"

About how my almost sister-in-law and the whole of Heaven consider me a musical freak? "No, thank you." She cringed remembering how the town had pushed her to arm's length after the lemonade and storytelling fiasco. Sure they'd been amused by her Rome-and-Mary-Lee ditty, but Lord forbid she create a ditty about any of them.

Shunned by society at the age of nine.

Not that she'd cared. She'd gladly stepped into the shoes of a social misfit. Being a recluse had enabled her unlimited time at the piano and minimal interaction with the judgmental public. She wondered, not for the first time, how she'd feel when she stepped onstage at the Desert Moon. What if the audience heckled and booed?

Stomach churning, she swung her legs over the side of the cot and focused on the rustic, one-room adobe, one of several stationhouses they'd visited since leaving Yuma. Exhausted, she struggled to pinpoint her exact location. "Where are we?"

"Midway twixt Gila Bend and Maricopa Wells." Mr. Wiggins stretched his back. "You best hurry, Miss. We're headin' out in ten minutes." He jerked his thumb at the planked table as he limped toward the front door. "We saved you a plate seein' you slept through breakfast. Can't offer you a bath, but there's a pail of fresh water near the hearth."

Paris waited until he had gone then tended to her morning rituals. Somewhat refreshed, she rifled through her carpetbag for a clean shirt, opting for Rome's lucky poker shirt. The sight and scent of the starched ruffled shirt caused her throat to constrict. She missed her brothers terribly. Silly, considering she'd only been away for a little over a week. And it's not as if she saw them on a daily basis. Rome and Boston spent most of their time tracking bandits. As a widower and state legislator, Athens had a young son and daughter and political aspirations that kept him on the go. London had inherited the Gilded Garrett Theater. Though they all called the Garrett estate home, Paris was the only one who spent the majority of her time under its three-story roof. She'd been so wrapped up in her quest to keep a childhood promise, she'd never imagined she'd feel homesick. Though in reality it wasn't Heaven that she missed. How could she miss a place where she'd never really belonged? She missed her brothers, her nephew and niece, and Emily—the people who made her feel special. Safe. For a moment her mind flashed to one other who had made her feel special and protected, and something altogether different.

Her heart fluttered at the thought of Joshua Grant. A bothersome man in more ways than one. Not wanting to dwell on his knee-melting kisses, she grabbed her carpetbag, snatched up a biscuit and hurried outside. Dipping her head to shield her eyes from the morning sun, she swept past her one and only traveling companion hoping to escape his notice.

To her dismay, the dandified blowhard kept pace. He relieved her of her bag, gently set it behind the stage then returned to her side and smiled. "It is without rival in simplicity, durability and ease of operation," he said, as though they'd been in the midst of a conversation.

"The vertical feed. That's what sets us apart."

Paris braced herself for a long-winded sales pitch. "That's terribly interesting, Mr. Hinklemyer, but—"

"Did I happen to mention we have an automatic bobbin winder?"

"Yes, you did." *Approximately a dozen times over the last two days.* "I appreciate your enthusiasm as to the superiority of your product, but as I said, I have no talent whatsoever with a needle and thread."

Mr. Hinklemyer pooh-poohed her admission with a dismissive wave of his plump, bejeweled hand. "Nonsense, my dear. Sewing is easy with the New Davis Sewing Machine."

Her polite smile drooped as the traveling salesman launched into another informative tirade. Mr. Horace Hinklemyer of San Francisco, California seemed to know everything there was to know about sewing machines. Paris had never seen the New Davis Sewing Machine, but she figured she'd be able to draw one with her eyes closed by the time they reached Florence.

"Dash! Look at the way our driver's handling my demonstrator model! Please excuse me, Miss Paris. I must see to its safe loading."

The chubby salesman waddled to the rear of the Overland Stage where his machine was being carelessly hefted onto a hinged, chain-supported platform. It landed with a thud and a clang. Mr. Hinklemyer voiced his complaints by swearing and slapping his gray felt bowler against his thigh. Moe Wiggins shrugged his indifference and spat a stream of tobacco juice past the salesman's slate-colored shoes. When he hoisted Paris's carpetbag aboard, it too landed with a thud.

Mr. Hinklemyer gasped.

Mr. Wiggins snickered. "Movin' out in two minutes."

Curbing a smile, Paris nibbled on her biscuit while waiting for the stationmaster to finish inspecting the relief team's rig. The Overland Stage line insisted on fresh horses every few hours. Desert conditions were brutal. Rocky terrain. Blistering heat. Exhausting for horses and passengers alike. Turkey Dan, Mr. Wiggins's side-kick, had succumbed to a mysterious fever the first day out. Ignoring his protests, Mr. Wiggins had left him to recover at Gila City, one of the many station houses situated along the route.

The one-room adobes were reasonably clean, the food decent, although the sleeping arrangements were cramped. Growing up in a well-to-do household, Paris was accustomed to spacious accommodations and the superb cooking of their longtime housekeeper. Nevertheless, she found an odd comfort in the simplicity and hospitality of the region. Each night the men had insisted on sleeping under the stars in order to allow her privacy.

Not that she'd slept all that much. Sheriff Joshua Grant kept popping into her thoughts, lecturing her reckless behavior. Accusing her of being on the lam. *Who are you running from?* Then she'd start feeling guilty for worrying her brothers. Darn him. If that wasn't bad enough, he'd monopolized her dreams. Dreams full of toe-curling kisses and singing angels.

"Do hurry, Miss Paris," Mr. Hinklemyer called from inside the coach.

Startled out of her cheek-flushing reverie, she rushed to the stage.

Out of nowhere, Burgess Riley appeared, stepping directly into her path. "Well now," he said, treating her to a bucktoothed grin, "if it ain't the little fireball."

What in the world was he doing here? She dodged right to avoid plowing into the bully's big-as-a-barn frame.

He nabbed her elbow. "I don't recall us bein' properly introduced. My name's Burgess. What's yours?"

Paris wrested her arm free. "Please, step aside, Mr. Riley."

"Mr. Riley? I'm touched." He stretched a beefy hand over his pea-sized heart. "You cared enough to ask about me."

"You're mistaken. I don't care at all. Now please step aside."

"Move it, Burgess, or climb on board," Mr. Wiggins called down from his driver's seat. "I've got a schedule to keep."

Burgess ignored the man and leaned closer to Paris. "You know, I cursed my horse when he went lame a ways back." He raked her body with a loathsome gaze. "Now I'm thinkin' I should have thanked the jughead."

Her stomach roiled with disgust. Why was he leering at her? Following Emily's advice, she'd dressed like a boy to deter such attention. Boston's trousers. Rome's shirt. London's fedora. Maybe Rome's shirt wasn't so lucky.

Burgess chuckled, a gruff, ugly sound that made her skin crawl. He opened the stage door and waved her inside. "After you, sweet thing."

She glared at the bearded skunk, refusing to be intimidated. She'd grown up with four brothers who'd taught her to defend herself with fists and feet. Unfortunately, she'd already used a couple of those moves on Burgess and wasn't sure if he'd fall for the same tricks.

Glancing over her shoulder, she scanned the dusty corral for Josh. Futile since he was halfway to wherever. Not that she needed him. Still, he did have a way with her oppressor. Like knocking his teeth out.

Ignoring the door he held open, she hastened to the front of the stage. Shielding her eyes from the morning sun, she tilted her head back and summoned Mr. Wiggins.

"What can I do fer ya, Miss?"

"I was wondering," she half whispered, "if I might

sit atop with you today? I'd surely enjoy the clear view. That is if you wouldn't mind the company."

"Gits mighty hot up here."

"I don't mind." Anything to avoid Burgess Riley. Not to mention Mr. Hinklemyer's endless sales pitch on vertical feeds and bobbin winding thing-a-ma-jigs.

Mr. Wiggins pursed his lips then spat a stream of brown juice in the vicinity of the lead horse. "Suit yourself."

Smiling at the Riley man's muffled oath, she scaled the stage and seated herself. The coach rocked with the bully's weight as he climbed inside. When the door slammed, Mr. Wiggins yip-yipped, and with a crack of the reins, set the team of four horses into a unified trot. A cloud of dust swirled behind them as the coach rolled out of the corral.

Paris looked over her shoulder and waved farewell to the stationmaster. She wondered if Josh had passed this way. He'd hinted that they'd be traveling in the same direction, yet she hadn't seen hide nor hair of the infuriating man.

Her disappointed sigh caught Mr. Wiggins's ears. "What is it, Miss?"

"Nothing," she lied. She couldn't stop thinking about him. His eyes. His lips. *His kisses.* Blast! Wasn't it bad enough that he haunted her nights? Now he was ruining her days.

Disgusted with herself, she swung back around and focused on the desert scenery. So different from the lush hills and valleys of home. So invigorating. The rough and wild landscape filled her with a sense of awe. If it weren't for a certain lawman sidetracking her thoughts every three seconds she would have composed a melodic tribute by now.

I'm an entertainer. Destined for the stage. Destined for greatness. No time for men. No time for kissing. She never thought she'd see the day when she'd issue a self-directed lecture.

Mr. Wiggins pointed out various sites. She was happy for the distraction. In the hours that passed, she found herself hanging on the driver's every word. She not only learned the founding history of Yuma, but she could tell the difference between a Prickly Pear and the Cholla cactus. Her favorite was the Giant Saguaro.

The Saguaro stood as high as fifty feet, some sprouting as many as a dozen arms from its prickly green body. According to Mr. Wiggins, a yellowish-white flower would bloom from its tops in May. The flower would develop into a fruit resembling a small reddish-brown pear somewhere about June. Paris doubted she'd be around to see that. May was a good eight months away. She'd be lucky if she made it eight days without her brothers closing in.

"Here I been carryin' on and ya' look as if ya' can

barely keep your eyes open."

She stifled a yawn. "Nothing personal. I haven't been getting much sleep."

"You're welcome to curl up on the roof if you like. The sun's hot as the devil's kitchen, but there's a good breeze blowin' today. We got a ways 'fore we reach our next relay station."

She hesitated, feeling bad for deserting the kind, old man in the middle of one of his stories.

"Go on," he insisted, nudging her in the side with his bony elbow. "I'll wake 'ya once we get to Maricopa Wells."

Too tired to argue, she worked her body around and climbed up over the shoulder high backrest. By some miracle she managed not to topple overboard as the stage bounced over the rocky mason track. She positioned herself as comfortably as one could on a stagecoach roof, and pulled the corner of a canvas cloth over her face to protect it from the baking sun.

Exhausted, the rhythmic pounding of horse hooves along with Mr. Wiggins's whistled rendition of *Jim Crack Corn* soon lulled Paris into a bone-weary sleep.

CHAPTER 5

"**S**ure you won't stay for some vittles, Sheriff Grant? I can rustle you up somethin' real quick like."

Thorn Butte's stationmaster was as well known for his longwinded story-telling as he was for his hospitality. If Josh stayed much longer, he'd be joining the lonely man for a walk down memory lane. "Much obliged, Ben, but I'm in a hurry to be on my way. Only stopped long enough to rest Buckshot and stretch my legs."

"Where you headin'?"

"Chance."

"Never been there."

"You haven't missed much." He gripped his saddle horn and vaulted into the leather seat, not bothering to elaborate. As far as he was concerned, the less thought he gave to his new life, the better. Besides, Ben's attention had drifted to a point on the horizon.

The stationmaster squinted against the noonday sun and scratched his head. "What in tarnation?"

Josh squinted in the same direction. "What is it?"

"The Overland Stage. But I ain't never seen Moe Wiggins drive a rig that hard. They're comin' in fast. Too fast."

An invisible knife twisted into Josh's gut. A knife held by Hank, I-told-you-so, Fedderman.

Paris was on that stage. Sure enough, somehow, some way, she'd gotten herself into another fix. The knife plunged deeper as a vivid image of Mason's runaway buckboard flashed in his mind. Fearing the worst, he raced his horse toward the rolling cloud of dust.

His heart leapt to his throat as he neared the careening stage. That wasn't Moe driving. It was that accident-prone hellion, and she was doing a damn poor job.

Closing in, he whipped Buckshot around and pulled up even with the rocking coach. Moe was either drunk or dead. Turkey Dan was plumb missing.

"*Glory, glory, hallelujah!*"

Paris was singing *Battle Hymn of the Republic* at the top of her lungs. "Are you crazy?" he shouted over the ruckus. "Pull back on the ribbons!"

"Are you blind? I *am* pulling back! It's the horses who aren't doing their part. *His truth is marching on!*"

"Stop singing!"

"Stop yelling!"

"Stop arguing!" A wide-eyed, chubby-cheeked man hung out the window. He shook a ringed finger at Josh. "Do something, man! I'm not ready to die! Oh, my Lord, my demonstrator model, my . . ."

The man's whining faded as Josh spurred Buckshot forward in line with the lead sorrels. He grabbed onto the rigging and, using all his strength, gradually slowed the lathered horses into a winded walk.

The coach rolled to a stop just shy of Thorn Butte's relay station. Ben hurried forward and took the snorting team in hand. The door slammed open and two men jumped out of the stage as though their seats were on fire.

Josh's gaze drifted over the unidentified whiner and landed on Burgess Riley. Why was he here, and where in the blazes was Turkey Dan? Though curious, he was more concerned with Paris. Peculiarly silent, she'd yet to budge from her rooftop position.

He dismounted and scaled the stage. To get to her he had to climb past Moe. A quick examination proved the driver dead, the reason unclear. Josh squeezed his bony shoulder before moving on to the uncharacteristically silent girl.

Even though she was dressed in trousers and a man's shirt, she looked feminine and fragile and, dammit,

that chafed. His heart hammered knowing how easily she could've been thrown from the coach. Mason, a
superior horseman, had met that very end, breaking his
neck in the process. Josh breathed easier, noting the
battered hat mashed down over her tangled hair. He
thanked God for that hat. It reminded him that underneath that ruffled gambler's shirt beat the heart of
a spirited lunatic.

"You can let loose of the ribbons, sweetheart. Ben's
got hold of the team." He gently pried the leather lines
from her hands, frowning at the welts marring her
palms. He wouldn't blame her if she cried, but hoped
she held strong. He'd never been good with weepy
women. "Where's Turkey Dan?"

"Gila City. Sick."

At least he wasn't dead, which is more than he could
say for Moe. He glanced at Paris and swore. White as
milk and trembling like a treed cat. "Safe to assume you
haven't driven too many rigs?"

She nodded, but didn't answer.

He tried a different route. "Mind if I ask why you
were singing?"

"Music soothes the savage beast."

Biting back a smile, he used the pad of his thumb
to wipe away the sweat on her upper lip. "Just a suggestion, but you might want to try a lullaby next time. You
sang as though you were leading those horses into the

heat of battle."

"This is all very touching," Burgess shouted from below, "but I've got a bone to pick with the one who was supposed to be driving this stage in the first place."

"Yes," the roly-poly man with the matching gray bowler and shoes whined. "What happened to Mr. Wiggins?"

Startled out of her daze, Paris lurched forward.

Josh caught her by the waist and held tight. "Nothing you can do, darlin'. He's gone."

A tear escaped through her lowered lashes, slid down her cheek, and smacked against his hand. Shit.

"The old goat picked a devil of a time to up and die!"

Josh glowered. "Shut up, Burgess, and give Ben a hand getting Moe into the stationhouse. You too, Mr. . . . "

"Hinklemyer. Horace Hinklemyer at your service."

Josh kept an eye on Paris as the men maneuvered the driver's body down from the stage and into the small wooden shack.

"I don't understand," she began in a shaky voice. "He seemed fine when I climbed up here to take a nap. Next thing I knew . . . "

Her voice cracked, but instead of giving in, she looked away and blinked back tears. The fact that she was holding strong did little to ease Josh's misery. Needing to comfort the both of them, he pulled her into his arms. He knew her tears would rattle him, but this was ridiculous. It felt like someone was squeezing his heart. What in the Sam Hill was wrong with him?

Had to be the circumstances. Moe's death. The runaway stage.

Breathing easier, he removed the girl's hat and smoothed away the long strands of hair plastered to her dusty, tear-streaked face. "Moe lived a long, full life, darlin'. My guess is his old heart just gave out. He wouldn't want you to fret."

"It's just that he was so kind. He asked me about my nightmare . . . offered me . . . biscuits. He saved me from Mr. Hinklemyer's bobbin-thing-a-ma-jigs and Mr. Riley's . . ." She choked on a sob and shook her head.

He was curious about the nightmare and Hinklemyer's bobbins, but it was Burgess's antics that roped and tied his interest. He stroked Paris's back, willing her to continue. "What did Burgess do?"

"Nothing," she said in a small voice.

Several dicey scenarios tramped through Josh's head. His patience slipped another notch.

He hooked a finger under her stubborn chin and looked directly into her red-rimmed eyes. "All right then, what did he *say*?"

"Nothing. I just didn't like . . . the way he looked at me, it made me . . . uncomfortable." Color returned full force to her face. She averted her eyes, used the heel of her hand to wipe them dry. "I'm blowing things out of proportion. I'm overly tired, that's all."

"Right." He believed that about as much as he believed she hadn't run away from home. It didn't take much imagination to guess why Burgess made her uncomfortable. The troublemaker had been a pain in his backside for going on two years. A bully for hire, the man spent most of his time committing crimes outside of his jurisdiction. Later, he'd stroll back in with a smug smile and money to burn. Aside from nailing him for setting fire to the livery and inciting numerous bar brawls, he hadn't been able to prove Burgess Riley guilty of anything more than pure meanness. Society would be safer with Burgess off the streets. Paris certainly would. Unfortunately, a man couldn't be locked away for making a woman *uncomfortable*.

As much as it rankled, Josh knew what he had to do. If Mason were here, he'd pop him in his ever-lovin' interfering snout. This was sure as shootin' his fault. "Come on," he ordered Paris, trying to keep the irritation out of his tone and failing. "Let's get you down."

Paris feared her knees would buckle when her feet touched the ground, but Josh's strong grip kept her upright. He guided her to a bench pushed against the stationhouse wall.

"Wait here. I'll be inside seeing to Moe's passage back to Yuma. I'll also have a few words with Burgess."

"I wish you wouldn't." Even though she'd only been

defending herself, she knew she'd made a dangerous enemy. "It might make things worse."

"Let me worry about that." He squeezed her shoulder before disappearing into the stationhouse.

Despite her frazzled nerves, her heart swelled to twice its normal size. He reminded her of Rome when he got all riled in her defense. Only her feelings for Josh were far from sisterly.

She blew out a shaky breath. This was absurd. Craving the attention of a man she barely knew. Then again, she hadn't been herself since she'd hit Yuma. Maybe there was something in the desert air. Even though the runaway team and Mr. Wiggins's sudden death had shaken her senseless, she couldn't believe she'd taken comfort in Josh's arms and given in to tears. She almost wished she'd been thrown and trampled by the horses. Sure, she'd be dead, but she'd still have her dignity.

She glanced at the door, worrying suddenly that Josh's *few words* would turn into a brawl. Not that Burgess didn't deserve a good beating. Just the same, it bothered her to think of Josh risking harm on her behalf. He'd already rescued her two or three times. As much as it pained her to admit, she'd be in a heck of a pickle if it weren't for Sheriff Joshua Grant.

Sharp voices pierced the stationhouse walls. The heated exchange ended with bone cracking against bone. Someone hit the floor with a thud.

Josh marched out of the stationhouse and kept going. "Come on."

Wide-eyed, she hurried after him. "You hit him?"

"What do you think?"

Right. Next question. "Where are we going?"

"I'm taking you to Florence."

"You are?"

"I am."

"You don't sound happy about it."

"I'm not." He patted his horse then readjusted the saddle.

His foul mood bewildered her. Moments ago he'd been so tender. So sweet. "I could wait here. For the next stage."

"Forget it." He gave the cinch a final tug and turned to her, hands on hips.

What had she done to deserve such a grim look? "Honestly, I don't mind—"

"Stop arguing."

"I'm not!"

"I'm a man who enjoys his sleep," he continued as if she hadn't spoken. "I refuse to spend my nights staring up at the stars wondering whether or not you've been thrown from a runaway stage or violated by the likes of Burgess."

"Those thoughts don't appeal to me either."

"Then it's settled."

"My valise—"

"—stays where it is. Ben doesn't have a horse to spare, so we have to double up. He'll put that overloaded satchel of yours on the next stage to Florence."

"I need my toothbrush."

"I'll get your toothbrush."

"And my sheet music."

His eyebrow shot up, a clear warning that he was fast losing patience. "Necessities only."

"My music is a necessity." These were her personal compositions. Her life's work. She couldn't, wouldn't leave them behind. Intent on standing her ground, she threw back her shoulders and cocked a stubborn chin, refusing to give in to a new batch of tears.

"For the love of . . ." Josh hustled to the back of the stage. He returned with her toothbrush, comb, soap, and a bundle of music. Muttering to himself, he stuffed her personal items into his bulging saddlebags. In one fluid movement he mounted the tall buckskin, leaned down and hoisted Paris up onto his lap. "Here's the plan," he grumbled into her ear. "I'll deliver you to Florence then you'll go your way and I'll go mine."

His close proximity momentarily obliterated her fear of the spirited horse. *If he moves a breath closer*, she thought, *he could actually nibble my earlobe*. Ever since she'd caught Boston nibbling on Lydia Ivey by the creek last summer, she'd always wondered what that would feel like.

"Agreed?"

She'd sworn she'd heard Lydia purr. "Pardon?"

"I'll go my way—"

"—and I'll go mine," she said, catching on. Nibbling earlobes? What was it about this man? He made her crave the most ridiculous things.

"Seeing it'll be just you and me for the next day or so we best forget what happened back in Yuma."

"You mean the kissing."

"Precisely." He urged the horse into a brisk walk.

She grabbed hold of the saddle horn and held tight. She'd never forget the kissing. No, sir. She had a sinking feeling she'd think about it at least twice a day for the rest of her life. But she wouldn't let him know that. "Don't flatter yourself. I haven't given you a second thought."

"Same here."

Was he serious? Had she been that forgettable? "I don't even like you," she lied, her pride wounded.

"The feeling's mutual."

"Good."

"Fine."

"*Fine.*" She swiped her hair out of her eyes and tugged her hat low. The last few days had been disastrous. The jail incident. The runaway stage. Burgess. She couldn't get her mind off of Moe Wiggins. Death

71

had a way of twisting her heart and turning it inside out. "So long as we understand one another," she mumbled.

"I doubt that I'll ever understand you, kid."

Closing her eyes against a vivid image of her over-protective brothers and the narrow-minded citizens of Heaven, she whispered, "You're not alone."

CHAPTER 6

Torture, Paris decided, is a subjective word. Emily sometimes wrote Medieval stories involving hideous contraptions like "the rack", one of several horrors inflicted on her less fortunate knights. Then there were the delicate agonies experienced by motivated artists. Such as listening to an all-thumbed oaf mangle *Buffalo Gals,* or not being able to play a piano for seven days and counting. Even worse were the secret tortures she never imagined would happen to her. Like being told *not* to think about kissing while forced to sit cozy with the very person who made you think of nothing *but*!

"How much farther?" she asked on a frustrated sigh.

"You know, kickin' never gets you anywhere unless you're a mule," Josh answered.

Although he sounded amused, the observation stung, making her feel like an impatient child. She didn't mean to whine, but she wasn't sure how much longer she could stand sharing a saddle. They'd been riding for hours. He'd spent most of that time in confounding silence, leaving her to contend with a fearsome inward struggle. With his strong arms fencing her in, his rock-hard torso pressed up against her back, her bottom snug up against his—well, best not to think about what her bottom was snug up against—all sorts of shameful thoughts riddled her mind.

Embarrassed, she leaned forward, putting some distance between their bodies. It didn't help. His forearms still rested on her thighs. His right hand, expertly guiding the reins, kept brushing her own hands as she refused to leave go of the saddle horn.

She was trapped. Much like when he'd pinned her against the jail cell wall.

Cheeks flaming, she glanced down at his long, tanned fingers recalling how they'd felt when he'd tangled them in her hair. When he'd held her captive, deepening a kiss that blew her mind to smithereens.

She swore she'd seen stars.

She fought the urge to turn in his arms, to press her mouth against his and explore heaven. God help her, she longed to rekindle the fire that had burned in her belly when he'd made her toes curl. How was she supposed to blot out what was quite possibly, no, definitely, a miracle? The earth shook. Angels sang.

Obviously, he hadn't been paying attention.

The notion stoked the rebel in her, dared her to ignore his warning and to thumb her nose at propriety. To shock him with a kiss that would haunt him for the rest of his born days. It would serve him right.

At least it would make them even.

The longer she endured this intimate position, the harder it was to resist the scandalous urge to make an impression he couldn't ignore.

Desperate for a distraction, she focused on the roadside scenery. Unfortunately, the territory had held little attraction since Thorne Butte. Gone were the mountainous peaks of Yuma, the mesquite with its feathery leaves, and the green masses of cottonwoods. Even the various forms of cacti were few and far between. The *Pedras Pintados*, or painted rocks as Mr. Wiggins had translated, had been intriguing. A pile of boulders heaped high to about forty feet. The smooth sides of the boulders were covered with rude carvings and hieroglyphics. According to Mr. Wiggins, some people believed that the images were painted by the Pima Indians. Others believed they dated back to a mythical race. Paris didn't know what to believe but she liked hearing the stories.

She had liked Mr. Wiggins.

Her heart pounded. *Don't think about that poor soul*.

As though sensing her distress, Josh squeezed her hand, which only heightened her anxiety. *Don't think about the man sitting behind you, those strong hands skimming up your arms, framing your face and . . .*

Veering away from wicked thoughts, she glanced at the multi-colored horizon. Another breathtaking sunset. Another awe-inspiring explosion of purple, red, and orange. Emily would adore these sunsets. Emily would adore Josh. Both suited the romantic stories the shy woman secretly penned. Yes, indeed, her imaginative, lovesick friend would most certainly consider Josh hero material. The way he'd overpowered the runaway stage and pummeled Burgess Riley, all for the sake of a damsel in distress.

Paris frowned realizing she was said damsel. She wasn't sure she liked to think of herself in those terms. She wasn't delicate or helpless. She knew how to use her fists and brains. How could she not with four intelligent, worrywart brothers? Still, she couldn't fight a fluttery feeling whenever she envisioned Josh rushing to her rescue.

Jelly limbs. Butter for brains. She'd read about these kinds of afflictions in Emily's stories. Cripes almighty. Was it possible? Was she was actually sweet on the man? The notion was horrifying. Logic told her to fight the attraction tooth and nails. What if he knew her brothers? What if he sabotaged her dream? But Emily's persistent voice whispered in her ears, urging her to take advantage of an enriching phenomenon. *Life experience inspires passionate prose*. Paris squirmed in the saddle, debating the confounding dilemma.

Josh locked one arm tight around her middle and squeezed. "Stop fussing."

His husky command and possessive hold stoked the embers glowing in her belly, making her skin burn from the inside out. "If you know what's good for you, you'll loosen your hold." She was two seconds from whipping around and making that memorable impression.

"Relax," he said, his warm breath fanning her ear. "I'm not going to bite."

Please do, she thought, flattening her lips to trap a blissful sigh. *Nibble my earlobe. Make me purr*.

Lord, she was pathetic.

Antsy, she elbowed him in the stomach. It was like nudging a stone wall. He eased back, but not before an image of his naked torso exploded in her mind. She imagined muscles, lots of hard, defined muscles, and groaned.

"Got a bee in your britches?"

"Never you mind about my britches," she snapped, grateful he couldn't read her mind. "I'm hot." Apparently the desert sun had warped her brain. Between the intense heat and her erotic musings, she felt plain dizzy.

He passed her his canteen.

"I'm not thirsty."

"Drink."

Arguing was useless. He was as bossy and as stubborn as any one of her brothers. Sighing, she took the canteen and swigged several mouthfuls of cool water. She hadn't realized she'd been so thirsty.

"Better?"

She was until she craned around to say, *yes, thank you*. Her gaze locked with his and her mouth went dry. "How much farther?"

"Contrary as a mule," he said, lip twitching.

"Better than being one."

"Are you calling me an ass?"

"If the shoe fits."

He grinned and her stomach flipped. Why did he have to be so darn handsome? Why couldn't he have a wart on his chin or hair growing out of his ears? Just her luck, he had to have the chiseled good looks of a Greek statue. Every time she looked into his twinkling eyes her heart skipped like a flat stone across a lake. His smile, on the rare occasion that he gave one up, turned her legs into overripe bananas.

"I wish you were ugly," she said without thinking.

"You say the strangest things." He shook his head. "Thank you, I guess."

"You're welcome," she mumbled, entranced by the playful gleam in his eyes. She wondered if he found her fetching, not that she was about to ask. His gaze roamed over her face, and she thought, just maybe he did. But instead of commenting, he jerked his attention to the horizon.

Instincts told her not to pry. They'd shared a heart-skipping moment—at least in her mind—why ruin it? "What are you thinking about?" So much for restraint.

"You don't want to know."

His tone revealed nothing, but then she remembered their awkward showdown back in Thorne Butte. He didn't like her, or so he'd said. How could she have forgotten? So he'd smiled at her. So he'd teased her. That didn't mean he harbored affection. Obviously, the attraction—and she hated to admit she was indeed attracted—was one-sided.

Anxious, she swiveled back around and grappled for another distraction. Anything that didn't have to do with Joshua Grant.

The Desert Moon. Yes, that would definitely do. She pursed her lips and concentrated on her dream with fierce determination.

Opera House seeking entertainers! *Hitch your star to the Desert Moon*!

She'd never given much thought to fate, but if that advertisement hadn't been a sign, she'd eat London's hat. Believing she was destined to become a prominent musical actress, Papa had begged her to reach for the stars. She'd promised to lasso the moon. Two days later, ten years ago this month, he'd been killed in a shootout at the theater. Her stomach pitched just thinking about the look on her mama's face when the sheriff had come to the door.

Not wanting to dwell on that awful moment, Paris imagined the mountain-based opera house. Would it resemble the Gilded Garrett, a three-story architectural wonder decorated in subdued red, creamy white, and brilliant gold? A prosperous and popular theater boasting a tasteful saloon, elegant conversation rooms and an impressive auditorium that seated up to a thousand patrons? She'd only been inside the Gilded Garrett a dozen times in her entire nineteen years, an amazing statistic since her family owned the establishment. Mama had been a formidable obstacle, considering San Francisco a bad influence on young children. Now that Paris was an adult, she had to contend with her brothers' old-fashioned values. It seemed as if the whole world frowned upon her frequenting the theater. Still, the Gilded Garrett was emblazoned in her memory, as were the few shows she'd had the privilege to view from backstage.

On second thought she couldn't imagine any theater as grand as the Gilded Garrett.

So as not to be disappointed, she lowered her expectations. Perhaps the Desert Moon was more in keeping with Percy's Poker Palace, the rollicking gambling establishment that sat on the outskirts of Heaven. Not that she'd ever seen the interior of Percy's, but Rome spent a good deal of time there when he was home. Given his taste for the finer things in life, certainly Percy's must be first rate. If she couldn't have grand, first rate would do.

A third and extremely unappealing thought occurred. What if the Desert Moon more closely resembled Hell's Drinkin' Hole? It was, after all, in the middle of nowhere.

Paris absentmindedly braided sections of Buckshot's coarse mane. The prospect of singing her original compositions in front of strangers was nerve-racking enough without those strangers resembling the ruffians she'd encountered in Hell's Drinkin' Hole. She'd prefer a sophisticated clientele, thank you very much. According to Rome, those who attended Percy's Poker Palace were well behaved and appreciative of any and all entertainment that graced its ornate stage.

She envisioned herself standing on an elevated stage, ornate or otherwise, the center of attention. Envisioned the audience scrutinizing her costume, waiting to be dazzled by her talent. She imagined herself in her mama's buttoned boots, and experienced a sharp pang of panic.

She'd inherited her mama's voice, but that didn't mean she'd inherited her charisma. Charisma, Papa had once said, sets apart the stars from the chorus girls. What if she lacked charisma? What if she froze? What if they booed? If she botched her opening night she wouldn't have to worry about the clientele, sophisticated or otherwise. She'd be terminated!

Brain buzzing with disastrous scenarios, she stiffened, knocking Josh in the chin with the back of her head.

"What's wrong now?"

"Nothing." *Hopefully*. The proprietor of the Desert Moon had promised her a job, but he hadn't designated the length of her engagement. Why hadn't she thought to ask for details? If she failed to impress M.B. he had every right to boot her out the door the next morning. She knew from London that an inferior performer could be as bad for business as secondary service. She couldn't afford to be an inferior performer. She was already an inferior songwriter.

How was she ever going to become famous if she didn't make a name for herself?

Her mind scrambled to rehash snatches of work-related conversations between her parents—specifically, various tactics to insure a successful performance. She needed to win over the audience the moment she stepped on stage, and she couldn't count on mesmerizing them with charisma if she had the stage presence of a tree stump. She needed to open with something tried and true. A popular song. A sing-a-long. A guaranteed crowd-pleaser.

Her musical hero sprang to mind. "What do you think of Stephen Foster?"

"Who?"

"Stephen Foster." She looked over her shoulder. "You know. The man who wrote *The Old Folks At Home*."

Josh palmed his hat to the back of his head, signaling she had his reluctant attention. "Can't say I know the song."

"Of course you do. Everyone does." She cleared her throat and sang, "*Way down upon the Swanee River*—"

"Swanee River." He gave her waist a playful squeeze. "Why didn't you say so?"

The affectionate gesture caused her breath to catch. She wondered, for the briefest of seconds, what it would feel like if he leaned in and kissed the back of her neck. Rattled, she launched into a nervous stream of chatter. "The actual title of the song is *The Old Folks At Home*, not Swanee River. In fact, Mr. Foster originally wrote about the 'Peedee River,' but decided it wasn't all that pleasant on the ears. Keeping in mind that he needed a two-syllable name, he picked up a Florida map, looked it over, and found the Swanee River. Thank heavens, right? Can you imagine?" She snorted then sang, "*Way down upon the Peedee River . . .*"

Josh rolled back tense shoulders and smiled. Her questionable sanity aside, Paris's voice flowed over him sweet and rich like molasses. Entranced, he waited for her to finish out the song. Instead, she launched into another story about Stephen Foster.

Had the sun struck her delirious? Although, this was Paris. She'd set herself apart from normal folk the moment she'd waltzed into a saloon in search of a piano. Creative people, musicians, artists, weren't they generally famous for their eccentricities? Maybe that was it. Maybe she was eccentric. Not that eccentric was much better than crazy.

"The lyrics. It's all in the lyrics. Well, not all. The melody counts, of course. It's a matter of finding the perfect blend. One must complement the other. I mean, as much as I admire Mr. Foster's lyrics, can you imagine if they'd been set to a melody of Mozart's?" She waved a dismissive hand. "What am I saying? You don't know Mozart."

"I know Mozart." Mason had been an avid fan. Though Josh preferred simpler melodies, he respected the composer's obvious talent. "Not personally, of course."

She chuckled. "You're full of surprises, Mr. Grant."

He merely smiled, thinking he was pretty damned boring compared to her.

"Wolfgang Amadeus Mozart," she continued in reverent awe. "An honest-to-gosh genius. It's not as if he plunked out a melody on the piano and then committed it to paper. No, sir. He heard entire operas in his head, complicated concertos and symphonies, he heard them in his head, and *then* committed them to paper. First drafts. Perfect drafts. Beautiful, soul-wrenching music."

Josh tried his best to keep up with her rambling. She'd been blessedly quiet up until this point, which he appreciated since he'd been preoccupied with a personal heart to heart, trying to dispel several worrisome thoughts. Some of them involved Fedderman and his hare-brained notion. Most of them involved Paris and her penchant for landing herself in precarious fixes.

In between it all he'd obsessed on the two passionate kisses he'd advised her to forget. Riding double only complicated his predicament. She felt delicate and vulnerable in his arms, prompting conflicting needs to protect and seduce. Every time a breeze kicked up he got a whiff of lilacs. Every time she shifted in the saddle her cute, little backside rubbed up against his privates. Her trousers left nothing to the imagination. Why couldn't she wear layers of petticoats and skirts like a normal woman?

Because she's not normal.

If not for the risk of overexerting Buckshot, he would have kicked the horse into a gallop. The sooner they reached Maricopa Wells and he got Paris off of his lap, the sooner he'd regain his sanity, for he was sure shootin' *loco* for even considering Fedderman's suggestion.

She'd make as good a wife as any.

Damn Hank for putting that thought in his head. Damn Mason for putting that marriage stipulation in his will. Ignoring the stipulation wasn't an option. It would mean forfeiting the Desert Moon to his no-account cousin, Niles Burke. The irresponsible cardsharp hadn't had the decency to attend his father's funeral. Not that Josh was surprised. Father and son hadn't been on speaking terms for years. Still, Mason hadn't had the heart to disinherit his only son. He'd bequeathed Niles half of his substantial windfall. The rest of his fortune, including the deed to the Desert Moon, had gone to Josh, provided he married in an allotted time frame. Even though the stipulation rankled, he wouldn't let Mason down, and Mason knew it. Damn the old coot.

Regardless, Paris was all wrong. Just because he wanted to bed her, didn't mean he wanted to share her bed for the rest of his life. You can't hitch up a horse to a coyote. She'd have him sprouting gray hairs before his time. The sooner he dumped her in Florence the better. She had her mission, whatever the hell that was, and he had Mason's. He had less than two weeks to court and marry. He wasn't worried about the time limit. Seth was well acquainted with the eligible women of the region. He'd point him in the right direction.

"My mind is constantly filled with music too," she continued in a soft, earnest tone. "Difference is, I'm not as gifted as Mozart, or as Stephen Foster, or as . . ." She shrugged and sighed. "That's partly why I answered the advertisement."

Instead of spurring Buckshot faster, Josh reined him in. "What advertisement?" A deafening silence had him massaging a telling twinge in his neck while his brain raced to fit together pieces of an irritating puzzle. He knew this songwriting thing was important to her. Hell, she'd stormed a saloon just to get a song out of her head. She'd nearly fallen apart when he'd suggested they leave her sheet music behind. This girl was fueled by passion. The kind of passion that made a person go to extreme lengths to achieve goals.

"What's in Florence, Paris?"

"What?"

"What's waiting for you in Florence? I need to know."

She squirmed in the saddle and tugged her hat low. "A position. Why do you need to know?"

His gut kicked, a dead sure sign of disaster. "What kind of position?"

She dipped her head and busied her hands. What the hell was she doing to his buckskin's mane? "I don't know what this has to do with anything," she muttered.

Quicker than she could fuss, he lifted her and settled her sideways on his lap. "Look at me." She reluctantly met his gaze and his pulse spiked. "You're a real pain in the neck, you know that?"

Hurt flashed in her eyes. "I don't mean to be."

Realizing he'd struck a nerve, he filed away her reaction, and persisted. "I believe you, but the fact remains. What kind of position?"

"Honestly," she huffed.

"Honesty would be nice. For once."

She squared her shoulders. "Very well. I've been hired to perform at an opera house."

"To perform?" He frowned, her revelation as unexpected as gun play in Bible class. He had a hard time envisioning Paris as a dance hall girl, between her tomboy appearance and her reckless behavior. Fact was, he didn't want to envision anything of the sort. "I thought you said you're a songwriter."

"I am. But I've decided to try my hand at being a musical actress."

"*Try?*" He massaged a dull throbbing due center of his forehead. "Meaning you've never been on stage? You have no experience?"

"Given my background, M.B. didn't seem to mind."

"Who's M.B.?"

"The proprietor of the opera house."

M.B. Opera House. Mason Burke came to mind, only Mason's gurdy was situated several miles North of Florence at the base of the Superstitions. Besides, why the hell would his uncle hire a west coast greenhorn when Phoenix and Tucson brimmed with experienced talent? "Got a name to go with those initials?"

"No. He just signed the telegram M.B."

Naturally. The throbbing progressed to full-blown headache. He'd been in Florence only seven days before, arranging Mason's burial, meeting with Seth and the lawyer, yet he hadn't paid attention to the town's pleasure palaces. Near as he could remember there were two gambling halls and maybe four or five saloons. No doubt, all of them boasted entertainment. He didn't know an M.B. Then again he didn't spend that much time in Florence. That was Seth's jurisdiction. "What do you mean, given your background?"

"My mother was a musical actress." She glanced away with a wistful sigh. "She could have been a star."

"You don't say." Now he was getting somewhere. "Where is she now?"

"She died of pneumonia when I was nine. Just a few months after my father was killed."

He blinked down at the back of her bowed head. Similar to his own story only he'd been twelve and his ma had gone first. "I'm sorry."

She shrugged indifference though her voice quivered with emotion. "It was a long time ago."

"What happened to your pa?"

"Shot by a stray bullet. Someone didn't like the comedian."

"Pardon?"

She met his gaze, hiked her chin a proud notch. "Papa

owned a theater. I may not have practical experience, but entertainment is in my blood. M.B. understood. I don't see why you can't."

"If I tried any harder I'd bust a blood vessel."

"Oh."

"How do you know this M.B. is an upright man? How do you know his intentions are honorable?"

"What are you implying?"

He dragged a hand over his face.

"Why are you so aggravated?"

"Why are you so trusting?" Swear to God, her innocence was his undoing. "Do you know how many women travel west in hopes of making their own way only to end up girls of the line?"

"What?"

"Seamstresses, nurses, teachers. Women with skills."

She stiffened. "Are you saying writing songs, playing the piano, and singing aren't skills?"

"Most of them find that they can't make a decent living," he plowed on. "The few that aren't lucky enough to snag husbands end up selling themselves in saloons, gambling houses, cribs." Exasperated, he gave her a gentle shake. "Girls of the line. Soiled doves. Prostitutes. Take your pick. By any name, it's a hard living."

Paris gawked at him. "Are you saying that someone wouldn't be willing to pay me a reasonable amount of money in return for my musical abilities?"

"For the love of—"

A rattling sound rent the air. Buckshot danced and reared.

Paris screamed and latched onto Josh, burying her face in his neck. Her piercing wail damn near struck him deaf. He drew his gun and shot the pesky diamondback, calming both woman and horse as he holstered his Colt. "Easy now."

"What was it?"

"A rattle snake."

"Is it dead?"

"Stone cold." He smoothed a comforting hand over the woman's trembling form expecting her to relax. Instead, she surprised him by bolting upright, attempting to slide from the saddle. "Hold up." He caught her, but she kept squirming. "Settle down, Paris."

She grabbed two handfuls of his shirt, her breath coming in short, panting gasps. Her fear seeped through the fabric, singeing his skin. Perplexed, he swept off her hat, stuffed it in his saddlebag, and cupped the sides of her face. "Listen to me. It's over. You're safe."

She bit her lower lip and nodded.

"You're all right." He cringed at the tears shining in her dazed eyes. She'd reacted similarly after the episode with the runaway stage. He'd thought it was because of Moe's death. But then he remembered she'd been shaken even before he'd announced the old man's passing.

"Talk to me, kid."

"I was bucked off of a horse two days before my tenth birthday," she said in a rush. "Broke both of my wrists. It hurt something awful. But not as bad as wanting to play the piano and not being able to. I never rode again. Never tried."

"Never wanted to take the chance."

She nodded, her hair tumbling forward in a mass of windblown tangles.

He tucked her hair behind her ears, marveling, yet again, at the depth of her passion for the piano. "So how do you get around? Buckboard? Buggy?"

"We live in town," she said. "So mostly I walk. It's not like I get around all that much anyway. I'm kind of a homebody. Or at least I was."

"Why didn't you tell me you're afraid to ride?"

"I'm not afraid."

He glanced down at her hands still entangled in his shirt.

She loosened her hold, but didn't let go. "All right. I'm nervous. I'm a coward. Are you happy now?"

He rolled his head left and then right, trying to ease the persistent twinge in his neck. "Not really." Why hadn't her brothers taken the time and effort to help her conquer her fear of horses? Unless they were considerably younger than Paris. He'd just assumed they were older. He didn't even know how many brothers he was dealing with. He'd purposely avoided in-depth conversation figuring the less he knew about her the less he'd care. Obviously there was a hole in that theory. "Put your arms around me."

"Why?"

Casting a baleful look at the heavens, he spurred Buckshot into a lope, grunting with satisfaction when she locked her arms around his waist. He eased the horse into a walk then pressed her head against his shoulder, willing her to relax. "First of all, you're not a coward. A coward wouldn't have taken on the Riley brothers or braved her fear of horses by wrestling a runaway team. A coward generally turns his back on dangerous situations whereas *you* run into them head on. If you're anything, darlin', you're one card shy of a deck."

She tensed. "Are you calling me daft?"

"Different," he said carefully. Sensing he'd exhausted the *job* subject, he veered toward another source of interest. "Let's talk about your brothers."

"I'd rather not."

"It wasn't a request."

"But—"

"And don't bother lying. You're not very good at it."

She let out a dramatic sigh. "Fine," she said, but he wasn't fooled. She wouldn't tell all, if anything. No doubt about it, she was a runaway with something to hide. Her brothers figured in and he wanted to know how.

"I'm assuming one or all of them raised you."

She nodded.

Less than specific, but he'd take it. "How many do you have?"

"Four."

"What do they do?"

She shrugged. "The usual stuff."

"Uh, huh. Married?"

"No. Was. No and no." She peered up at him. "What about you? Have you ever been married?"

He met her gaze. "No. You?"

She snorted. "Marriage isn't in my past or future."

"Sure it is. You just haven't met the right man."

"I could meet the most wonderful man on this earth and I still wouldn't marry."

Odd talk for an attractive young woman, though he shouldn't be surprised. This was, after all, Paris. She was . . . different. "Don't you ever want to have children?"

"I don't need a husband for that."

What the hell? "How old are you?"

"Nineteen."

"And your brothers?"

"Thirty-two, thirty, twenty-seven, and twenty-five."

Four *older* brothers. "Any one of them ever take the time to talk to you about how it works between a man and a woman?"

She pushed off his chest and studied him with an

arched brow. "You mean sex?"

She was either the most naïve or the worldliest woman he'd ever met. *Sex.* From her mouth to his ears, that three-letter-word worked as effectively as foreplay. He marveled at his instant erection, hoping she didn't notice, although how in the hell could she miss it? He felt as big and hard as a petrified mesquite. "I guess they also skipped the lecture on decorum."

She rolled her eyes. "I've been lectured on every subject imaginable."

"Then you should know better than to talk about relations in mixed company."

"You brought it up."

"Unfortunately."

She furrowed her brow. "We are talking about sex, right?"

"For the love of . . . Stop squirming," he ordered through clenched teeth.

"Your gun's poking me."

"That's not my gun."

"Then what . . . ?" Her eyes widened in realization. She had the nerve, Christ almighty, to grin. "Oh."

"Not another word," he warned in a gruff voice. If she commented further so help him he wouldn't be held accountable for his actions. He spied Maricopa Wells up ahead and kicked Buckshot into a gallop knowing it would distract the woman.

A brazen, cute-as-a kitten, accident-prone virgin. How in the Sam Hill was he supposed to turn her loose on the hell-raising men of Florence?

CHAPTER 7

We'll camp here for the night."

Paris surveyed the surrounding area while Josh dismounted. Sand. Rocks. Shrubs and cactus. Not a glimpse of civilization. Illuminated by a brilliant full moon, the desert terrain struck her as lonely and bleak. The eerie howl of a distant animal augmented the ghostly scenario. If she weren't so blasted exhausted, she'd be spooked. "Are we lost?"

"No." He sounded amused that she would even suggest the notion.

"We're going to sleep out in the open?"

"Yes."

"Why?"

"It's a surprise."

She wasn't in the mood for guessing games, but she was less eager to spend another minute in the saddle. She was beyond bone tired, and weary of holding her body rigid in an effort to avoid physical contact with her companion. "So long as it involves solid earth and a blanket."

He smiled kindly, squeezed her thigh. "Come on down."

"Gladly." Muscles screaming, she slid from the saddle. Her legs buckled like an accordion.

Josh scooped her up before she hit the ground and deposited her on a nearby boulder. "Rub some feeling back into those legs, walk around. The longer you sit, the more they'll cramp." She caught a glimpse of concern in his gaze—although it could have been annoyance—before he turned his attention to hobbling his horse.

She massaged her right thigh, focusing on their assuredly uncomfortable sleeping arrangements. Josh had been especially prickly since she'd slipped and mentioned the advertisement. Could that be the reason he'd bypassed the last station? "Why didn't we spend the night at Maricopa Wells? Was it that important to push on? Are you that desperate to get rid of me?"

"Were you that desperate to sleep on Leroy's cot?"

She wrinkled her nose. "You have a point." Though hospitable, the stationmaster looked and smelled as though he hadn't bathed in months. No telling when he'd last washed his blankets. She had to admit the way he'd fussed over her had given her the willies. Better to brave the great outdoors than Leroy Mink. Besides, it's not as if she'd never slept outside. When they were little, she and Boston frequently slept under the stars. It was one of her fondest memories. They'd stare up at the glittering sky and talk about their dreams. His dreams were numerous and seemed to alter weekly, but hers was always the same. She wanted to make her papa proud. Out of all of her brothers, she expected Boston would be the least irritated with her for trying to make that happen. Still, there'd be the dickens to pay when he and Rome caught up with her. At least she assumed it would be the two of them. Athens had the boys and London had the theater. They wouldn't just up and desert their responsibilities, would they? She cringed at the thought of all four brothers storming the Desert Moon.

Anxious, she pushed off of the boulder and tested her wobbly legs. Weak, but working. Keeping an eye out for snakes, she circled the boulder to stretch her calves and thighs. A cool breeze whispered across the rugged land, making her teeth chatter. The temperature had dropped with the sun. Grimy, chilled, and exhausted, she'd give anything for a hot bath. She'd spent the last three days making due with rainwater sponge baths compliments of the relay stations. Given Leroy's filthy state, she wondered if he even owned a rain barrel.

Swiping her sleeve over her dusty face, she watched as Josh tended to Buckshot, mesmerized by the man's moonlit form. Her gaze roamed over his broad shoulders, strong back and narrow waist as he removed the bedroll and saddlebags. She smiled when she un-cinched the saddle and lowered it to the ground, giving her an admirable view of his backside. He was a striking man, head to toe, front and back.

He turned unexpectedly and caught her staring.

Mortified, she braced herself for an arrogant remark, but he simply massaged the back of his neck then set to gathering dried brush. She eagerly pitched in, determined to keep naughty thoughts at bay. It proved a difficult task what with their shoulders and hands brushing time and again as they reached for the same tinder. By the time they'd built the small fire she felt as jumpy as a cat in a room full of rockers.

Kneeling beside him, she spread her hands in front of the flames. She wasn't sure if they trembled because she was cold or nervous. She wasn't sure of anything just now. Since meeting this man, she hadn't been herself. Fighting mental and physical exhaustion, she glanced sideways at him, wondering about his surprise. Should she be concerned? After all they were alone, which was highly inappropriate, yet her stomach quivered with excitement rather than dread.

The flames crackled and glowed, shedding golden light on his exquisite features. Foster's *Beautiful Dreamer* blared in her ears and she nearly swooned. *Why* did he have to be so handsome? Why did she have to be smitten? She ached to throw her arms around his neck and to kiss him till her lips hurt, but he was dead set against kissing and she wasn't fond of rejection. Hugging her knees to her chest, she bowed her head and hummed a verse of *Turkey in the Straw*. Anything to drown out Foster's romantic ballad.

Comforted by the fire's warmth, her limbs grew heavy, the music in her head fading to a distant drone. She wasn't aware that she was falling asleep until Josh gave her a gentle shake. "Not yet, kid." He grasped her hand and pulled her to her feet. "Come on."

Jerked out of her dozy state, she stumbled alongside him as they picked their way through a precarious path of cactus and rocks. "Where are we going?"

"It's a surprise." He tugged her to a stop.

Paris blinked, squinted in the direction he pointed, and blinked again. "Is it a mirage?"

"Nope."

"But a lake? In the desert?"

"Hot springs."

That explained the mist rolling off of the shimmering pool of water. It looked . . . magical. A leisurely bath in a hot spring? A chance to soak away the desert dust

as well as her aches and pains? He may as well have presented her with brand new, state-of-the-art piano!

"The springs are famous in these parts," he said,
leading her closer. "Rumor has it these waters soften
the skin and soothe the nervous system. Does wonders
for stiff muscles."

Appreciative tears stung her eyes. How could he
be so infuriating one moment and so thoughtful the
next? She turned to thank him, but her voice stuck in
her throat.

"This was supposed to make you happy."

"I am happy." And confused. She'd survived nineteen years without ever once being seriously attracted
to a man. Why now? As if pursuing her papa's dream
wasn't challenging enough, now she had to contend with
all these physical yearnings and desires? It was as if she
were being tested . . . or punished. Was this some sort
of karmic payback for defying her brothers?

Josh caressed her cheek, cursing the queer tickle
in his throat, the erratic beating of his heart, and the
damned circumstances. What was it about this girl?
Strong yet vulnerable. Infuriating yet intriguing. He
studied her sweet face, that sassy mouth, and marveled
that he'd kept himself in check all day.

Giving in to pent-up desire, he pulled her into his
arms and indulged in a lingering kiss. His pulse spiked
when she wrapped her arms around his neck and melted

against him.

She'd make as good a wife as any.

Easing back, he soaked in her moon-drenched face, his heart hammering against his chest. He knew what he had to do, had decided for certain back at Maricopa Wells after witnessing Leroy Mink's blatant lust. He just didn't know how to approach the subject.

He tugged at her shirt collar. "Take off your clothes."

She slapped away his hand. "Excuse me?"

Well, damn, that hadn't come out right. "I'll fetch your soap. Take off your clothes and get in the water." Needing to collect his thoughts, he set off for camp. "I won't be long."

He quickened his pace not wanting to leave her alone any longer than necessary. She had an uncanny knack for getting into trouble which was the main reason he'd finally succumbed to Fedderman's phantom nagging.

That and her opera house revelation. He'd be damned if he'd leave her at the mercy of a smarmy saloon operator and his drunken, randy patrons. As soon as they got to Florence he'd track down a bible-thumper and figure out the rest from there.

He heard a splash and relaxed. Good thing she worked fast. Seeing her naked would surely snap what little control he had left.

He rifled through his saddlebag in search of the wildcat's soap. Meanwhile his thoughts strayed south.

If she was half as enthusiastic about lovemaking as she was about kissing, she'd burn up a man's bed. Maybe marrying an impetuous crazy woman wouldn't be *all* bad, so long as he checked his heart at the church door.

Snagging the bar of soap, he lifted it to his nose and sniffed. Lilacs. A scent favored by his mother. A gentle woman who'd died of consumption when he was twelve. Broken hearted, his father had drunk himself to death not long after.

Another advantage to marrying Paris. Love had nothing to do with it.

Clutching the soap, he walked back to the spring, pausing a few feet from the edge to admire the magnificent view. Only her head was visible, surrounded by an ethereal mist, her petite body hidden in the depths of the rippling water. She hummed a haunting melody and smiled up at the moon. Lulled by her siren song, he fantasized about smoothing his hands over her slick, bare curves. Breasts. Hips. Thighs. Envisioned kissing her, seducing her, claiming her wild spirit.

His knees wobbled.

Lust, he told himself as he felt the world shift. Safe and simple lust.

Paris glanced away from the moon, her latest composition dying mid-verse when she spied Josh standing near the lapping edge of the springs. "Oh!" Her cheeks flooded with embarrassment. Instead of fighting the dangerous attraction, she'd been fantasizing about his hands, his mouth, the way he'd suckled her tongue. "How long have you been there?"

"Not long."

"Did you find the soap?"

"I did." He passed the bar back and forth from hand to hand as though stalling. "How's the water?"

"Divine." Between his heated kiss and the magical spring, her body felt blissfully relaxed. Her mood oddly calm. He, on the other hand, looked miserable. She studied his rigid posture and expression. Had the journey been taxing on his body as well? Being a man, and a stubborn one at that, he'd no doubt suffer in silence. Would he turn her down if she invited him in for a soothing swim? Given their mutual attraction, dare she be that reckless?

Life experience inspires passionate prose.

She smacked her palm against the side of her head. *Shut up, Emily.*

"Water in your ear?"

"Mmm." She swiped her wet hair out of her face and assessed the situation. The spring was wide and deep. They could soak on opposite sides. Meanwhile, maybe she'd get a glimpse of his bare chest. Look, but don't touch, she told herself. Surely that would be inspiration enough. Her skin prickled in nervous anticipation. "Are you going to bring that soap to me?"

"Better I should toss it."

"It's dark. What if I miss?"

He leaned forward. "Swim closer."

So much for being subtle. "For goodness sake, Josh. Come in for a swim."

He shifted his stance. "Not a smart idea."

"Three long days on the trail and you're telling me you don't have any aches?"

"Oh, I have an ache."

"Then you'll benefit from a soak in the hot springs."

"I'd benefit from a swim in a cold lake."

She started to respond then shut her mouth as the words sunk in. She'd overheard London make a similar remark to Rome after catching one of Victoria Kensington's theatrical performances. Her oldest brother fancied the British actress. Not knowing Paris was listening, Rome had cast an obscene comment referring to London's private parts.

She thought back on Josh's physical state when she'd been sitting on his lap. The memory filled her with mixed emotions. Curiosity, pleasure, trepidation, but mostly an odd sense of power. If she was going to experience life, it felt good to be somewhat in control. Blaming Emily for her sudden boldness, she cleared her throat and waved him in. "Don't let a little thing like that stop you."

He chuckled, a low rumble in his chest that sent a

delicious shiver down her spine. "There's nothing little about it, darlin'."

Her eyes widened and her tongue got all tied. "Really? I mean . . . that is . . . we're just talking about a friendly swim, right?"

"Are we?"

Was she? She wrung her hands under the water, growing more flustered by the minute. She wanted him to take advantage of the soothing waters. She did. But if she was honest with herself, she also wanted him to take advantage of *her*. She'd been fantasizing about him all day, her curiosity piqued to a fever pitch. She shrugged. "We're both adults."

"That we are." He grumbled something to the stars, swiped off his Stetson and tossed it and the soap to the ground. Quick as lightning, he shucked his boots, holster, and shirt.

"I, um, should probably turn around," she stammered, entranced by his spectacular chest and arms. "Or at least close my eyes," she squeaked as he went for the buttons of his pants. She swiped her hand over her perspiring brow as he stripped. "Oh, my." The moon shone as bright as the noonday sun illuminating his form in all its naked glory.

He leaned over to scoop up her soap. "I thought you were going to close your eyes."

"I thought you'd be wearing unmentionables." She

watched him wade into the water, reminding herself that she'd skinny dipped with her brothers when she was four. Only she wasn't four and he wasn't her brother. He was . . . a work of art. Broad shoulders. Sculptured chest. Hard stomach. Hard thighs. Hard . . . She tempered a squeal of shock by submerging herself in the springs.

When she came up for air, he was standing next to her, his lower half safely concealed beneath the water line. His wondrous chest glistened with droplets of water. Forcing her gaze upward she focused on his face. Her mouth raced ahead of her brain. "You're beautiful."

He smiled at that. "Sunsets are beautiful. Women are beautiful. Men? Not beautiful, hon."

She begged to differ, at least where he was concerned, but she didn't argue. If the moon had any sympathy, it would disappear behind the clouds and save her from making any further observations.

"Turn around."

With her back to him, she wouldn't be tempted to comment on his physical attributes. "Good idea." She swirled around and paddled toward the middle of the spring, willing the magical waters to do something about her suddenly out-of-whack nervous system.

He nabbed her by the waist and hauled her back. "Speaking of unmentionables . . ."

She'd been too shy to strip completely, retaining her bloomers and chemise. "They needed washing," she explained lamely, her insides seizing when he buried his hands in her hair. He massaged her scalp in a slow, sensual motion. She blinked. "You're washing my hair?"

"Do you mind?"

"No. I . . ." Her mind went blank as his hands slid to her neck, over her shoulders and down both arms. Goosebumps prickled her exposed flesh. Her legs quivered and her arms went limp. Holding her steady, he massaged her weary muscles, shifting the soap from one hand to the other while working his own special magic.

She closed her eyes, giving over to the glorious sensation, happy that she'd shunned propriety. His touch was everything she'd dreamed of, well worth the risk to her reputation. Not that she was worried overly much as they were utterly alone in a godforsaken desert.

Her heart soared with an empowering sense of freedom, urging her to embrace the moment. New and powerful sensations pummeled any lingering reservations. The night air chilled her face, and yet she felt so hot. So deliciously languid. Sighing, she allowed him to pull her flush against his sinewy front. She felt his male hardness pressing into her backside. Felt his hands skimming her breasts. Felt the soap bounce off of her thigh, landing near her foot. She felt . . . "Sick. I think I'm sick."

His hands stilled. "Your stomach?"

"Actually, it's more like an ache. And it's . . . lower."

She felt him smile against her neck. "How much lower?"

She opened her mouth, but nothing came out.

"Show me."

She couldn't. She shouldn't. But phantom Emily was screaming in her ear, egging her on, not to mention her own restraint was non-existent. There was *definitely* something in this desert air! Dizzy with yearning, she clasped his hand and pushed it down the front of her soaked chemise. Lower . . . lower . . .

He pressed his hand over her nether region. "Here?"

She gasped, shocked, but curiously pleased. "Yes."

"Want me to ease that ache, darlin'?"

She swallowed hard. *Experience life.* "Yes."

He loosened the ties on her drawers and slid his palm beneath the thin fabric, his hand like fire on her bare flesh. "Are you sure?"

No! "Yes!" She gasped as his fingers caressed her intimate folds. "Yes!" Tensed when he applied pressure to the center of her ache and rubbed. Waves of sheer ecstasy washed over her, overwhelming her, causing her blood to burn, her limbs to quake. "Oh, Josh. I . . . I . . . "

He increased the pressure as well as the pace. "Let yourself go, honey." His mouth grazed her ear.

Let herself go? She was coming apart! She grasped his forearms and squeezed. Her legs quivered. Her heart pounded as her body tightened and pulsed. "I can't breathe."

He sucked on her earlobe.

And just like that she exploded into a million pieces. Those pieces shattered into smaller pieces, raining down on her like stardust in her mind's eye. Exhausted, her knees gave way. If it weren't for Josh's strong embrace, she'd slip under the water and drown for sure. "No wonder Lydia Ivy purred."

He laughed softly. "What?"

"Nothing." She gasped for an even breath, marveled at an odd sense of relief. "That was . . . " her sluggish mind groped for the appropriate word, " . . . amazing."

Josh smiled, thinking very near the same thing. He'd barely touched her. She'd peaked faster, more intensely, than any woman he'd ever pleasured, and suddenly all he could think about was getting her in bed. "Actually, the amazing part comes later."

"When?"

"Soon."

"How soon?"

"As soon as we're hitched."

There was an ominous moment of silence followed by a shriek. She whirled around to face him. "What did you say?"

He probably should have phrased it a little differently. Maybe in the form of a question. Although knowing her views on marriage, he wouldn't have liked her answer.

Better to give her no choice. "As soon as we're married." He ignored her horrified expression, assuring himself he could wait that long.

"I told you I don't believe in marriage!"

"I don't expect that matters now."

"Just because you . . . It's not like we . . . " She slapped him.

He ignored his stinging cheek, but held her at arm's length, just in case her knee got into the act. "Just so I'm straight, was that for pleasuring you or proposing?"

"Proposing, of course."

"Of course." He should've known this wouldn't be easy. Grasping her shoulders, he gave her a little shake. "What am I going to do with you?"

She wrenched out of his hold and stormed toward dry land. "What you agreed to do. Drop me off in Florence. That was the plan."

He was hot on her wet heels. "The plan's changed."

"Not my plan. I have a dream to fulfill."

"So do I. Maybe we can help each other out."

"Not if it involves wedding vows." She snatched up her boots.

"Give me those." He yanked the shoes from her hands, turned them upside down, and shook.

"What are you doing?"

"Checking for scorpions."

"Oh."

Frowning, he handed back her boots. What would she do without him? "Dammit, woman, you *will* marry me."

"I can't." She jammed her bare feet inside her boots while suspiciously eyeing her trousers.

Josh picked up the jeans and shirt, shook them out then passed those to her as well. "Give me one good reason."

She clutched her balled-up clothes to her chest. "I'd make a lousy wife."

"That goes unsaid."

"I can't sew."

"We'll manage."

"*Or* cook."

"I'll teach you," he snapped, donning his pants and boots.

"It won't help. I'm telling you I'm no good in the kitchen."

"So, you can make up for it in the bedroom."

Her mouth dropped open. "You're despicable." Nose in the air, she turned and marched toward camp.

All right. He deserved that. She was, despite her fiery demeanor, respectable. He'd known since their first kiss that he was dealing with a virgin. A naïve hellcat ripe for seduction or rape. In a region where the men greatly outnumbered the women, her chances of escaping the territory with her innocence intact was pitiful to none. Cursing, he snatched up his shirt, holster, and hat, and set after her. She needed a protector. He needed a wife. That was that.

"I'm not marrying you!" she shouted over her shoulder for good measure.

"That's what you think," he grumbled under his breath. Hellfire, he could feel the gray hairs sprouting.

He found her pacing around the fire, her trail-ragged clothes clutched to her chest, her wet chemise and drawers plastered to her goose-pimpled skin, leaving nothing to the imagination. She looked panicked, flushed, and enticing as hell.

"I should have slept with Leroy," she railed in a trembling voice. "I mean . . . you know what I mean!"

He stalked past her, resisting the urge to throw her down and to take her then and there. "Take off your clothes."

"Stop saying that!"

He rooted through his saddlebags, pulled out a clean shirt, and tossed it to her. "You'll catch your death. Take off those wet clothes and put on my shirt. Don't worry. I won't look." Lord knows he'd seen too much already. Christ, he ached to touch her again. To taste her. Bed her. His entire being quaked with restrained desire.

"But—"

"Just do it," he snapped.

"Fine."

He turned his back and set to laying out the bedroll. It was either that or turn her over his knee. He'd never struck a woman in his life, but, by God, Paris frazzled his patience worse than a two-year old. Maybe she didn't run away. Maybe her brothers kicked her out. He could damn near imagine her driving them to it and could almost forgive them.

"I'm finished," she said in a small voice.

Wondering at her contrite tone, he turned, hands on hips. He swallowed hard at the sight of her wearing his shirt, her bare legs visible from the knees down. The clingy chemise was almost preferable.

"I'm sorry for losing my temper," she said, braiding the front section of her wet hair. "Considering what we, how you . . . " She nibbled her lower lip. "Offering marriage, well, it was very noble of you."

He clenched his jaw hard enough to crush walnuts. He felt far from noble just now, imagining her buck naked under his shirt.

"But it's not necessary. No one need know what we . . . how you . . . " She gestured toward the springs, her cheeks bright red. "What happened back there."

He tugged possessively at her shirt collar. "*I* know."

She dipped her chin in embarrassment. "Maybe you could forget."

"Not likely." He sank down on the bedroll, bringing her with him.

"I can't sleep with you," she said when he stretched out on his back.

"Yes, you can." He pulled her flush against him and covered her with a blanket, hoping she was too drained to argue.

She punched him in the shoulder. A coyote howled and she changed her tune right quick, latching onto to him real tight. "All right," she groused. "But only because there's one bedroll between the two of us. And because it's cold and we should probably keep each other warm. Just don't get any funny notions."

Kind of difficult with her lying half-naked in his arms. "Such as?"

"Such as thinking my sleeping with you means anything. I won't marry you. I can't."

"So you said. I'm still waiting to hear a good reason."

She yawned. "I made a promise."

"Not to get married?"

"To reach for the stars."

He didn't know what to make of that. "Is this about succeeding where your mama failed?"

"She didn't fail. She didn't try." She snuggled closer, her limbs heavy and her words slurred from exhaustion. "She chose marriage instead of fame."

He frowned down at the top of her head. "Fame is fleeting, angel. And rarely worth the heartache."

"I don't have a choice."

"Why not?"

"It's my destiny."

He smoothed his hands over her face, pondering her whimsical declaration. Her steady breathing and heavy limbs signaled that she'd fallen asleep. However, her slumber was far from restful. Her fingers drummed softly on his chest. She moaned, snatches of words coming out in a slurred drone. " . . . by chance their lips did meet . . . both would fight . . . whose heart . . . "

He realized suddenly that she was singing and playing the piano in her sleep. Her music—an all-mighty opponent. He preferred an in-the-flesh rival. But no, matter. In the end, he'd prove the victor.

"Brace yourself, honey," he whispered to the sleeping minx in his arms. "Our dreams are about to collide."

CHAPTER 8

Florence.

Under normal circumstances, Paris would have appreciated the lush landscape. The surrounding mountains. The trees. The grass. So much green after days of brown. But circumstances were far from normal.

She was sharing a saddle with a delusional man. Josh truly expected her to marry him. What's worse, the notion was vaguely appealing. This was all Emily's fault. She didn't explain all the possible ramifications and consequences of *experiencing life*!

Sleeping in his arms last night had been a dreadful mistake. Waking in his arms had been her heart's doom. With her cheek pressed against his bare chest, their legs and arms entangled, all sorts of wicked thoughts had lazed through her sleepy head. She'd opened her eyes, and oh my, even with his hair tousled and his clothes rumpled he stole her breath away and filled her heart with song. But it was the feel of his hands upon her face—gentle, yet possessive—the intensity of his gaze when he searched her eyes—puzzled, yet entranced—that did her in. With Josh, she didn't feel like a musical freak, or a fragile little sister. With Josh she felt like a woman.

Her skin tingled when she remembered the way he'd pleasured her in the hot springs. She shouldn't have allowed him the intimacy, what's worse she shouldn't have enjoyed it. She certainly should not be yearning for an encore. He'd promised her *amazing*. Never had she wanted anything so badly.

Except for fame.

My little girl is destined for greatness. Her papa's decree echoed in her ears, and as always, made it harder to breathe. The pressure to make a name for herself, to make her mark on this world, was suffocating at times and yet she'd never once questioned her goal.

Until recently.

Not that she was seriously considering Josh's bungled proposals. He'd ordered instead of asked, and wasn't a man supposed to get down on one knee, or give a girl flowers, or something? No, indeed, she was not getting hitched. She'd wanted success a whole lot longer than the thrill of his touch. Still, this morning when he'd started talking about making babies, reminding her of her adorable nephew and niece, she'd wavered. To think that he had that kind of power over her. *Nibble my ear, and I'll say yes to anything.* That's what really had her in a snit.

Frustrated, she'd blurted out that she didn't understand why intimacy and marriage had to go hand in hand to which he'd responded, "You're giving me a headache."

First she was a pain in his neck, now she affected his head.

Maybe that's why he'd finally fallen silent on the subject. Maybe he'd concluded that, for the sake of his health, the sooner he ditched her, the better.

That thought should have cheered her. Instead, panic jittered through her veins. She straightened in the saddle and tried to distract herself with Florence's unique charm. The town's streets were shaded on either side by rows of cottonwoods. At their roots, along the sidewalks, flowed babbling streams, suggesting there was a river nearby. She noted a schoolhouse, a church, two hotels, various restaurants and numerous saloons, and wondered suddenly how Chance would compare in size.

Chance.

The gravity of her situation weighed mightily on her already heavy heart. She'd lied to Josh, naming Florence as her final destination. Any minute now he'd ask her where he should drop her specifically. Then what? She chewed her bottom lip and braided the top portion of Buckshot's mane.

Josh leaned forward, overwhelming her with the masculine heat of his big body. "Nervous?"

Warm breath teased her earlobe and her eyes nearly rolled back in her head. "What makes you think that?"

He stopped dead center of the bustling street, covered her nimble fingers with his callused palm, and gave them a calming squeeze. "What's the name of M.B.'s gurdy?"

Her heart thundered in her ears, the warmth and strength of his grip causing her stomach to flutter with a thousand butterflies. She hated that he could make her world tilt with a simple touch. She whipped around, intending to blast him for complicating her life, and made the mistake of looking into those seductive eyes. Her heart skipped and her thoughts evaporated. She cupped his sinfully attractive face and kissed him full on the mouth.

He sat stock still, no doubt shocked by her boldness, allowing her a brief moment of exquisite control. She caught his bottom lip between her teeth, suckled ever so gently, and then, just as he'd done to her last night, teased open his mouth with her tongue. He groaned, deepening the kiss, and causing a blessed heat to flicker in her belly. Ignited, she bested his passion, determined to make a lasting impression. This was, after all, goodbye.

A wolf whistle pierced the air, followed by applause. Josh broke away from her with a muttered curse.

They'd attracted a crowd.

Uh oh. She hurriedly slid from the saddle, her knees buckling when her feet hit the ground. Was she ever going to master riding? Luckily, Josh caught her upper arm, holding her steady.

"What are you doing?" he demanded in a raspy voice.

"You can leave me here," she answered, a bit breathless.

"The hell I can."

She backed away on wobbly legs, excusing herself when she bumped into a group of gawking, weathered cowboys. They smiled and winked. Blushing, she looked back to Josh. He scowled at the men, causing them to quickly disperse.

"I'll just pick up my carpetbag," she rambled, edging near the stage depot. "After that I'll meet with my employer, then get settled somewhere, and then, well . . . I don't want to hold you up and well, this is Florence and you did say once here you'd go your way and I'd go mine. If I could just have my sheet music—"

"Not so fast." He dismounted, roped Buckshot to a hitching rail then bore down on Paris, dark eyes flashing.

"About that kiss . . . " She stepped onto the raised boards. "I'm sorry. I know I shouldn't have . . . I just wanted to say . . . "

"Yes?" He backed her against the outer wall of the post office.

"Thank you," she croaked. "I just wanted to say, thank you. For," she fluttered a hand, "everything."

"You're welcome. What's the name of M.B's gurdy?"

She blinked up at him, cheeks blazing. Why was he being so persistent? Didn't he understand this was it? The end? Goodbye? Why was he making it so difficult? "Honestly, I don't want to bother you—"

"I'm already bothered." He braced his arms on either side of her and dropped his face close to hers. "What's the name of the opera house?"

She placed her palms against his chest and shoved. He didn't budge and she didn't remove her hand, marveling how their hearts pounded in tandem. "People are staring," she whispered, fidgeting under his intense regard. "*Men* are staring. They're going to get the wrong idea."

"You should have thought of that before you kissed me in the middle of the street. What's the name of that opera house?"

"I'm not going to the opera house just now." If she didn't escape, and fast, she was going to snap. She wanted nothing more than to come clean—as he'd pointed out, she wasn't very good at lying—but if she told him the truth, he'd no doubt insist on escorting her to Chance. As they couldn't seem to keep their hands off of each other, and as he seemed to think that constituted a walk down the aisle, it didn't strike her as a smart idea. "As I was saying, I'll wait here for my bag—"

"Then you'll be waiting all night."

"Excuse me?"

"The next stage won't arrive until tomorrow."

"Oh." She hadn't thought of that. Defeated, she let out a weary sigh.

"You're exhausted and you look like you caught too much sun." With an enigmatic look, he pushed off of the wall and tenderly grasped her elbow. "Let's get you settled in a hotel."

She didn't argue. She couldn't leave for Chance until her bag arrived, and after a week on the trail, the prospect of a clean, soft bed was too tempting to pass up. Every muscle in her body ached, including her heart. That goodbye kiss had been a stupid mistake. Instead of satisfying a fierce yearning, it only intensified her misery. She wanted more, and she couldn't have more because she couldn't have Josh. She was headed for the Desert Moon and he was headed . . . she didn't know where he was headed. For someone so intent on knowing her life, he'd been suspiciously quiet about his own. Curious, she wondered aloud, "Why did you turn in your badge?"

"My uncle died and left me his business, which entailed shucking my old life for a new one."

His curt tone deterred her from probing too deeply. "I'm sorry about your uncle," she said, heart thumping. She'd yet to recover from Mr. Wiggins's passing and now this. She didn't want to pursue the sad subject, but wanted to lend her support. "Were you close?"

"He was like a father to me."

"What about your real father?"

"He died when I was a boy."

She cringed at the bitterness in his voice, and though she yearned to comfort him with a hug, she refrained. As he'd pointed out, she'd already made a public spectacle of herself. Instead, she patted his hand. "I miss my papa, too."

Before he could comment, two scrawny men clad in dusty overalls staggered out of a saloon, directly into her path. The bowlegged man openly leered. The bearded man smoothed his filthy hands over his greasy hair and belched. "Hey, pretty lady. My name's Harley Fox. What's yours?"

Josh glared at the man. "Get lost, Harley." He cocked a thumb at his friend. "You, too."

The puny drunks took one look at Josh's imposing stance and stumbled over each other hitting the street.

Paris frowned up at her self-appointed protector. "You didn't have to be rude."

"Shooting them would have been rude." Stone-faced, he nabbed her hand and hastened her down the walk.

Florence offered visitors two hotels, the Elliott House, and the less imaginatively named *Florence*. Business boomed for both of the hospitable establishments. Paris had visions of sleeping in a stable when the Florence informed them there was no room at the inn. She feared they'd fare no better at the equally bustling Elliott, so she was relieved when Josh sauntered toward her brandishing a key. Maybe once she was settled in her room he'd finally leave her alone. A bubble of hysteria rose in her throat, her heart heavy at the thought of never seeing him again, even though she knew it was for the best. Breathing deep, she assured herself that she was simply wrung out from the week's events. Once Joshua Grant was out of the picture, her life would go back to normal. Her dream, her one true focus.

"Room number nine," he said, squiring her up the stairs and down the hall.

Freedom, she thought. Relief. Sanity. She nabbed the key out of his hand. "Thank you for everything. Good luck with . . . whatever." She waved a sloppy farewell over her shoulder as she limped ahead, wincing with each aching step. She didn't look back. The prospect of saying goodbye for good was unexpectedly devastating.

Heart in her throat, she stopped at the room marked number nine and stuck the key in the lock. It jammed. She wiggled and shimmied the key, but to no avail. "Darn." She dropped her forehead to the door, fought the overwhelming urge to cry . . . and lost.

His hand closed over hers. A second later, the door swung open and he swept her up in his powerful arms. The same arms that had comforted her after Mr. Wiggins's death. The arms that had kept her safe when Buckshot reared. Without a word, he carried her across the threshold and gently laid her on the plump bed.

She blinked up at him through a bleary haze of tears. "I don't know what's wrong with me." She hiccupped and sniffled, dragging her sleeve across her running nose. "I don't usually cry this much. Honest."

"You've had one hell of a week." He placed his hand on her cheek. "You're wrung out and overheated."

"I'm fine."

He raised an unconvinced brow, tugged off her boots and covered her with a quilt.

His tender actions only made her cry harder.

"I know you're anxious to see M.B.," he said, "but it can wait until tomorrow. You'll feel better after a sound night's sleep."

She hiccupped and nodded. It would have to wait. M.B. was in Chance. Her anxiety mounted at the thought of her stage debut. She swiped at a new flood of tears, feeling like a blubbering idiot. "You should probably go," she croaked. "We shouldn't be in a hotel room alone. It's inappropriate."

"So was that public display."

"I didn't want you to forget me."

"Trust me, sweetheart. That's impossible." He braced his hands on either side of her head and leaned down. His gaze burned into hers, searching, prying, making her feel exposed and vulnerable. "What exactly is your dream?"

Her heart drummed as she grappled for a sane thought. "To fulfill my papa's dream."

He didn't flinch at her cryptic answer, nor did he relent. "Is he the one who told you you're destined to become a musical actress?"

She swallowed hard, remembering a similar conversation with her brothers. She'd bared her heart and they'd ripped off her head. Mostly, they'd cursed papa. She wasn't up to a repeat performance. She merely nodded.

"Shouldn't passion play into one's destiny?"

Why was he being so dense? "I thought we'd settled this. I can't marry you, Josh."

He smoothed her hair from her tear-streaked face and smiled. "I'm talking about your songwriting."

"Oh." Embarrassed, she tried to focus on his words rather than his tempting mouth. "What makes you think I don't long to sing and dance in front of a sold-out house?"

He brushed his lips across hers, just enough to beckon the seductive groan of a cello. "I'm beginning to understand how you tick."

Heaven's citizens congregated in her mind to wag judgmental fingers. *I can't believe you invited Goofy Garrett. If only you'd praised God instead of Boston's blueberry pancakes. Incorrigible snoop. Musical freak.* Her voice trembled. "No one understands how I tick."

"Maybe I'm special."

"I don't want you to be special." But even as she said it she knew it was too late. A haunting melody took root. Lyrics budded.

A love song.

"This can't be happening." She averted her gaze in an effort to harden her heart. "You have to go. It's for the best. Honest. You don't want me. I'm a danger to your health."

After a long moment, he straightened and headed for the door. "I could always track down your brothers."

Panicked, she shot upright. "Please don't."

"Why not?"

"They'd kill me."

CHAPTER 9

What do you mean it burned down?" Blood pumping, Josh had swung by the front desk to ask the innkeeper the whereabouts of the nearest bible-thumper. In the next breath, he'd asked about M.B.

First things first.

By the time he was done with the gurdy owner, Paris wouldn't have a job. He refused to feel guilty. Songwriting was one thing. Singing in a gambling hall for the benefit of gun-wielding drunks was just plain begging for trouble. He understood her motivation. How could he fault her for living another man's dream when he was doing the very same thing? Difference was he had a strong sense of self. He knew his purpose in life. Whether he was riding with the Rangers or dealing

Faro at the Desert Moon, he'd keep the peace. He was a lawman same as Paris was a songwriter. Only she didn't have faith in her talent, didn't know her own heart. He blamed her damn brothers.

They'll kill me.

Bastards.

"I mean there was a fire," Mr. Loss said, jolting him out of his mental rant. "A big one. Wasn't owned by an M.B., but it did feature the best in entertainment." He glanced over Josh's shoulder. "Ain't that so, Sheriff?"

Well, hell. Josh turned, knocking elbows with the impeccably dressed man who'd claimed the innkeeper's attention. Sporting a black frock coat and matching plainsman hat, Seth Wright had two inches on his own six feet. The blond-haired, green-eyed-lawman possessed an eye-for-an-eye reputation, a flair for fashion, and a drier-than-dirt sense of humor. Twice he and Josh had vied for the same dove. Twice Seth had won. According to the sporting ladies of the greater Southwest, Seth Wright was a looker and a lover of the first water. Not that he gave a gopher's ass. "Seth."

"Josh." Sporting a lopsided grin, the lawman thrust out his big hand in greeting. "What are you doing back here?"

"Business of sorts." He gripped his friend's hand in a warm shake.

"Legal matters," Seth ventured. "Don't tell me Niles

is contesting the will?"

As far as he knew, his cousin had yet to learn the terms. Seth had tracked down the professional card-sharp at a gambling house in Phoenix to inform him of Mason's death. Niles acknowledged the wire but skipped the funeral and the reading of the will. Something about a lucky streak. "You mean he finally showed?"

"The day after you left." Seth snorted in disgust. "Man's slimier than the underside of riverbed rock."

He quirked a knowing eyebrow. "No need to be diplomatic on my account."

"In that case, your cousin's a snake. A cocky bastard with the morals of a pig. I take that back. Pigs have more morals." He shook his head. "How in the hell did the apple fall so far from the tree?"

Josh had an idea, but no proof. "Been asking myself that question for years." Taken in by Mason after his pa died, he'd had the displeasure of bunking with his cousin for a year. At twelve years old, he'd been convinced he was sleeping with the devil. How else could you describe a boy whose favorite pastimes included tying lit firecrackers to a steer's tail and picking off cats with his slingshot?

Two years Josh's senior, Niles had been hell-on-wheels since the day he'd learned to walk and had been rolling over his mother ever since. Short on patience and lacking maternal skills, Celia Burke gave up early on, letting her son run wild. Mason wasn't home enough to be a steady influence, but when he was around he did his best to drum morals into his only son. Futile as far as Josh was concerned since the boy was plain and simple a bad seed. He ran away a year later, much to Josh and Celia's relief. Mason tracked him down, but he didn't bring him back. Though he never outright said, Josh knew Mason had sadly concluded Niles a lost cause. "So he met with the lawyer?"

"Walked in smiling . . . "

"Walked out cussing a blue streak."

"Pretty much." Seth flattened his mouth. "He's up to no good, Josh."

Niles and trouble went hand in hand. Nothing new there. However, the concern in his friend's eyes piqued his interest. "Know that for a fact?"

"I do." Seth tucked his thumbs in his pockets. "Been meaning to follow up, but I'm knee deep in an investigation."

"The fire," Mr. Loss said, jumping back into the conversation. He'd been so quiet, Josh had forgotten he was there. "Sheriff suspects arson," he said, eyes twinkling. He braced his hairy-knuckled hands on the hotel's front desk. "So, have you two known each other long?"

Seth smiled, his emerald gaze glittering with brotherly affection. "Sheriff Grant and I go way back. Two years with the Arizona Rangers policing desperados along the Mexican Border. Another two with the Special Ranger Force trying to bring law and order to Texas." He glanced sideways at Josh. " Now *that* was a helluva challenge."

"Heck of a history," Loss said, duly impressed. "Arizona *and* Texas Rangers?"

Seth slapped Josh on the back. "Kicked some serious miscreant ass."

Josh glanced at the lawman, wondering at the colorful jaunt into the past. He wasn't the sort to brag. Maybe his friend wasn't keen on discussing his investigation in front of big-eared Loss. He winked at the innkeeper, cocked a thumb at his friend. "Seth was one of the best."

"Don't doubt it," Loss said. "He's one heck of a sheriff. Speaking of which, did I hear right? You're a sheriff too?"

He clenched his jaw. Knowing he wasn't the law anymore was difficult enough. Admitting it to Seth . . .

"Yeah, yeah, I know," Seth said, saving him the trouble. "Turned in your badge. Fedderman wired me." He shook his head. "If that don't take the rag off the bush."

"That cuz you're getting married?" Mr. Loss asked.

Seth's eyebrows shot up, disappearing under the low brim of his hat. "You're getting married?"

Now would be the perfect time to let Seth in on the *wife* stipulation. If Josh didn't marry, and soon, Mason's property would revert to Niles. Seth would understand his agenda, although he'd have plenty to say. Maybe that's why Josh kept his mouth shut. "It's complicated."

"Preacher Davis is out at the Jenkins Ranch," Mr. Loss explained. "Heard tell Bo Jenkins is on his deathbed."

"Bo's too stubborn to die," Seth told Loss then gaped at Josh. "God almighty. I just saw you nine days ago. You didn't say a word. When? Who?" He scraped his knuckles along his jaw. "Ah, hell. Don't tell me . . . "

"What?"

"Not Paris Garrett."

Josh frowned. "You mean, Getty."

"The girl you tangled with in Yuma? Piano girl?"

"That's the one." He reached around to massage a severe twinge in his neck, wondering how Seth knew Paris—and how *well* he knew Paris.

"Garrett," Seth repeated, shaking his head. "How the hell did you end up with her? According to Fedderman the two of you had words. You took off for Chance. She hopped the stage for Florence. He asked me to keep my eye on her once she got to town. A runaway, he said. When the stage didn't show today I figured it busted a wheel and got off schedule. Happens often enough."

Josh swept off his hat. "Moe Wiggins's heart gave out."

Mr. Loss clucked his tongue. "Well, that's plumb awful."

"Sorry to hear it," Seth said. "Moe was a good man." He squinted at Josh. "So what? You rescued Miss Garrett from the perils of the desert, offered her a ride, and somewhere along the way had the harebrained notion to get hitched?"

"That's the most romantic thing I have ever heard," Mr. Loss said, blowing his nose into a red kerchief.

Seth rolled his eyes. "Where is she, Josh?"

Not liking the tone, he set his hat on the desk and folded his arms over his chest. "Why?"

"Room number nine," Mr. Loss offered.

"This is damn awkward." Seth removed his hat, slapped it against his thigh. "I'm here to arrest that girl."

Josh glanced at the deserted stairs. Tuckered out as she was, Paris had most likely fallen asleep. Still, to be on the safe side, he grabbed his friend's elbow and dragged him across the hotel lobby, away from the stairs and the gossipy innkeeper. "Come again?"

"I'm not the only one Fedderman contacted. He came across an urgent telegram regarding a runaway, put two and two together, and immediately replied. The wires have been burning up for two days. This one came this morning." He pulled a telegram out of his coat pocket. "You might want to sit down."

"Just give me the damned thing." Josh unfolded the note and read. He was incredulous midway through. Seething by the end.

URGENT. KEEP PARIS UNDER
LOCK AND KEY. ON OUR WAY.
ROME GARRETT

Josh gnashed his teeth. No wonder she got agitated every time he brought up her brothers. "Son of a bitch."

"Dime novels love Rome Garrett, *and* his brother Boston." Seth reclaimed the telegram, folded it into a neat square then tucked it back in his pocket. "Couple of frontier heroes. Two of Wells Fargo's best. I can't believe you're mixed up with their sister."

"Neither can I." Josh didn't know which pounded harder, his heart or his head. Hoodwinked by a five-foot-two maverick. Needing some fresh air, he pushed past Seth, stepping out onto the hotel's wide veranda. He braced his hands on the railing, leaned forward, and breathed deep. Serenity, however, was not in the air.

The sun set low in the sky, signaling another day's end. Respectable folk, family folk were heading home. The night belonged to the gamblers, rowdies, and whores: the wild folk, the lonely folk. The kind of folk Rome and Boston Garrett tangled with on a daily basis. For sure and for certain the kind they didn't want their little sister mingling with. Which probably meant they didn't approve of her dream. Which was why she'd run away. He gripped the railing tighter. If he wasn't so all-fired ticked at her for misleading him, he'd actually admire her determination.

As for her brothers mistreating her, he wasn't sure what to think. Granted, two of the four were legends, but even legends have a dark side. And they *had* instructed Seth to toss her in jail.

Whatever the case, the pain in his neck had graduated to a royal pain in his ass. Albeit it a fetching pain. Sweet Jesus. Her kisses, her passion, her pretty little freckled face haunted his every thought.

Seth brushed past him and leaned back against the corner post. "So Miss Garrett," he said, hitching back his coat and withdrawing a cheroot from his vest pocket. "Is she—"

"Very."

"Did you—"

"No."

Seth struck a match and lit the slim cigar. "Too bad." He blew out a stream of heady smoke. "At least that would've been worth dying for."

"Meaning?"

"Heard about that kiss. Middle of Main Street. Ned Jasper said you steamed up his spectacles and he was standing twenty feet away."

"Took you long enough to bring it up."

"Took me this long to realize it was you." Seth furrowed his brow. "You've never been one for public displays."

"Yeah, well, there's a first time for everything."

"You compromised the Garretts' little sister, Josh. They're going to hunt you down and, guaran-damn-teed, you'll be shakin' hands with St. Peter two minutes after. What were you thinking?"

Thinking? Hell, she'd kissed him senseless. "They won't have to hunt. We'll be in Chance. Send them on."

Seth bumped up the brim of his wide-brimmed hat, the tip of his cheroot glowing in the dusk. "We?"

He turned and settled back against the railing. "She's coming with me."

"Now hold up," Seth said, pushing off the post. "Rome Garrett—"

"Wants you to hold her prisoner. I'll be damned if I'll let you lock her up for however long it takes them to get here."

"Give me some credit," the other man huffed, dropping the cigar, and crushing it under his boot. "Like I intended to chuck her in the calaboose."

"What *did* you intend?"

"To take her into custody."

"Over my dead body." It's not that he didn't trust his closest friend. The man treated women like European royalty. However, it was that very trait, coupled with his notable looks and sense of humor, that generally had women tripping all over themselves to win his favor. The thought of Paris falling prey to that natural

133

charm set his teeth on edge.

"Well, what do *you* intend?"

"To marry her." The fact that she kept fighting him on the matter rankled. Any other woman would've agreed in a heartbeat. Then again, Paris wasn't like any other woman.

"You didn't even know her real name until five minutes ago."

"Doesn't matter." He'd mentally discarded the eligible women of Florence as he'd already settled on Paris. He didn't want to examine his all-consuming need to protect her from the big, bad world. This union was beneficial to them both. Period.

"You love her?"

"No." He liked her, cared for her, sure as hell lusted after her, but he'd be damned if he'd allow himself to fall in love. Love twisted life into a confounding knot. "But, she loves me." Hence his ability to wrangle her into marriage with a guilt-free conscious.

"She tell you that?"

He thought about her uninhibited kisses, the besotted look in her eyes. For sure and certain, that girl wore her heart on her sleeve. "In a roundabout way."

"Uh huh. Like I was saying, I'm thinking it might be best if I keep an eye on her until her brothers get here. You can discuss marriage proper like with them."

Josh braced his hands low on his hips, his thumb

brushing the butt of his .45. He'd be damned if he'd let Paris's misguided quest, her brothers, or Seth stand in his way. "You don't want her," he said, lowering his voice to an ominous drawl. "She's *loco*."

"Crazy?"

"As a sheepherder." He glanced at the toe of his boot trying to focus on his plan, which despite the turn of events, hadn't changed. He needed a wife and she needed a protector. At least now he knew the truth, well, most of it anyway. "You know the name of every saloon operator in Florence?"

"Sure."

"Know an M.B.?"

"Can't say I do."

"What about the fella who ran the opera house that recently burned?"

"Arnold Tucker. A respectable proprietor with an impressive nose for fine entertainment. The Lucky Lady went up in flames around three in the morning last week. Two days after you left for Yuma." He frowned. "The day after Niles got into town."

Seth's implication was clear, though Josh couldn't wrap his mind around the charge. Niles was a mean cuss to be sure, but he couldn't imagine him burning down a building full of sleeping doves and performers. "Got motive? Proof?"

"No, on both counts, but hear this. Tucker loaded

up whatever he could salvage along with his prized employees, including doves, dealers, and entertainers, and relocated in Chance."

Josh digested that bit of news, stymied by Tucker's choice of locales. Chance wasn't even on the map. Population fifty-some, though growing daily as all boomtowns did. Still, why not Phoenix or Tucson or, hell, Prescott? "Nothing wrong with a little competition," Josh said, trying to harvest the root of Seth's suspicions.

"Except when your vindictive bastard of a cousin is part owner of that competition."

Pay dirt. "Niles went into business with Arnold Tucker?"

Seth nodded. "Used part of his inheritance to buy out the Mercantile. He provided the building. Tucker provided the rest. Heard they opened their doors night before last."

"That's what you meant when you said he was up to no good."

"Basically."

"Hmm."

"Hmm?" Seth braced one hand on the veranda's post, cocked his head. "What the hell does that mean?"

"It means I'll reserve comment until I speak with him." He'd learned long ago that things were rarely black and white. Though that's exactly how Seth saw the world.

"Lottie Evans broke both of her arms jumping out of a second floor window to escape that fire. If Niles was involved—"

"I'll let you know if I pick up on anything."

Seth grunted, definitely unappeased.

"Back to why I'm in town," Josh said, mentally juggling his problems. "You're positive you don't know anyone with the initials M.B.?"

"Milton Beane. He runs the livery. Mary Black. She's married to Vic Black."

"Never mind. Paris probably lied about the proprietor's name same as she lied about hers. She didn't want me to know her name, fearing I'd make the connection to her brothers. Didn't want me to know where she was heading in case I figured out who she was, assuming I'd inform her brothers. Which I would have if I had known who they were."

Seth scratched his forehead. "I'm confused."

"Welcome to my life."

Mr. Loss rushed the veranda, a mischievous gleam in his eye. He passed Josh his Stetson.

Josh thanked him.

Loss nodded but made no move to leave.

"Was there something else, Percy?" Seth asked.

"I thought, that is . . . " The man fiddled with his bow tie. "Not that it's any of my business . . . "

"Spit it out."

Loss adjusted his spectacles, cleared his throat. "Yes, well, *Mrs.* Loss just saw to it that a hot bath was delivered to room number nine for Miss Getty."

"Garrett," Seth corrected.

"Paris," Josh insisted, not wanting it to get back to her yet that he knew her real name.

Loss cleared his throat, obviously confused. "Yes, well, according to my wife, that young girl had been crying her eyes out."

Josh ignored Seth's steely glare. "Go on."

"Miss . . . Paris asked Mrs. Loss if she knew what time the next stage left for Chance."

Josh pushed his hat to the back of his head. What the hell?

"The stage doesn't go to Chance," Seth said.

"That's what Mrs. Loss told her," the innkeeper continued. "Miss Paris asked Mrs. Loss if she knew of anyone traveling that way."

Seth looked at Josh. "You're traveling that way."

"I know that, dammit." Why would she be interested in visiting a one-horse mining town? Unless . . . "I don't believe this."

"What?"

"I understand your distress," Mr. Loss said. "You don't have to worry about me or Mrs. Loss wagging our tongues. We know all about lovers' spats. We have 'em all the time. I just thought you'd like to know so you could buy your fiancé some hair ribbons or gumdrops or something." He pushed his spectacles higher on his nose and smiled. "You know, to smooth things over so you can kiss and make up."

"Thanks," Josh grumbled.

"One last thing," Mr. Loss said, backing toward the door. "She wanted to know if me and the missus had a piano. Mrs. Loss told her, no. Next Miss Paris asked the most peculiar favor."

"Directions to the nearest saloon?"

Seth gawked at him. "She wouldn't."

"I should've tied her to the bedpost."

Mr. Loss turned beet red. "Course Mrs. Loss didn't offer directions," he said in a rush, "but as you can see the Sand Spur is right across the street."

Seth waited until Loss disappeared back into the hotel then turned to Josh. "Guess you weren't kidding about her being weak north of the ears." He sighed. "All right. What have we got? Chance. Opera House. M.B. Are you thinking what I'm thinking?"

"Unfortunately."

"What's the connection?"

That there *was* a connection boggled his mind. He'd never believed in fate, but by God if this wasn't a glowing example . . . Josh relayed the information in a disbelieving drone. "Paris answered a newspaper advertisement. An opera house seeking entertainers. She received a telegram in return offering her a job."

Seth nodded, putting two and two together. "A telegram signed M.B."

"Mason Burke."

"I take it she doesn't know Mason's, well . . ." Seth cleared his throat, " . . . gone."

Josh's gut clenched at the thought of his uncle pushin' up daisies. "Guess not."

"Or that you're his nephew."

"Definitely not."

Seth furrowed his brow. "You gonna tell her?"

"Eventually."

"Not sure I like the sound of that."

"Didn't figure you would."

Seth scratched his chin then rubbed the back of his neck. "Guess that makes you her employer."

"Guess so."

"Awkward."

"Yup."

Seth nodded toward the Sand Spur. "Buy you a drink?"

"You can buy me a bottle."

CHAPTER 10

Strangers passing in the night, by chance their lips did meet. Though they shared a moment's fire, the kiss was incomplete."

Paris lay in the center of the bed, staring up at the ceiling, singing the lyrics that had been ringing in her ears for over an hour. She wanted to scream.

"*Fate conspired to lend a hand, desire became their curse. Both would fight against the fall, whose heart would be lost first?*"

The prophetic verse played over and over in her sluggish mind, refusing to blossom and grow. Her head throbbed. Her throat burned. Her entire being ached. The hot bath, though it had calmed her frazzled nerves, had failed to soothe her trail-weary body. What she needed, as Josh had pointed out, was a sound night's sleep. Unfortunately, she wasn't going to get a wink of rest with a song stuck in her head. If Mrs. Loss didn't come back with the change of clothing she'd promised, and soon, she'd be forced to scout out a piano in her underthings. Cursing herself for allowing the woman to cart off her trousers and shirt for washing, she closed her eyes, and tried to focus on something other than the haunting ballad Josh's kisses inspired.

"Strangers passing in the night, by chance their lips did meet. Though they shared a moment's fire, the kiss was incomplete."

She snatched the pillow from beneath her head, pressed it over her face, and screamed.

A knock sounded at the door. Groaning, she flung the pillow aside, pushed herself upright and dragged her stiff legs over the bed. Five grueling days across the desert. Between the journey, the multiple mishaps, and her vexing attachment to Josh, no wonder she'd been so weepy. As he'd pointed out, she'd had one heck of a week, and it wasn't going to end until she got this darned song out of her head.

"Miss Paris? Are you in there?"

"Coming." Ignoring her aches and pains, she padded barefoot across the warped wooden floor, grimacing when she caught a glimpse of herself in the mirror. Puffy eyes. Tangled hair. Reddened face. She looked like something the cat coughed up. Good thing she wasn't out to impress anyone. She cracked open the door, faint with relief. "You came back!"

A portly woman with graying hair and wrinkled, sun-browned skin stood on the threshold, a bustled emerald gown cradled in her pudgy arms. "Of course I came back, dear." Smiling, Mrs. Loss shuffled into the room, using her elbow to shut the door behind her. "I'm sorry it took me so long, but you're a tiny thing and I wanted to make sure I borrowed the perfect gown." She held up a magnificent silk taffeta for inspection. "What do you think?"

Fighting a bout of dizziness, Paris grappled for a polite way to express her dismay. She'd be courting trouble if she walked into a saloon wearing *that* fancy, low-cut get-up.

Mrs. Loss cupped her chin and leaned close. "Gracious, girl, you're sunburned. I noticed you were pink when we spoke before, but now . . . " She whistled. "Does it pain ya'?"

"A little." Paris shoved her bed-mussed hair off of her face, wincing as her nails scraped tender flesh. "I know I look a fright."

"Nonsense, dear. You look lovely, just red and puffy. We can fix that with a dose of chamomile tea."

Paris dabbed at the sweat trickling between her breasts. Even with the window open, the tiny hotel room was stifling. "I appreciate your offer, but it's a little warm for hot tea."

Mrs. Loss smiled kindly. "It won't be hot, and you won't be drinking it. We'll sponge cooled chamomile tea over your face and you'll feel right as rain."

Strangers passing in the night, by chance their lips did meet. Though they shared a moment's fire, the kiss was incomplete.

"Blast!"

"Or . . . " the old woman drawled, "we could try vinegar. Doc Farley swears by vinegar."

It's not that," she said in a rush. "I've got this song . . . it's stuck . . . and . . . " She eyed the gown, sighed. "It's a beautiful dress, Mrs. Loss. I'd be honored to wear it for the evening. Would you mind helping me? I'm in a hurry." The sooner she visited the saloon, the sooner she'd get some sleep. Three minutes with a piano. That's all she needed. Ten at the most. Her hands tingled in anticipation.

Mrs. Loss placed the gown on the bed and laced her into a corset. "Are you all right, dear?"

She grabbed hold of the bedpost, feeling positively ill. Either the corset was too tight or she was delirious with exhaustion. "I'm fine," she said, even as her vision blurred. "Just hot."

"I'll fetch you a glass of cool water." The woman crossed the room in a blur of ruffled calico. "Are you meeting your fiancé for dinner?" she asked, sounding as if she were calling from the next room.

"My what?" Paris blinked to bring the woman back

into focus.

Mrs. Loss poured water from a large-mouth pitcher. "Your fiancé," she said, floating back toward Paris and placing a glass of water in her tingling hands. "I assume that's why you're getting all slicked up. Mr. Grant is taking you out to dinner to make up for whatever he said to make you cry."

Dazed, Paris tried to make sense out of the woman's rambling. *Fiancé?*

"You caught yourself a handsome one, sweetie." Mrs. Loss urged her to step into a petticoat then pulled the multi-layered slip swiftly to her waist, clasping the waistband tight. "Handsome *and* romantic. Mr. Loss told me how Mr. Grant rescued you from some mishap and how you fell in love, and—"

"Fate conspired to lend a hand, desire became their curse. Both would fight against the fall, whose heart would be lost first?"

"That's lovely, dear. Is it a poem?" The woman gathered up Paris's hair, twisting it into a loose knot. "Maybe Preacher Davis can include it in the ceremony."

Yellow dots danced before her eyes. "Preacher Davis?" The room spun.

"The gospel sharp who'll be performing your wedding."

The water glass crashed to the floor.

* * *

The Sand Spur was eerily quiet. Fifteen men tops, aside from Josh, Seth, the pianist, the barkeep, and a lone dove occupied the stale-smelling gurdy. Three wranglers stood at the bar, nursing warm beers. Josh and Seth lingered at the far end, opting for whiskey. The rest of the men took up three tables near the front door, half-roostered and immersed in various card games. The dove sat at the third table, acting as a slicked-up gambler's good luck charm.

Seth spun his empty shot glass on the polished mahogany bar. "I'm beginning to think you don't know the Garrett girl as well as you claim."

"She'll be here." He signaled the bartender for another bottle. When he'd warned her against seeking out M.B., he hadn't considered her obsession with the piano. Wrung out as she was, he'd expected her to fall asleep soon after he left. "She must have a song stuck in her head."

Seth poured them both another shot. "What?"

He nodded to the upright across the room. "The only way to get a song out of her head once it sticks there is to give it life." Christ, had that been a mere week ago that she'd offered that warped explanation? How had she managed to get under his skin in so little time?

"I can't believe she'd risk getting pawed by a bunch of cowpokes just to get to a piano." Seth set the bottle aside with a disgusted growl. "You *should've* tied her to the damned bedpost."

"She'd find a way to drag the bedpost. She's that determined when it comes to her music. Just let her get it out of her system." Then he'd confront her about Chance.

"Can't." Seth lit up a cheroot. "Her brothers are against her performing in a saloon and so am I." He blew out a blue plume of smoke and gestured toward the scruffy clientele. "These boys are easily riled. I don't need the headache."

"Who does?" Josh nursed his drink. He'd given himself a whopper figuring out how he was going to deter her from singing at the Moon. Between her sweet face and sultry voice she'd have the miners worked into a lustful lather by mid-song. After a calming shot of whiskey, he'd decided his best course was to lay his cards on the table. As his wife she could play the Moon's piano to her heart's content, but he'd be damned if he'd allow her to prance around on stage serenading an audience of lonely drunks.

"You're not going to honor Mason's telegram, are you? The men of Florence are saints compared to those hellraisers in Chance."

"I'll protect what's mine." Those hellraisers would treat his wife with respect or suffer the consequences.

"She's not legally yours. Yet," Seth added with a frown. "You are going to wait for Preacher Davis to get back before you drag that girl off, aren't you?"

"When do you expect him?"

Seth shrugged. "Depends on how long Bo Jenkins hangs on."

"I can't hang around here indefinitely. Oscar Pike has been running the Desert Moon on his own for three weeks now. He's good, but he's no match for Niles. If my cousin is cooking up trouble, I'm the one to douse the fire. Just send the preacher up to me as soon as he returns."

"I hate to ask, but where is Paris going to stay?"

"With me."

Seth ran an exasperated hand over his clean-shaven jaw. "You better hope Davis gets there before the Garretts, otherwise they're liable to shoot you dead. I'd hate to see that happen."

"I'd be more worried about my shooting the Garretts."

"Shit. You don't honestly believe they'd hurt their little sister."

"Not physically, but emotionally . . . " He studied the amber liquid in his glass. "Someone twisted her priorities. Don't even get me started on her cock-eyed opinion on relationships."

"Run that last one by me again."

"Let's just say she's . . . open-minded."

"That sounds like trouble."

"With a capital T."

"I don't mind telling you none of this makes a lick

of sense." Seth drummed his fingers on the bar while studying Josh for a long, annoying minute. "There's something you're not telling me."

"Would you leave me the hell alone?"

"You said you don't love her. Claim she's loco. So why are you all-fired intent on marrying her? Hasn't your life been turned upside down enough?" He swiped off his hat, and leaned in, green eyes sparking. "You're a lawman, Josh. Keeping the peace. Protecting folk. It's what you do. Who you are. Now you're moving to a boomtown to run a damned opera house. I know you feel like you owe Mason, but trading your life for his? Ain't that carrying gratitude a bit far?"

"It's not your business."

"You're my friend. I'm making it my business. I've held my tongue until now, but hell! You actually think you'll be able to stand behind that bar and abide by the lawlessness that abounds in Chance?"

"I aim on doing what comes naturally."

Presently Mr. Loss busted through the swinging doors, bow tie and spectacles askew. He near about tripped over his own two feet trying to get to them. Red-faced, he sputtered for a full five seconds before Seth slapped him on the back. "Spit it out, Percy. What's wrong?"

"It's Miss Paris." Loss pinned Josh with a frantic look. "You better come quick."

* * *

"*Don't you ever, no, no never, even if you think you're clever, don't ignore the Doc. Ooh-ooh-ooh. Doc knows what's best. Drink, eat and rest, or else.*

"*He will wonder, then he'll ponder, he will even travel yonder for the perfect cure. Ooh-ooh-ooh. Doc knows what's best. Drink, eat and rest, or else!*"

"She's delirious," the doctor said, laying his palm to Paris's burning forehead.

"I'm not delirious," she said, her voice a raspy scratch. "It just came out." Josh sat to the left of her bed. A stranger, a tall fair man with vivid green eyes, sat to her right. She was afraid to look at Josh. What if he had that expression? The one that said, "*She's crazy.*" The hurtful expression perfected by the majority of Heaven's citizens.

The green-eyed stranger chuckled. "You've been immortalized, Doc."

Unimpressed, Doc Farley snapped shut his worn black bag. "She's suffering from heat exhaustion and a pesky fever. Get her out of that stifling contraption. Cover her body with cool, wet cloths, and make sure she drinks lots of sassafras tea. Mrs. Loss should be up with a pot momentarily." Snagging his bag, he turned to take his leave. "Fetch me if you need me."

"*Ooh-ooh-ooh. Doc knows what's best. Drink, eat and rest, or else.*"

"Delirious," the doctor said, then shut the door.

"Stop ogling," Josh ordered Green Eyes as he jerked the quilt to her chin.

"I'm hot," she complained, shoving the blanket to her waist. Swear to heaven if she didn't get out of this corset, and soon, she was going to suffocate.

"I'm not ogling," Green Eyes said. "I'm admiring. Beautiful *and* a sense of humor." He grinned, displaying a set of endearing dimples. "Now I understand."

"Understand what?" she asked. The stranger was really quite handsome, she realized. Though not as striking as Josh.

"My friend's fascination."

"With what?"

His grin broadened. "You."

A wave of depression washed over her, rivaling the dizziness that had committed her to bed. "He's not fascinated. He's just being noble."

She heard Josh grunt as he yanked the quilt back up. She tried to fling it aside, but he shoved her hand away.

"What do you mean?" Green Eyes asked.

She pouted, wishing Josh would hold her hand instead of batting it away. Darn him. "He only wants to marry me because of what we did."

"Hush, Paris." Josh lifted strands of damp hair from

her face, his gentle touch kicking her temperature higher. "You're delirious."

"No, I'm not. I'm hot." Didn't he know he was making her miserable?

Green Eyes frowned down at her. "Specifically, what did you do?"

She struggled to sit up, groaning at the effort. Her head felt as big and heavy as a two-ton boulder. "Who are you?"

"Seth Wright." Josh pushed her back down on the bed. He lay a damp cloth to her brow. "Say goodbye. He's leaving."

"Not until Mrs. Loss gets here," the other man said, eyes intent on her face as if waiting to catch her in a lie. "Why does Josh want to marry you?"

"He made me purr."

He glanced up at Josh. "That so?"

She tugged on Seth's shirtsleeve to get his attention, beckoning him to lean closer.

"He's fine where he is," Josh protested.

Seth winked at her. "What, darlin'?"

She didn't know why she was confiding in this man. Maybe because he reminded her of Athens. Athens would definitely make this dreadful hurt better. He knew all about matters of the heart. She could barely get the words past the dratted lump in her throat. "Tell Josh he wasted his time contacting the preacher."

"He's standing right next to you, sweetheart."

"I can't look at him."

"Why not?"

"I can't think straight when I look in his eyes." She quirked a sad smile. "When he kisses me, angels sing."

The stranger looked to the heavens, or maybe he was rolling his eyes. She couldn't tell. His tone, however, was most amiable. "Seems the angels might be in favor of this marriage. Why aren't you?"

"I have to be someone."

"You are someone," Josh snapped.

Why did he sound so cross? "I have to be a star," she told Seth.

"Do you want to be a star?"

She imagined herself center stage, strutting and posing, wooing nameless strangers with dramatic monologues and dynamic songs. Her body shivered in rebellion. "Not really."

Seth massaged the back of his neck just as she'd seen Josh do a hundred times. "Then why bother?" he asked.

My little girl is destined for greatness. Her eyes misted. "I promised."

Someone knocked on the door. Paris felt herself drifting away. Her head swam and her limbs tingled. Voices blended and blurred. Someone wanted Mrs. Loss to look after her. Mrs. Loss didn't mind. Josh minded. He told everyone to get out. Seth, at least she thought it was Seth, told Josh he was digging his own grave. Was he sick?

"I want Josh," she croaked. Now why had she said that? He was her doom.

She heard a muffled curse, reluctant goodbyes, followed by silence. Blissful, peaceful silence.

Someone whipped the quilt aside. She sighed, enjoying a brief rush of cool air. She forced open her heavy lids, locking gazes with Josh for the first time this evening. The unexpected tenderness in his eyes caused her to smile. "Did anyone ever tell you you're beautiful?"

He laughed softly, rolling her to her side. "Just you."

"What are you doing?"

"Getting you out of these clothes."

She opened her mouth to object but couldn't think why. She was burning up. Mrs. Loss had dressed her in layers of frilly underthings, and though she appreciated the effort she couldn't wait to shed the suffocating garments. "Thank you," she said, fumbling with the waistband.

"I'll get it, honey."

"I like Mrs. Loss."

"So do I." He quickly ridded her of the cumbersome petticoat and tossed it over a chair.

"She thinks we're getting married."

"We are." He unlaced her corset, blessedly easing the pressure on her ribs.

"Mama and Papa were married," she said, trying to keep the panic from her voice. "They fought all the time." Before she knew it, she'd been stripped down to her chemise and bloomers. She felt immeasurably cooler, but not cool enough. "I'm thirsty."

"Mrs. Loss brought tea. Sassafras for fever. Chamomile for sunburn. I think we'll go with the sassafras." He stood and walked toward the rosewood bureau.

She shimmied out of her unmentionables and fell back on the damp sheets. "That's better."

"Ah, hell," she heard him say, as her eyes drifted shut and shades of the past enveloped her consciousness.

"What did you think, Songbird?"

"Miriam's monologue was swell, Papa." Paris applauded as the dramatic actress took her bows. *Several members of the audience threw flowers at her feet and the actress, famous for her emotional outbursts, blew kisses in return. "But I liked Julio best."*

William Garrett regarded his young daughter with amusement. "The singing juggler?"

Paris fidgeted on her backstage stool. "He was funny."

"You liked his rhymes."

She nodded, rolling her eyes when Miriam's leading man draped a silk cape over her shoulders and gently escorted her from the wings to her dressing room. Miriam, unlike Julio and the other novelty performers, was a snob.

"His lyrics are not half as witty as yours and you are only

six," said Papa.

Paris wasn't sure what "witty" meant, but from the twinkle in Papa's eyes, she guessed it was good.

"You are going to excel in the theater, Songbird. You're destined to be a musical actress, just like your beautiful mama. Only you'll stick with it."

She hopped off the stool, turning her back on the Gilded Garrett stage. She couldn't imagine performing in front of all those people, but she'd very much like to help behind the scenes. "I'd rather play the piano, Papa."

"And you shall. You'll compose clever melodies and perform them on stage. Why, with your talent and wit you could write quite an amusing opera. You are going to be a star and I am going to be the happiest man on earth." He came up behind her and tugged her pigtail. "You want to make me happy, pumpkin, don't you?"

* * *

"I want to make you happy," Paris mumbled, tossing and turning and making Josh insane.

"Then lay still," he said, swabbing wet cloths over her naked body. Not that she heard his order. She was sleeping, though fitfully. Dreaming. Although the way she thrashed about he'd peg it more for a nightmare. Much like his life the past two hours.

A herd of morbid thoughts had stampeded his mind

when he'd first laid eyes on her feverish body. Like the memory of his mother succumbing to consumption. Thankfully, Doc Farley had been a stone's throw away. Thankfully the diagnosis hadn't been worse. Still, he blamed himself for her fragile state. He should have protected her better from the sun. His punishment, severe by any healthy man's standards, included ministering her firm young body.

"Can you teach me to juggle apples and sing rhymes at the same time?"

The corners of his mouth lifted. "What the devil are you dreaming about?"

Her eyes fluttered open. "Josh?"

"Right here, honey."

"I'm cold."

His hand stilled. "What?"

She shivered then turned onto her side and snuggled up against him.

His brain seized. A knock on the door had him swearing and on his feet. He peeled off the damp cloths, pulled the covers over her, and tucked the quilt tight around her trembling form.

Percy Loss greeted him at the door. "I know the missus brought you some tea, but this is even better." He held up a tall glass of steaming amber liquid. "My miracle remedy."

Josh lifted a suspect eyebrow. "What's in it?"

Mr. Loss smiled. "Hot whiskey, lemon, and water. Cures just about everything."

It would certainly knock her out, a blessing, given her restless state. "Thank you." He took the glass and shut the door before the loose-lipped innkeeper could get an eyeful. Walking back to the bed, he coaxed Paris into a sitting position. "Sip this."

"It smells disgusting." She gulped down the remedy, shuddering as she passed him back the empty glass. "Tastes awful. Guess that means it's good for me. At least that's what London always says." She fell back on the bed. "I'm still cold."

London, he surmised, was another brother, and wouldn't appreciate what he was about to do. Or maybe he would since it was for her wellbeing.

"Remember that," he told himself as he shucked his clothes and crawled under the covers with the naked girl. "This is for her, not you."

She draped her arm over his bare chest and threw her right leg over his thighs, pressing her soft thatch of curls against his hip. Every muscle in Josh's body tensed.

"I'm not a freak."

He frowned down at the top of her head. "Who called you a freak?"

"Did I show you the telegram?"

He assumed she was referring to the wire she'd received from Mason. "You can show me tomorrow."

"M.B. isn't in Florence," she said in a small voice. "I lied. I'm sorry. It's just that . . . I didn't know you then."

He hugged her close. "We'll talk about it tomorrow." *When your mind's not jumping tracks every three seconds.*

"Seth is nice."

"You think so, huh?"

"Is he married?"

He cursed a pang of jealousy, threaded his fingers through her silky hair. "No. Why?"

"I'm thinking he might be perfect for Emily."

"A friend of yours?" His relief was immense and damned annoying.

"My best friend. She's been forever in love with Rome. But he won't give her the time of day."

"Bastard."

"What?"

"Nothing. Try to go to sleep." He stroked her smooth, flushed curves, hoping to soothe her, trying not to admire her perfect breasts, her slender thighs. Ignoring the way she fidgeted, grinding her womanly mound against his upper thigh. She was hot, wet, and, as Doc Farley noted, delirious. Making love to a fever-ish woman was out of the question and yet it was all he could think about.

"Josh?" She snuggled her face into the crook of his neck.

He held her tight, groaning when she shifted, her

knee brushing his erection.

"I don't feel right."

"I know, sweetheart." He prayed for her fever to break, for Mr. Loss's miracle remedy to kick in. He wouldn't get a wink of sleep this night, but he would rest a helluva lot easier if she would just conk out. "It'll pass. Think about something else."

Sighing, she drummed her fingers on his chest. "All right. I thought of a good reason."

"For what?"

"For not marrying you."

"I'm all ears."

"Marriage equals broken hearts and dreams," she whispered, her fingers dancing over his abdomen.

He sucked in a breath, nabbing her hand before her fingers jigged lower. "I won't break your heart."

"Maybe I'll break yours."

Since he didn't aim on giving her his heart, that wasn't a worry. "I can take care of myself."

"Really?" She slid her hand from his grasp and traced the jagged scar on his shoulder. "How'd you get this?"

"Tangling with an obstinate bandit."

"Rome and Boston tangle with bandits too. I wonder if they have scars."

"Probably." Desperados rarely gave up without a fight. He wondered if she realized how freely she was talking. Wondered if he could take advantage. "About your brothers—"

"Touch me." She snagged his hand and placed it at the sweet junction between her legs.

If she'd meant to distract him, she'd done a fine job. Hellfire, would his punishment never end? "Not now."

She wiggled against his fingers and moaned. "I like that."

The muscle in his cheek jumped as he summoned every ounce of decency in his bones. Either Mr. Loss's remedy was lethal or she had zero tolerance to whiskey. "You're not in your right mind."

"According to Heaven, I've *never* been in my right mind."

Heaven? Was she citing religion? Did she think sex was a sin? Shit. One more thing to beat herself up over. He tried to pull his hand away, tried to be a gentleman, but she refused to cooperate. She continued to wiggle against him, wrapping her free hand around his shaft. He clenched his jaw and cursed a silent blue streak.

"Do you fancy me?" she asked, her fingers gliding over his stiff rod.

If he weren't in such misery, he'd laugh. He rolled on top of her, forcing her to release him. Hoping to distract her, he devoured her with a starving kiss.

"Touch me," she pleaded, when he allowed her to come up for air. "Please?"

A naked woman. In bed. Begging for pleasure. How

had every man's dream turned into his personal nightmare? Giving up, he showered her with lusty kisses and stroked her, wanting to drive her into oblivion. It took a total of three minutes. She exploded under his touch, writhing, moaning his name, and, a split second later collapsed against him in exhaustion.

Damn. He'd never known a woman to peak so easily. What would it be like when they actually made love? If she wasn't so ill, swear to God, he'd pack her off to that preacher tonight.

Another knock came at the door. He tried to get up, but she had her leg anchored over his thighs. "Just a minute!"

"Go away," she mumbled, her voice slurred from the liquor.

He snagged his shirt off the nightstand and managed to button her into it, but when he tried to push out of bed, his legs got tangled in the sheets. Paris groaned, the knocking grew louder, and he lost his composure. "We don't need any more whiskey!"

The door swung open and Seth stepped into the room, a shotgun swinging at his side. He took one look at Josh's naked state and swore.

A man wearing a black suit, with a skinny, white-banded collar stepped in behind him, and calmly shut the door.

Josh was trying to jam his legs in his trousers when

the preacher opened his bible.

Seth cocked a wry grin. "You'll thank me when the Garretts show up on your doorstep."

Josh didn't argue.

CHAPTER 11

Mrs. Loss thinks we're getting married.
We are.

Last night trickled back in distorted fragments, intensifying Paris's foul mood. Still suffering from whatever had ailed her, she fought the urge to retch. Every step of her horse's trot drove a railway spike into her sluggish brain. Frantic to reach her destination, she grimaced against the splitting headache and pressed onward. The more distance she put between her and Josh, the better.

"How long before we get to Chance?" she asked.

"At the pace we're moving?" Harley Fox slowed his sorrel's gait to match her mare's. "Better part of the day."

She ignored the prospector's sarcasm. She couldn't

care beans about his surly disposition. He was passing by Chance on his way to the Superstition Mountains and that's all that mattered. Clenching the saddle horn for dear life, she urged the mare on a little faster, praying all the while that she wouldn't lose her seat and tumble to the hard ground.

This morning she'd awoken, half naked, her body tingling. She'd hugged a pillow and breathed in Josh's distinct scent of sandalwood soap and leather. Her cheeks burned as erotic images flooded her mind. Josh unlacing her corset . . . crawling into bed . . . smoothing his hands over her skin.

Although the specific details blurred, she knew she'd acted scandalously. Now, with her goal as close as the next town, her childhood promise was in serious jeopardy.

When Mrs. Loss had knocked on her door bearing a selection of second-hand shirts, and news that Josh was out shopping for *their* new home, she'd made a split second decision. Ten minutes later, she sneaked out the back door, talked the livery owner into selling her his daughter's horse and enlisted Harley Fox, who'd just saddled his own mount, as her guide.

By the time Josh discovered her missing, she'd be halfway to Chance. He'd be too fed up with her antics to follow. At least, that's what she kept telling Harley.

The sound of thundering hooves caused her escort to swivel in his saddle. "Dad-burn it! I *knew* it!"

Paris didn't need to turn around to know that Josh was bearing down. She could feel his fury radiating across the desert plain, prickly and as intimidating as any one of the surrounding cacti. Sweat trickled down the side of her face, and she didn't think it was due to the mid-morning sun. Her fear of horses paled volumes in comparison to her apprehension of facing Josh's wrath. Swallowing hard, she dug in her heels trying to urge Sunny into a record setting gallop. The horse refused to cooperate, holding to a trot.

A shrill whistle rent the air, nearly splitting her aching head wide open. Sunny stopped cold. Were Paris not clinging for dear life, she would've flown over the horse's head. When she looked up to find Josh glaring at her, jaw clenched, chest heaving, she wished she'd taken that dive. Unconsciousness would be preferable to the blistering lecture coming her way. She just hoped he didn't do something rude. Like shoot her.

Harley reined in his horse. "I know," he said, casting Josh a sour look. "Get lost."

"Wait!" she called, when he turned to leave. "I paid you to escort me to Chance!"

The prospector dug in his vest pocket and passed her the cash she'd paid him up front. "Ain't worth dying for, lady."

Three seconds later, Harley was gone and she faced Josh alone. Lordy, he was imposing. So tall. So broad.

His unshaven jaw clenched tight. Wearing a stone-gray duster over a black vest and a blood-red shirt, he looked dark and dangerous, and mad enough to chew a bucket of nails without cracking a tooth.

He hadn't said a word. Not to Harley. Not to her. His silence heightened her anxiety. She threaded her fingers through Sunny's mane. For the life of her, she couldn't look him in the eyes.

"How are you feeling?"

Like I've been dragged through the bush backward. "Better, thank you."

"Let me know when you're one-hundred percent so that I can give you the spanking you deserve."

"You don't mean that."

"You're right. Tell me when you're *ninety* percent." He leaned closer, the sheer force of his presence causing her to tilt sideways in her saddle. "Do you ever think before you act?"

She blushed profusely, feeling guilty for a dozen reasons.

"What the hell were you thinking riding into the desert with a stranger?"

She wished he would bellow. The controlled tone set her nerves on edge. "Harley isn't a stranger," she said, braiding another portion of Sunny's mane. "We met him yesterday when he stumbled out of the saloon and winked at me."

"That doesn't ease my mind." He wrapped his

hand around her busy fingers and squeezed. "Look at me, Paris."

The warmth of his hand seeped through her skin, causing her stomach to coil into a familiar knot. *Touch me.* She jerked her hand away, blasting him with the full force of her anxiety. "I can't marry you!"

"Did I ask?"

"What?"

"Did I just ask you to marry me?"

She blinked at him, thoroughly confused. "But Mrs. Loss said . . . and I thought . . . after last night . . . what we . . . did."

"Which was?"

If her cheeks burned any hotter they'd be on fire. "It."

He furrowed his brow. "It?"

"Must I explain?"

"If you want me to understand what you're talking about."

"We were naked."

"For medicinal reasons."

"We slept together."

"Actually, you slept. I had things on my mind."

She threw up her hands in exasperation. Had she only imagined they'd been intimate? Wait a minute. Someone had called her delirious. Maybe it *was* her imagination!

"Who called you a freak?"

His question took her aback. "What?"

"Last night you said, *I'm not a freak*. I want to know who put that notion in your head."

"Mary Lee Bernbaum."

"Who's Mary Lee Bernbaum?"

"My almost sister-in-law." When he reached around to rub the back of his neck, she figured she'd better explain. "It was one of life's most embarrassing moments. Up until now, that is. The annual Lemonade and Storytelling Social picnic. I made Mary Lee angry. She called me a musical freak." She shrugged. "The whole town pretty much agreed."

"Are you telling me you're an outcast in your hometown?"

She couldn't fathom why he looked so angry. It's not that the townfolk walked around calling her vicious names. Her brothers would never stand for that. They simply kept their distance and regarded her with "that look." "If you heard one of my ditties, you'd understand."

"What's a ditty?"

"That's what my brothers call my musical rhymes. I don't plan them ahead of time. They just pop out. A slice of life in catchy song."

His eyes danced with understanding. "You sang one of those last night."

She groaned. "I did?"

"Uh huh."

"About who?"

"Doc Farley."

"Was he insulted?"

"Why would he be insulted? It was amusing."

The breath whooshed out of her lungs. "You liked my ditty?"

He nodded. "So did Seth."

"Seth?" The name sounded vaguely familiar, but she couldn't put a face to the name.

"The man you want to match up with your friend, Emily."

She remembered then. A fair man with emerald-green eyes. He reminded her of Athens. "Oh, him. I said I wanted to match him up with Emily? I *must* have been out of mind. She wouldn't have Seth."

He looked surprised. "She wouldn't?"

"Absolutely not. She's hopelessly in love with . . ."

"Yes?"

"One of my brothers." She was relieved when he didn't ask which one, but had to wonder what else she'd blabbered last night. She started to ask, but then another question popped into her head. "How did you know where to find me?"

"Seth." He glowered again, making her sorry she'd asked. "He was passing by the livery and heard Milton Beane trying to explain to his seven-year-old daughter why he'd sold her horse to the pretty, crazy lady."

Paris's shoulders slumped. She'd been particularly

nice and wholly reasonable with Mr. Beane. "Why did he think I was crazy?"

"Because you gave him a ridiculously high IOU for that nag."

Her misfit heart ached for the swayback mare. "Sunny is not a nag. She's gentle."

"She's a year away from being put out to pasture." Josh cupped Paris's chin, narrowed his eyes. "*You* are a genuine pain in the ass."

Unnerved by his touch, she nudged away his hand. "It would seem as though I'm affecting more of your body parts daily."

"That's an understatement."

"All the more reason why we should part ways. I'd hate to cause you anymore trouble."

"I can't imagine that's possible."

"In that case, I'll be going. It was kind of you to be concerned, but as you can see, I'm fine. If I hurry maybe I can catch up with Harley."

His right eye twitched. "I'll escort you to Chance."

He was almost whispering now. That couldn't be good. Feigning ease, she leaned down to adjust her left stirrup. "I wouldn't want to put you out."

"Too late. And for the record, M.B. stands for Mason Burke."

"You know M.B.?"

"He was my uncle."

She would've slid right out of the saddle if he hadn't caught her and pushed her upright. He leaned down and finished adjusting her stirrup while she assimilated the shocking news. M.B. was his uncle? But hadn't his uncle died? Yes, he had specifically said his uncle had died and left him his business. "Oh, no."

Josh straightened, a devious gleam in his eyes.

"But that makes you my—"

"Employer."

"Which makes this—"

"Interesting."

"Awkward." She frowned. "When did you figure it out?"

"Last night."

In her delirium she must've mentioned Chance or the Desert Moon. Or maybe she'd shown him the telegram. He'd simply put two and two together. "How can fate be so warped?"

He grinned while urging Buckshot north. "Are you coming?"

She didn't know which was more disturbing. Never seeing him again or seeing him every day. Logic told her to swing Sunny in the opposite direction. But with Emily shouting in one ear and Papa in the other, rational thought was impossible. She couldn't imagine why she wasn't more upset. Maybe because there was no real need to panic. It'll be all right, she told herself. Everything happens for a reason. Trusting her instincts, she reined Sunny alongside Buckshot, casting Josh a wary glance. "About last night . . ."

"Fuzzy on the details, huh?"

Her cheeks burned. "Will you clear it up for me?"

He didn't look at her or smile but, she'd swear to heaven, he was amused. "Eventually."

* * *

He'd married a lunatic. True, he hadn't put up a fight when Seth had barged in with the preacher. As he saw it his friend was doing him a favor, saving him the trouble of having to try to reason with Paris. How did one reason with a woman who dreamed about juggling apples and singing rhymes, and professed that she didn't need a husband to have babies? He hadn't the slightest idea or the inclination. He'd wanted the deed done for his sake as well as hers, and he didn't much care that they'd resorted to trickery. Thanks to the fever and Loss's miracle remedy, she'd been incoherent when she'd mumbled "I do." And she'd only said those words after Seth had prompted, "So do you really hear angels sing when Josh kisses you?"

Josh refused to feel guilty. He couldn't, however, help but question his sanity. He'd actually thought, as ill as she'd been, that she'd sleep until noon. He'd thought it was safe to do some shopping, supplies for Mason's, no, his, no *their* house. Thought he'd have time to arrange for a buckboard so she wouldn't have to brave another day in the saddle. He'd thought that they'd discuss their shotgun wedding over a late breakfast. He'd even braced himself for a public tantrum, but he sure as hell wasn't prepared for the news that his bride had skipped town with a prospector. Hellfire, he'd nearly punched the messenger. Seth had laughed, assuring him Harley was harmless, and wishing Josh luck because he was going to need it. His wife was *loco*.

She was also a beautiful, determined young woman. He glanced at the petite minx riding next to him. Sunburned cheeks. Bed mussed hair. Baggy trousers cuffed over her dusty boots, a faded yellow shirt and an ill-fitting brown vest. Most women wouldn't be caught dead in men's clothing. Most women would have spent the day in bed recovering, wrung out from the fever, whiskey, and five days on the trail. He knew she had to be hurting and yet she'd hit the ground running. Literally. Negotiated a mount and an escort, conquered her fear of horses and lit for Chance, aiming to fulfill her papa's dream. He had to admire her dedication, which was just about the only reason he hadn't shaken the stuffing out of her. That and the fact that he'd been so damned relieved to find her safe.

As payback, he'd meant to level her with the news

that he was the owner of the Desert Moon. She'd barely flinched. His only consolation was that she didn't remember the whole of last night. For sure as certain she didn't remember promising to honor and obey. His mouth curved into a wicked grin. He'd let her stew for awhile. She deserved to suffer a little after scaring the devil out of him.

Thunder rumbled in the distance, a prelude to a nasty rainstorm. Paris seemed oblivious to the darkening sky, lost in her thoughts as their horses trotted over miles of terrain, bringing them nearer their destination. Either she was still trying to fit together the pieces of last night's puzzle or she was plotting her retaliation. Not that he would let her back out of this marriage. What was done was done. At some point she'd realize her heart and recognize that she belonged with him rather than bouncing from stage to stage. He hoped, for the sake of his mental health, that it was sooner rather than later.

He looked to the horizon. To his future.

The Superstition Mountains loomed ahead. Desert flora dotted the rugged slopes, softening the craggy range's otherwise forbidding appearance. Wonder flowed through him as he studied the magnificent view.

He imagined Mason admiring a similar vista the evening of the accident. How easy it was to allow one's mind to wander in the face of such raw beauty. Had the old man been daydreaming about the opera house he'd built at the base of those peaks? Or maybe contemplating the legend of the Apache's thunder gods or the mystery of Peralta's lost gold mine? Since the day he'd stumbled upon the abandoned treasure that had made him a wealthy man, his uncle had become obsessed with the myths and tales surrounding the Superstition Mountains. Had his obsession contributed to his death? Had he been so distracted that he simply hadn't reacted swiftly enough when his horses bolted? It was the only explanation that made sense. Guiding Buckshot through a dense patch of jumping cholla, mesquite, and palo verde trees, it was plain that the man's team couldn't have gotten far at a dead run. Mason must have been thrown from the buckboard almost immediately.

Josh rolled back his tense shoulders. He thought he'd put his uncle's death in perspective. An accident. God's will. But traveling his last route, seeing the Superstitions as he'd last seen them, brought the absurdity and unfairness of it all back to light. His gut clenched thinking he was only minutes away from taking up where Mason had left off. Due to a quirk of fate he'd been handed a new life. He realized with sudden clarity that it was up to him to make the most of it.

"Are you thinking about your uncle?"

Paris's soft-spoken inquiry caught him off guard. He kept expecting her to ask him about the Desert Moon, the size of the stage or the make of the piano. Her

accommodations and salary. The length of her engagement. It struck him as uncharacteristic that she wasn't
the least bit curious, but maybe she was too nervous to
ask. They hadn't discussed their relationship, professional or personal, since he'd intimated that she still had
a job. Truth told, she had a right to be nervous.

"Mason took a day-trip to Florence to pick up a
supply of liquor," he finally said. "He was on his way
back to Chance when something spooked his horses.
The buckboard flipped and he broke his neck. Happened somewhere around here."

"That's terrible."

She shivered and he wondered if she was thinking
about her mishap with the runaway stage.

"One minute you're here, and the next . . . " Her
voice caught. "It's not fair. People shouldn't have to
leave this earth until they've realized their dreams."

Spoken like a passionate artist. Ignoring the hitch in
his heart, he reached over to caress her cheek. "Honey,
if you're fretting over Mason you can stop. He realized
his dream. He built the Desert Moon."

She stared hard at the craggy mountains, her voice a
ragged whisper. "What about Mr. Wiggins?"

"I could tell you stories about old Moe that would
make your ears blush. You needn't worry that he died
unfulfilled." He tucked her hair behind her ear. "I'm
thinking you're upset about someone else. Someone you

knew a little better than Moe and Mason."

She reined her horse to a stop.

He shifted in the saddle, noting with pride how comfortable she looked sitting astride the mare. He respected anyone who faced their fears. Riddled with insecurity and misguided loyalty, Paris faced her demons on a daily basis. He no longer thought of her as reckless so much as absurdly brave. Her courage terrified him at times, but it was wholly admirable. Like now. She looked apprehensive, but when she squared her shoulders and stared him dead in the eye, he knew to brace himself for a blow.

"I have four brothers," she blurted out. "London, the oldest, inherited the Gilded Garrett. He's an ace accountant and has Papa's eye for talent. He's one of the most respected theater owners in San Francisco. Athens is a state legislator, a dynamic politician and the devoted father of a little boy and girl. My other two brothers are the best in their field." Her cheeks flushed but she didn't look away. "They've been on the cover of more dime novels than, well, they've been on a lot of covers."

"I guess that makes them pretty famous," he said, amazed that even now she felt it necessary to withhold the Wells Fargo agents' names. Ridiculous since she'd just revealed her last name by mentioning the Gilded Garrett. In addition, every sibling had been named after a major city. Dime novel heroes? He'd have to be an imbecile not to come up with Rome and Boston Garrett. He didn't take the insult to heart. The fact that she thought she could pull something over on him was damned amusing.

"All of my brothers are extremely accomplished," she went on.

"I'm sure your pa wouldn't have loved them any different if they'd done less," he said, getting to what he guessed was the heart of the matter.

She lowered her lashes. "My brothers didn't get along very well with Papa."

"Why not?"

"They thought he neglected Mama."

"Did he?"

"It wasn't his fault that we lived so far away from the theater. He wanted to spend more time with us. He must have said so a thousand times." She glanced up, her eyes shimmering with hero worship. "He was a wonderful man."

Josh wished he could feel that way about his own pa. It was hard to worship a man who forgot he even had a son after his wife died. He resented his pa for drinking himself to death. For not being stronger. For not loving him enough to want to stick around. Yet wasn't he to be admired, even a little, for adoring his wife so much that he couldn't live without her? A week ago that thought wouldn't have even crossed his mind.

"That's why I can't let him down. He asked so little of me, Josh, and I promised. Promises are sacred."

An invisible hand squeezed his heart. "What did you promise, honey? Specifically."

She gripped the saddle horn. "If I tell you, do you swear you won't yell?"

"I won't yell."

"Or curse Papa?"

"What did you promise?"

She took a deep breath, let it out. "On my ninth birthday, well, the day after because he'd gotten tied up at the theater and missed my birthday. Not that it mattered," she added.

"Go on."

"He told me how proud he was of me. How I was destined to become a famous musical actress. He asked me to reach for the stars. I promised to lasso the moon. M.B.'s, Mason's, advertisement read: *Hitch Your Star to the Desert Moon.*" She reached over and squeezed his hand. "Don't you see? It's a sign."

Fate.

"Two days later Papa was killed. Ten years ago this month. When I saw the advertisement . . . " Her eyes misted. "Thank you for letting me appear at the Desert Moon."

He closed his eyes and swore.

"I know you're not happy about me singing in a

saloon," she plowed on. "But the Desert Moon is an opera house. And I'm sure Chance is a lovely town."

He near about choked. "Chance is a mining town. There's nothing lovely about it."

"How can you say that?" She smiled while gesturing toward the jutting, imposing range. "Just look at those mountains. They're beautiful."

He shook his head at her unique perspective. Maybe she wouldn't mind the primitive town and rustic log house after all. "Beautiful or not, those mountains are treacherous. Thunderstorms. Flashfloods. Bobcats, bears, Gila monsters, scorpions, and snakes. A man once said everything in the Superstitions bites, stings, pricks, or eats meat. That man was right."

"What's a Gila monster?"

"A big, ugly lizard with powerful jaws. Let's just say you don't want to make him mad."

She laughed. "You're just trying to scare me."

Damn straight. "This is a rough patch of territory, Paris. Wild terrain. Wild men. I want you to remember that, and I want you to listen to me once we get there. No wandering off. No midnight excursions."

"If by excursions you mean traipsing off in search of a piano, that won't be a concern. There's a piano at the Desert Moon." Her smile slipped. "Isn't there?"

"As I recall it's a pretty fancy upright." Mason had taken pride in giving him the grand tour each time he'd visited the Desert Moon during and after construction. Unfortunately, due to professional obligations, he'd only made it to Chance three times in the last six months. His only solace was that he'd never seen his uncle happier.

He gazed into Paris's soulful eyes, thought about her determination to keep a childhood promise. Her loyalty, her passion, her courage. On the surface they couldn't be more different, but their inner convictions, what made them tick . . . It was as if, in some bizarre way, they were kindred spirits. Was it possible Mason had done him a favor by willing him the Moon and a wife?

"Paris."

"Yes?"

"Why did you tell me about your brothers? Your pa? Why now?"

"I've been thinking it over all day, and I decided since we'll be working so closely together, and you've been so kind to me, I thought I should be . . . you know . . . honest."

If that didn't beat all. He swept off his hat and dragged a hand through his hair. "You and I need to talk."

"About my position at the Desert Moon?"

"About last night."

CHAPTER 12

Paris suppressed a flutter of panic. Maybe honesty wasn't all it was cracked up to be. She'd spent the past few hours trying to conjure a vivid account of last night while Josh rode along in aggravating silence. Now that he was ready to fill her in on the scandalous evening, she wasn't so willing to hear. Judging by the knot in her stomach, she'd be happier carrying on in blissful ignorance.

She still reeled from the fact that he, and not M.B., was the proprietor of the Desert Moon. The only consolation being that he was willing to honor his uncle's telegram. Maybe he did understand her after all. Allowing her to pursue her aspirations, in spite of his obvious reservations, was certainly a good sign. Of course they hadn't discussed details, but she figured there'd be plenty of time for that after they reached the opera house.

"Tell me one thing," she said, willing her voice not to crack. "Did we . . . were we . . . together?"

He reached across the space that separated them and grazed his thumb along her bottom lip. "Trust me, honey, when we make love, you won't forget one amazing second."

His searing gaze melted her bones. Had he not steadied her, she would have swooned. When. Not if. And it would be *amazing*. Except . . . "Given our new relationship, I'm not sure that being intimate would be . . . appropriate."

"Given our new relationship it's extremely appropriate."

She didn't understand. Thinking straight was difficult when he looked at her with such blatant desire. "London says it's dangerous to mix business and pleasure."

"He's probably right."

"And you said . . . before we . . . you wouldn't . . . unless . . . we were married." If only she'd remembered that earlier, she would've saved herself a day full of worry.

"About that," he said, reaching for her hand.

Thunder and lightning clashed against the darkening sky, setting the scene for something ominous.

Like a proposal.

Heart pounding, she jerked away, squealing with relief when she spied the perfect diversion. "Is that

Chance?" Not waiting for an answer, she kicked Sunny into a lope and headed for the flickering lights.

"Stick close," he called, but Sunny had already broken into a gallop.

Paris tried to slow her, but apparently the horse was equally eager to reach their destination. They cleared the edge of town just as a trio of brawling men burst through the front door of a two-story building. One man flew over the hitching rail and plowed into Sunny, knocking Paris out of the saddle. She landed on her backside, dazed and winded, amidst a deafening flurry of bullets. She circled her wrists. Once . . . twice . . .

Cursing, Josh scooped her up and hauled her out of the direct line of fire.

"Are they crazy?" she wheezed, when he dumped her behind a rain barrel.

"No, that would be you!" He jammed a finger in her face. "Dammit, I told you—"

"Sunny!" She popped up from behind the barrel and squealed. That stupid horse stood in the midst of gunplay, calmly drinking out of a water trough. "They'll kill her!"

Josh gave two short whistles. The palomino took her cue, joining Buckshot on the sidelines.

Paris drew a breath of relief. "Why are they shooting at one another?"

"They're drunk," he shouted over the fiery exchange.

"Don't imagine they mean any harm. They're shooting at the cactus, not you. Unfortunately, excessive amounts of whiskey affect a man's aim."

"Well, make them stop!" A bullet zinged by, embedding itself in the prickly body of an innocent saguaro. "You're a sheriff. They have to listen to you!"

"*Was* a sheriff." He put his hand on top of her head and mashed her down behind the barrel. Drawing his Colt, he darted into the fray.

She shoved back her fedora and peeked over the barrel's rim. Excitement skittered down her spine as she watched Josh weave his way toward the hell-raising cactus-slayers. He dodged a slew of renegade bullets without flinching, his confidence and experience apparent when he calmly advised the men to holster their weapons. She nearly fainted when a lone bullet sliced through the crown of his Stetson.

In a flash, he shot the revolver out of the offender's hand and disarmed the remaining two hooligans. One drunkard was crazy enough to take a swing. Josh ducked the roundhouse, knocking the man cold with a swift uppercut. Stunned by their friend's misfortune, the other two staggered back into the saloon.

Ignoring her shaky legs, Paris stood and marched toward the scene. "You could have gotten yourself killed!"

"You told me to make them stop." He bent over to retrieve his ruined hat. Straightening, he stuck his finger through the hole. "A good hat, shot to hell."

Bothered by his casual attitude, she knocked her hand against his Stetson, pointing out, "Better your hat than your head."

He grinned. "Worried about me, darlin'?"

"No," she lied. "From that arrogant smirk on your face, I'm guessing you actually enjoy giving troublemakers their due." Just like Rome and Boston. Likening him to her brothers in this instance helped to soothe her concerns. Experts with their fists and guns, they came out on top every time. Still, the thought of Josh being shot made her physically ill. That was definitely the last time she'd ask him to interfere.

Her heart easing from her throat, she squinted down at the crumpled drunkard, wincing at the awful stench wafting off of his soiled clothes. "Don't they take baths around here?"

"I guess they get around to it once a month or so."

"That's disgusting." She flinched when more shots rang out. This time they came from inside the saloon. "Please tell me that's not the Desert Moon."

"Used to be the mercantile. Now it's the Lucky Lady. The Desert Moon sits at the opposite end of the street."

Paris's mouth gaped open as she made a visual sweep of the uncultivated area. Did four false-front log structures and various framed tents constitute the makings of a town? "Lovely."

He laughed. "Welcome to Chance, darlin'."

In lieu of a red carpet, the rumbling sky split open and poured rain.

Josh hauled her up and ran for the covered veranda of the Lucky Lady. "Stay here where it's dry. I'll stable the horses, snag a slicker, then we'll head on down to the Moon. Last thing I need is for you to catch cold."

She started to point out that she was already soaked to the bone, but he'd already crossed the street. Stuffing her wet hair up underneath her hat, she turned toward the sound of a rollicking tune. The pianist was quite talented. Perhaps that meant he'd be more gracious than the rude oaf she'd encountered back in Yuma.

Lured by the music, she slipped through the Lucky Lady's front door, shimmied sideways and flattened her back against the wall. There was scarcely enough space for a body to turn around. Men of every shape and size filled the converted mercantile wall to wall, gambling and drinking the obvious source of amusement. More than half puffed on cigars or cigarettes, creating an eye-tearing haze while painted ladies circulated throughout the room, polluting the air with cheap perfume. Between the cigars and the cologne, the stench was overwhelming. The obscene language was shocking, the décor lacking, but the entertainment, she had to admit, was quite excellent.

She stood on her tiptoes, trying to get a better look at

the trio of musicians seated in front of the elevated stage. Someone nabbed her arm and she threw a blind punch.

Josh caught her wrist and blasted her with a heated glare. "What are you doing?"

"Checking out the competition," she said, breathing easier now that he was here. The Lucky Lady gave her the willies.

"I told you to stay put."

"You told me to stay dry. The veranda roof leaks."

He sighed and slipped a protective arm about her shoulders. "Let's get out of here."

A musical fanfare rang out over the din causing Paris to dig in her heels. The noise level dipped to a buzz of excited murmurs. "Wait." Her skin tingled with anticipation. She stared up at the stage, flooded with cherished memories of some of her papa's variety shows. "It must be someone special. Please," she added when he seemed intent to leave.

"Five minutes."

A dandified host sauntered across a four-foot make-shift platform taking center stage. Tall and lanky, dressed in a dapper dove-gray suit, his short, brown hair slicked back with pomade, his posture and manner-isms branded him an arrogant man. Rubbing his palms together, he took stock of the audience while the musi-cians played on. Paris tensed when he looked their way, his attention clearly on Josh. Fancy Pants winked, his smile as cold as a frozen pond.

Paris shivered and glanced up at Josh. He acknowl-edged the man by touching the brim of his hat. "Who is he?" she asked. "He doesn't look very—"

"Quiet, boy," a man hissed.

Josh shifted his arm to her waist and pulled her close.

"And now the moment you've all been waiting for," Fancy Pants announced in a broad theatrical voice. "She's the Darling of Denver, the Kitty of Kansas City. She's the gal with the golden voice. Let's hear it for Red Adams!"

Deafening applause accompanied boisterous hoots and shrill whistles. Two men parted a plush green cur-tain, revealing a gorgeous woman with an eye-popping figure. Her magnificent bosom spilled over a low-cut, ruby velvet costume. Her hair, an artfully arranged mass of fiery, auburn ringlets, grazed her bare shoulders. Even her lips were painted the color of cherries.

Paris blinked at Red Adams in stunned wonder. Beautiful, brazen, full-figured. *This* was her competi-tion? Her only hope was that the woman couldn't sing her way out of a pickle barrel. The instrumental trio, consisting of a piano, banjo, and fiddle, finished their intro, whereafter Red chimed in with the opening lyrics to *You Naughty, Naughty Men*. Paris' heart sank to her toes. Red was a first-class vocalist.

"She's not all that great," Josh whispered sympathet-ically in her ear.

"She's better than great." Red handled the stage and the rowdy audience with the grace of a seasoned professional. Paris had no practical experience. No training. She'd actually planned on winging it. Was she crazy?

She pressed a hand over her churning stomach. Maybe if she *eased* herself into the show at the Desert Moon. Yes, that was it. Maybe she could talk the house pianist into allowing her to accompany a couple of the other acts, just to get her stage-feet wet. She could practice in the afternoons and then, after a couple of weeks, she'd make her starring debut. Josh wouldn't mind if she took it slow. She was relatively certain he'd be thrilled if she didn't perform at all. But that wasn't an option.

Red belted her last note, ending with a dramatic bow.

Several men threw coins on the stage. Others shot bullets at the rafters. The woman was a rousing hit. Fancy Pants introduced the next song while motioning Josh forward.

"Come on," he said, taking her by the elbow and maneuvering her through the crowd. "I need to talk to someone."

"I was afraid you were going to say that." Personally, she'd seen and heard more than enough. She didn't want a closer look at the woman who made her feel like a no-talent blockhead. She certainly didn't want Red to get a closer look at her. Dressed like a boy and soaked clean through, she was hardly at her best. Unfortunately, Josh didn't seem to notice her dragging her feet. He steered her closer to the stage, nudging aside smelly drunks as easily as a horse's tail flicks away flies. Did these same men patronize the Desert Moon? "So much for a sophisticated clientele."

Just when she thought things couldn't get more depressing, Red launched into Foster's *Old Folks at Home*. The crowd eagerly chimed in. "Perfect," she muttered. "She stole my opening song." At least she had the satisfaction of knowing her intuition had been dead on. The sing-a-long was a rousing crowd-pleaser.

Two seconds later they were standing in the wings. Aside from the tasseled velvet curtain, the performance space lacked style and imagination as did the rest of the room. No painted backdrops. No stage lighting or comfortable seating. Overall, the Lucky Lady was drab. Everything was makeshift—the bar, the stage— but apparently the only thing anyone cared about was the entertainment. On and off stage. "There's more to running a successful theater than pretty faces and frilly costumes," she noted aloud.

"I agree, my dear. That's why I sent my partner to Phoenix to make a few essential purchases." Fancy Pants stepped off of the stage and extended his callus-free hand in greeting. "Niles Burke. And you are?"

She stared at his long-fingered hand, struck speechless by his gold pinkie ring. It was the gaudiest piece of jewelry she'd ever seen. Wait a minute. *Burke*? Was this man related to Josh's uncle? She sized him up in a heartbeat. An arrogant bully. He was handsome, though not as handsome as Josh. And, like Josh, his eyes were sable brown. However, when she met this man's gaze her stomach didn't flutter, it turned. She took an unconscious step back.

Josh interceded, shaking Niles's hand and making the introductions. "Niles, this is Paris. Paris, this is my cousin. Mason's son. He's part owner of the Lucky Lady."

Paris blinked. If he was Mason's son then why hadn't he inherited the Desert Moon? From Niles's icy smile she had a feeling he wondered the same thing. "Pleased to meet you, Mr. Burke." Although that felt like a lie.

Niles studied her face, his expression warming to cordial. "The pleasure is all mine," he bellowed over the music. "What brings you to Chance?"

"Josh," she said, without thinking.

He crossed his arms and gloated. "That so?"

Josh reached out and grasped her hand, giving it a supportive squeeze. "What brings *you* to Chance, Niles? Since when are you interested in making an honest living?"

"I take it you stopped by Florence. Talked to Wright."

"He filled me in on a few things." Josh angled his head. "Missed you at the funeral."

"Mason didn't." The man slid a cigar from his inner

jacket pocket and lit up. "I think he made it pretty clear what he thought of me."

"He left you a fortune."

"*Half* of a fortune. But that's water under the bridge."

The nerve in Josh's jaw ticked. "Is it?"

"Maybe we should talk somewhere else," Paris whispered, mindful of the escalating tension. Whether she liked Red or not, it was rude to carry on not three feet away from where the woman performed.

"Friendly warning, cousin," Niles said, ignoring her suggestion. "Some of the men in this region are less than thrilled about having another lawman in their midst."

"Ex-lawman."

"Officially, maybe." Niles spit a sliver of tobacco from his tongue then huffed a disgusted breath. "You're a chip off my old man's block."

"I aim on keeping the peace, if that's what you're driving at. In which case I'll issue a friendly warning of my own, *cousin*. Keep your rowdy clientele in hand. I can build a jail in a day if need be, and I won't think twice about filling it with your patrons if they get out of line."

Niles slid a hand deep into his pocket and rocked back on his polished heels. "Last I knew, drinking and whoring weren't out of line."

"If you can't run a respectable business, just keep the flying lead to a minimum."

"That's like asking a man to scratch his ears with his elbows. How do you propose I accomplish this monumental feat?"

"Have them check their guns at the door. Man's got no business waving his piece around when he ties on a bear."

Between the cryptic statements and unfamiliar lingo, Paris was having a hard time keeping up. "Why on earth would a man tie himself to a bear?"

Niles laughed. "Just a colorful phrase for drunkenness, little girl."

Pride smarting, she fixed him with a confident glare. "I'm not a little girl. I'm a performer full grown."

"You don't say." The music stopped and the audience erupted with applause. Niles glanced toward the stage. "Maybe I can fit you into the show. I'll talk with Red and—"

"I'm already spoken for. Thank you, anyway." Looking past Niles, she caught sight of what she thought was a familiar face staring at her from behind the green velvet curtain. The face disappeared before she could decide if she was seeing things. Burgess Riley couldn't be in Chance. He was on the Overland Stagecoach and the coach had yet to arrive in Florence. It wasn't possible, was it? She thought about asking Josh, but he'd want to investigate, and she'd learned her lesson on that score. She glanced up at him. "Can we go now?"

"Sure, honey."

"So that's how it is." A slow, lecherous grin spread across Niles's face.

Paris saw Josh clench his fist. Worried that he was setting to knock that grin off of his cousin's face, she tugged him into the crowd. "Good luck with the Lucky Lady, Mr. Burke."

"Don't involve her in this, Josh," he shouted in reply.

Paris felt Josh tense. For the first time since she'd met him, she sensed that *he* needed *her*. It was a powerful good feeling. Giving his hand a reassuring squeeze, she yelled back, "I'm already involved."

CHAPTER 13

He could hear her wheels turning.

If he had any sense, he'd fess up, tell her they were married, and that he had no intention of allowing her to perform. Surely that would derail his wife's assuredly dangerous train of thought. Instead, he nudged Paris over the Desert Moon threshold, battling a flash-flood of emotions.

He hadn't realized how much he despised Niles until the man had issued that veiled threat. Hadn't realized how deeply he cared for Paris until she'd lashed out in his defense. Neither realization sat well.

Seth was right. His cousin **was a vindictive** bastard, his intentions as obvious as his tasteless jewelry. If he couldn't have the Desert Moon, neither could Josh. But why go to the trouble of running him out of business? Why not set the place ablaze, as Seth suspected he'd done with the original Lucky Lady, and be done with it?

Plainly, Niles wanted to watch him struggle and suffer. Question was, how far would he go to exact his revenge?

Don't involve her in this.

I'm already involved.

He thought about the vehemence in Paris's voice, the way she'd squeezed his hand, as if to say, *don't worry. I'll protect you.* She'd gotten the way of things twisted in her mind. She was the one in need of protecting, and yet her silent decree wrapped around his heart like a thick blanket, warming him to his bones. The sensation proved unsettling.

Almost as unsettling was the possibility that she was in danger. What the hell had he been thinking bringing her into this volatile situation?

A clap of thunder rattled the front window's stained-glass pane. A gust of wind slammed shut the door. Swiping off his Stetson, he sleeved rainwater from his face and noted the room's occupants, his mood foul as the weather.

Two old men sat in the corner hunched over a checker match. Oscar Pike stood behind the bar immersed in a game of solitaire. The barkeep looked up from his cards, smiled at Josh, and then focused on Paris and frowned. He immediately disappeared into the back room.

Josh glanced down at the wildcat, who this moment more closely resembled a drowned kitten. He cursed when she stifled a sneeze. "I'm taking you to the log house to get dry."

She waved off his concern. "I've been dying to see this place. What's ten more minutes?"

He appreciated a stalwart countenance, but this was ridiculous. She hadn't fully recovered from a fever, and yet she'd refused the slicker and rushed up the street, mindless of the driving rain in her haste to get to the opera house. She was soaked to the skin and her boots were sodden and caked with mud. If she caught pneumonia, swear to God, he'd strangle her.

He expected her to make a mad dash for the piano. Lord knows she'd acted recklessly in the past in a bid to tickle the ivories. Instead she stood stock still, arms folded, toe tapping, silently assessing the deserted opera house.

That couldn't be good.

He scanned the dimly lit interior, wondering how the Desert Moon stacked up to the Gilded Garrett. Was Paris pleased or appalled by what she saw? He honestly couldn't tell. It bothered him that he cared, but dammit, he knew the time and sweat Mason had invested in this rustic place. Now that he was here, he felt humbled that his uncle had willed him, what to his mind, represented the mother lode at the end of an honest man's rocky life.

A sturdy pine bar lined the left side of the two-story establishment, complete with a stocked back bar. Gaming and dining tables occupied the first half of the main floor, followed by rows of theater seating. The second floor boasted balcony seating, kerosene sconces, and scenes from Shakespearean plays in gilded picture frames. The elevated stage stood at the far end of the room, its painted backdrop depicting a full moon rising over the Superstitions. Flush against the stage sat an elaborately carved upright piano. He didn't know much about the instrument, except that, according to Mason, it rivaled a Steinway.

He knew the moment she spied the East-coast import. She clasped her hands to her chest and squealed. So why didn't she make her move? Needing a drink and space to breathe, he snagged her hand and pulled her across the room. From the expression on her face he assumed she approved of the upright. In no mood to be charmed, he ignored her fetching smile and plopped her down on the padded stool. She reverently skimmed her fingers over the keys, summoning an awkward tickle in his throat. He suddenly felt as if he were intruding on an intimate encounter. "Ten minutes," he said, then stalked to the bar.

He didn't have to worry about anyone pestering her as there were exactly three men in the opera house and he knew each one. Barky Bob, the former owner of the mercantile, his tall, spindly friend, Tom Noggins, the proprietor of the livery, and Oscar, who'd emerged from the backroom carrying a blanket and steaming mug of coffee. "For the lady," he said, passing Josh on his way to the piano.

"Mighty thoughtful of you, Oscar." He bellied up to the bar, an impressive structure that Mason had constructed with his own two hands. Ignoring a wrench in his gut, he set down his hat, nodding at the barkeep on his return. "Desert Moon's more spacious than I remember."

"That's cuz there ain't no people in here crowdin' it up." The big man rounded the bar and poured Josh a whiskey. "I'm glad you're here, Sheriff."

He grasped the man's hand in a friendly shake. "Sorry it took me so long." He didn't know Oscar well, but Mason had been fond of the six-foot-seven bear of a man. Dependable, trustworthy, and hard working, he'd helped his uncle build the Desert Moon from the ground up. Josh was pleased he'd agreed to stay on. "You can drop the formalities. I'm not the law anymore."

Oscar nodded. "Who's the pretty gal?"

"My wife." He'd offered the information, knowing the news would spread, and hoping it would keep the lonely rowdies in line. He hadn't expected the admission to roll so easily from his tongue or to feel so natural. Now all he had to do was break the news to Paris.

Oscar smiled. "Plays the piano right nice, don't she?"

"Yes, she does." He didn't recognize the song, but he liked it. The melody was simple, but pleasing, although she couldn't seem to get past the one passage. If this is what it was like when she had a song stuck in her head, he sympathized.

"We could use a piano player."

Josh didn't care for the direction of this conversation. "I thought Mason hired someone last month."

"Your cousin Niles," Oscar scowled then spat on floor, "stole him away, along with the fiddle player. Not to mention the acting troupe that arrived three days ago. Mason hired them as a result of a newspaper advertisement. Also hired some high-falutin' singer from San Francisco. Soon as she arrives, Niles," he spat again, "will no doubt steal her, too."

"Over my dead body." He downed his whiskey, signaling for a refill. "Anything else?"

"He stole our cook."

Josh shook his head. "I'm surprised he didn't snatch you."

"Oh, he tried," Barky Bob said, waddling up to the bar. "Oscar spit in his eye."

"Yup." Tom moved in on the other side of Josh. "Spit right in his eye." The man snickered.

Josh's lips twitched. It hadn't escaped his notice that Oscar spit on the floor every time he uttered his cousin's name. He motioned to the man for three more glasses, poured them all a drink. "I appreciate you gentlemen patronizing the Moon."

"Least we could do for Mason," Barky Bob said. "He was our friend."

"Sure do miss him," Tom added.

Josh had summoned emotional distance the moment he'd scaled the steps of the Desert Moon's wraparound veranda. He couldn't shake the sick feeling that Mason had cashed in his chips too soon. Couldn't help but feel that he'd been cheated. But then life was rarely fair. Forcing a smile, he raised his glass in a toast. "Here's to loyalty."

They tossed back their drinks in unison.

Barky Bob cocked a fat thumb over his shoulder. "Who's the boy?"

"That ain't a boy," his crony said. "It's a girl. Take the specs off the top of yer head and put 'em where they belong, for cripes sake."

Barky Bob slid his spectacles down, resting them on the tip of his bulbous nose. "She's dressed like a boy."

"That's Sheriff Grant's wife," Oscar said.

"I'm not the law—"

"She always dress like a boy?" Tom asked.

"Mostly," Josh said. He'd never thought to ask her why, exactly. Dressed in a potato sack, she'd still incite fantasies. He didn't much care what she wore, although he had to admit, seeing her in that corset last night had spiked his pulse to the stars.

"That's probably a good thing," Oscar noted. "Considering there are a lot of lonely men in this town."

"Speaking of lonely," Josh said, indicating the empty room. "How long has it been like this?"

Barky Bob groaned. "Since Niles and Tucker opened the doors to that sin-house."

"And whose fault is that?" Tom asked his friend. "You're the one who sold them the building."

"*You* try turning down that kind of money. Figured I could run my business just as well out of a tent. Besides, I thought I was doin' a favor for Mason's son. Didn't know the smooth-talkin' varmint was gonna turn my building into a sin-house."

Tom snorted in disgust. "I'm just glad Mason ain't here to see it."

"Niles," Oscar turned and spat, "is tryin' to run you out of business, Sheriff."

"I gathered. And call me Josh." He eyed the mirrored back bar. Hordes of bottles lined the shelves. "It's not a lack of liquor that keeps the men away."

"It's the lack of women," Barky Bob said.

"Sportin' women," Tom clarified.

Josh rolled his glass between his palms. "I hadn't planned on importing any Calico Queens. Mason's goal was to civilize this town in hopes that some of the miners would import their wives and families. I aim on honoring his vision."

Barky Bob raised his gray, scraggly eyebrows. "You aim on taming Chance?"

"Aim on doing what comes naturally."

"Glad to hear it, Sheriff," Tom said. "Merely pointin' out the drawin' card of the competition. Scenery's a might more pleasant at the Lucky Lady."

"And more satisfyin' on a randy man's loins," Barky Bob added. He frowned then. "Don't your woman know another song?"

"She seems stuck on that one part," Oscar noted.

"She's drivin' me crazy," Barky Bob said.

Josh laughed. "One of her special talents."

✷ ✷ ✷

Paris slumped forward in frustration, hitting a clunker chord and bonking her forehead against a piano worthy of Mozart. Featuring intricate carvings, inlay, and marquetry, the Weber Upright had been especially designed for the 1876 Centennial Exposition in Philadelphia. She'd seen pictures. She never dreamed she'd have the pleasure of sampling its wonder.

Unfortunately, there was no pleasure to be had. She was blocked. The love song that had driven her to distraction all of last night and most of today eluded her beyond the first verse. Questions swirled in her mind instead of lyrics. Worries in place of melodies.

The Desert Moon exceeded her expectations. It wasn't nearly as elaborate as the Gilded Garrett, or as large, but the design and décor were charming. It plainly offered liquor and gambling, and the stage, with its paneled proscenium arch, exquisite backdrop, and foot lighting, rivaled that of a major theater.

So why did everyone frequent the Lucky Lady? Aside from the two elderly gentlemen, the giant barkeep, and Josh, the Desert Moon looked as empty as a poor woman's cupboard. Was Red that much of a draw? Was the liquor better or lower in price? Were the barmaids prettier?

Come to think of it, where were the Desert Moon's barmaids?

Clutching the blanket the curly-headed giant had draped over her shoulders, she rose and blinked at the stage. Where were the entertainers?

Where was the pianist?

Surely other performers had answered the advertisement. Was she the first to arrive? Would Josh expect her to sing and play the piano to bring in a crowd? To compete with Red Adams? The notion turned her stomach. She envisioned the beautiful, curvy vixen and then considered her own freckled, unpainted face and less than voluptuous figure. She wasn't . . . qualified. Nor did she have a full night's repertoire. She'd been set to ease her way into the show. To work up her nerve, to hone her stage persona. No, indeed, for all her former bluster, she was not ready to take center stage.

Besides, what if she performed and instead of drawing in customers, chased them away? Business was bad enough. Unlike Niles, she wanted to help, not harm Josh. She hadn't worked it all out in her mind, but she had the distinct feeling those two were longtime rivals. Now they were owners of competing establishments.

This moment the odds were stacked in Fancy Pants' favor. What did a lawman know about running a theater?

She, on the other hand, knew plenty!

Charged with excitement and purpose, she tossed off the blanket and rushed the bar.

"Maybe we should reconsider," said the rail-thin man. "Maybe you should get a dove or two. How else are you gonna compete? Maybe one cat with special talents. A saucy gal with big—"

Josh cleared his throat, alerting the men to her presence. Placing a possessive arm about her shoulder, he indicated each man with an introductory nod. "Tom Noggins, Barky Bob, Oscar Pike . . . this is Paris."

"Pleased to meet you gentlemen." She knew she should shrug off Josh's arm, since she didn't want to give his friends the idea that they were sweethearts, but comfort squashed good sense. His big body radiated a blessed heat that caused her to sidle even closer. "I have an idea."

"How come you're dressed like a boy?" Barky Bob asked, scrutinizing her head to toe.

"Because I was traveling alone and wanted to avoid male attention." She shivered and sneezed. "Now, about my idea . . . "

"You're chilled." Josh rubbed his palm up and down her arm.

"Fetch her a brandy," Tom told Oscar.

"I don't—"

She doesn't—"

"—drink," they answered as one.

She frowned up at Josh. How did he know she didn't partake? "And I'm not chilled," she told him before he could drag her off in search of dry clothes. "But I do have an idea."

"A painting!" Oscar slapped a Goliath-sized palm to the polished bar. "We could hang it above the back bar. A gigantic painting with a carved, gilded frame. Clouds and trees and half-naked women." He glanced at Paris, his ruddy cheeks deepening a shade. "I mean, since we ain't havin' the real thing."

"I like the sound of that," Tom said. "The half-naked women part. Not wholly indecent, yet tantalizing. Might work."

Her temper flared. "I was thinking—"

"Your face looks flushed." Josh smoothed her wet hair off of her cheek.

She batted away his hand, shrugged off his arm. "I'm fine. Now this idea of mine—"

"Forget it."

Her mouth dropped open. "Shouldn't you listen to what I have to say before shooting me down?"

"I know what you're going to say, and the answer is, no."

"How could you possibly—"

"You've got a one-track mind."

Insulted, she crossed her arms over her stomach. "Fine. If you don't want my help—"

"I don't."

"I do." Oscar turned pleading eyes on Josh. "Lack of business might not hurt you much as finances go, but it might kill me. Can a body die of boredom?"

"Git yourself a couple of doves," Tom offered. "Prettier ones than Tucker and Burke's. That'll fix their wagon and keep Oscar here entertained."

"No more doves!" Barky Bob snapped. "We're tryin' to clean up this town, remember? I'm hopin' to send for my Gilda real soon. God fearin' woman that she is, she'd have a conniption fit if her new town was overrun with workin' gals!"

"*Barky Bob was a grumpy old cuss, a grumpy old cuss was he. He squawked all day and he groused all night, but the man wouldn't hurt a flea.*" Paris clapped her hand over her mouth. Of all the times for a ditty to come out! She wanted these men to take her seriously, instead she'd pegged herself, and yet again, as a musical freak.

Oscar Pike's eyebrows shot to his hairline.

She didn't dare look at Josh.

Tom Noggins smiled and swatted his red-faced friend on the shoulder. "She has you pegged."

She shook her head, fingered the hem of her shirt. "Sorry about that. I was . . . inspired."

Barky Bob slowly turned, puffed up his chest. "I inspired a song?"

"Yes, well . . ."

He cleared his throat, stuffed his pudgy hands in his pockets and gave her his full attention. "You mentioned some kind of idea. Let's hear it."

"I bet it's creative," Tom said, eyes bright.

Oscar placed his forearms on the bar, leaned forward. "Creative is good."

It took her a couple of seconds to realize they weren't laughing at her or looking at her as if she'd lost her marbles. They were encouraging her to speak her mind. It felt awkward. No, it felt *good*. She smiled. "Actually, I have a couple of ideas."

Josh threw back his whiskey and folded his arms over his chest, making it clear he wasn't open to suggestions.

She didn't care. She was going to offer them anyway. Her brain was zinging with two or three winners. She rubbed her hands together, perched them on her hips. "I could be wrong, but it appeared to me that there's more to the Lucky Lady's allure than a few girls on the fence."

"Girls of the line," Josh corrected, leaning back against the bar and crossing his left boot over his right.

She ignored him and gestured to the back bar. "We have liquor. A man could get chickened here same as down the street."

Barky Bob and Tom looked at one another.

The left side of Josh's mouth hitched up. "I think you mean roostered, darlin'."

"Chickened. Roostered." She waved a dismissive hand. "We also allow gambling."

"Same as the Lucky Lady," Oscar said.

"So what are we missing?" she plowed on.

"Doves!" Tom shouted.

"Entertainment," Barky Bob said.

Tom screwed up his bearded face. "That's what I said."

"A gimmick," Paris said.

Oscar smiled. "Someone like Red Adams."

Josh locked gazes with her, stormy eyes needling in with an intensity that made her skin prickle. "You are *not* performing on my stage."

That's not the gimmick she had in mind. In fact, it's what she hoped to delay. But, dang it, how dare he go back on his word! Did he doubt her talent? Had he listened to her struggling with that one verse, deciding her skills as a pianist were limited? She hadn't been aware she'd been auditioning! Blood simmering toward boil, she matched his glare. "We have a contract."

"No, we don't."

Incensed, she dug Mason's telegram out of her pocket and slammed it on the bar. "Are you going to go back on your uncle's word?"

He unfolded the soggy paper, scanned the message and then passed her back the wire. "I'll honor his word."

"So I can perform."

"Didn't say that."

"But—"

"Telegram says you're hired. Didn't specify the job."

"But—"

"No wife of mine is singing in a gurdy."

"I don't care *what* happened last night," she blasted. "Hell will freeze over before I marry you!"

"Then the devil's wearin' long-johns."

Oscar scratched his head. "I'm confused."

"So am I!" She thought Josh supported her dream. She wanted to help *him* achieve success. Though Lord knows why she should care since he was the most arrogant . . . most infuriating . . . She stomped her foot in frustration. "You said you'd honor M.B.'s word!"

"I don't need a singer."

Tom looked over at Barky Bob. "Are you following this?"

"What *do* you need?"

"Aside from a wife?" Josh asked.

She nodded.

"A cook."

"I'll take it."

Josh pushed off of the bar, his voice ominously low. "But you don't cook."

She smirked. "You should have remembered that before you offered me the job." If he thought he was going to manipulate her into marriage, he had another think coming. She was going to help turn the Desert Moon around, and when she was good and ready, *he* was going to let her perform. Or swear to heaven she'd . . . she'd . . . She sneezed. Twice.

"That's it." Josh hauled her up over his shoulder and strode toward the back door.

Mortified, she smacked his broad back. "Put me down!"

"Want me to tend to your horses?" Tom called.

"Much obliged," Josh said, without breaking stride. "The buckskin and palomino."

"Got any luggage?"

"Just the saddlebags."

"I forgot my carpetbag!" Paris realized, her temples throbbing as the blood rushed to her head.

"Seth's bringing it tomorrow along with the buckboard of supplies I purchased this morning."

Supplies for *their* home. Her heart raced like a spooked rabbit. "What are you doing? Where are you taking me?"

"To bed."

"I'm not sleepy."

"Then I'll have to tire you out." He stalked out the door, into the night and across a small patch of land.

Luckily the rain had eased. Not so her misgivings. From her upside down position, she couldn't make heads or tails of where they were going. "Put me down this instant, you bone-headed brute, or I'll make you always and forever sorry!" She pummeled his back. "Do you hear me?"

"The whole town hears you." He scaled two steps and shoved through a door. "Lower your voice."

"Make me!"

He kicked the door shut and set her down, angling to strike a match to a kerosene lamp.

Golden light flooded the room, illuminating his enigmatic expression. The air crackled with tension. Why, oh, why had she blurted that childish challenge? Wringing her hands, she backed deeper into the excessively furnished sitting room, nearly tumbling backward over a Boston rocker. "On second thought, I am quite tired." She feigned a loud yawn. "If you would direct me to a hotel . . . "

"Chance doesn't have a hotel."

"Then I'll sleep at the Desert Moon. There must be accommodations for the help."

"You'll sleep here. With me." He advanced, backing her flush against the wall. His hot gaze ignited a fire in her belly that fanned out and singed her nether region. Her entire body tingled in anticipation even as her heart pounded with dread. Her mind emptied of everything but song and sensations.

He tangled his fingers in her hair.

Lovers sleeping in the night. Their hearts and hands entwined. One has given up the fight. Lost body, soul, and mind.

Ground his lower region against hers.

One holds onto fear and doubt. Won't say the words aloud. Both afraid of what could be forever and for now.

He played her like a newly tuned piano, striking all the right chords with a kiss that seduced her heart. Music that had failed her back at the opera house gushed forth with an intensity that left her shaking. Or perhaps the telling lyrics were at fault for her trembling. Blindsided by a staggering realization, she shoved him to arms' length.

He pinned her with an arrogant stare, causing the music to falter along with her pulse. Her knees gave way and her butt hit the floor. She glared up at him, her lips swollen from his arduous assault. Her heart pounding with a mixture of lust and outrage. "I hate you."

"That so?" He scooped her up, stalked into the next

room, and dumped her onto a massive bed. Covering her body with his own, he kissed her thoroughly, his hands laying claim to her subtle curves.

Struggling only intensified the friction between their bodies. Her nipples hardened beneath the pressure of his muscled chest. Within seconds, fury succumbed to passion. His hand slid between them, working the buttons of her shirt. She tore her mouth from his, her voice a ragged whisper. "What are you doing?"

"Getting you out of these wet clothes."

Hadn't he performed a similar deed last night? Erotic images flashed behind her closed lids. He suckled her earlobe, and her mind went blank. Her entire being shuddered with licentious desire.

Lifting his head, he gazed down into her heavy-lidded eyes. "Sure you're not just a little fond of me, sweetheart?"

She was more than fond of him.

One has given up the fight. Lost body, soul, and mind.

She was in love.

She turned away, not wanting him to see the truth in her eyes. "This is terrible."

"Oh, I don't know." He rolled off of her, smoothing his palm down her chemise until it came to rest between her legs. "Think of the amazing benefits."

"But you won't let me experience the amazing part unless I agree to marry you." She wanted him to tug down her trousers, to feel his hand upon her flesh, to take her mind off of the fact that her stomach was tied up in knots.

He brushed the back of his hand over her cheek, sending a sweet shiver down her spine. "We have to talk."

"Sheriff, come quick!"

"For the love of Pete." Josh snatched up a spare quilt, covering her just as Oscar skidded over the threshold.

"Whoa!" The barkeep lowered the kerosene lamp to knee level. "I'm sorry . . . I . . . "

"It's all right, Mr. Pike," Paris stammered, hoping to downplay the uncomfortable moment. Honestly, she was grateful for the interruption. Well, sort of. "We were just negotiating my rooming situation."

"Negotiating, my ass." Sporting a severe frown, Josh turned his attention to the barkeep. "What is it?"

"You best come quick." Oscar averted his gaze from the bed. "There's been a shooting at the Lucky Lady."

"It's not Mr. Burke, is it?" Paris shuddered to think that another one of Josh's relatives had suffered harm.

Oscar shook his head and spat over his shoulder. "We should be so lucky."

Josh pushed off the mattress, adjusted his holster. Clearly he meant to investigate. He'd warned his cousin about the "flying lead." It occurred to Paris that even though he was no longer official, he still behaved like a lawman. Apparently, protecting others was in his blood.

She remembered suddenly how he'd once voiced his concerns about her singing on stage in front of rowdy drunks. She thought about the cactus slayers. The patrons shooting at the rafters after Red's performance. *Whiskey tends to affect a man's aim.* She thought about her papa, and cringed. Was it possible that Josh had forbidden her to perform at the Desert Moon, not because he thought she lacked talent, but because he worried about her welfare?

But, of course! It was in his nature to protect.

An affectionate warmth spread through her as she watched him stride after Oscar. He had her best interest at heart.

Looking over his shoulder, he cast a parting threat. "You better be here when I get back."

Sighing, she gave him a mock salute knowing . . . she wasn't going anywhere.

CHAPTER 14

It was well past midnight by the time they got Cobb Sprite buried. His partner had wanted the deed done and over. "Things happen," he'd said. That statement stuck in Josh's craw. This *thing* wouldn't have happened if Lucky Lady patrons had been required to check their guns at the door, or if Niles had kept an eye on his clientele. A professional gambler, he knew how quickly a friendly game of poker could turn sour, but instead of overseeing his establishment, he'd been diddling Red Adams in the back room.

Josh had come by that information after a few inquiries. As to who had actually pulled the trigger, the miners weren't talking. Everyone, including Cobb's partner, claimed the shooting was an accident. It's not as if Josh had the power to do anything even if it had been a true crime.

He wasn't the law anymore.

The fact rankled more than ever. Doing what came naturally was a tad more difficult without a badge. Niles made sure it was almost impossible, reminding every man within earshot that the nearest official lawman presided several miles south in Florence. Josh let it lie, knowing that the *official* lawman would be in town come mornin', and that he had a low opinion of the very man throwing about his name.

Frustrated, he dragged through the front door, stopping short when he spied Paris. He'd been relatively certain she wouldn't bolt, although a small part of him had worried. The only predictable thing about the wildcat was that she was *un*predictable. Finding her asleep, slumped over Mason's roll top desk, was an almighty relief. He couldn't fathom chasing after her in this mood. He'd had it up to his eyeballs with her penchant for misadventure and the havoc it wreaked on his nerves. At first he'd simply thought her accident prone. After a full week in her company he knew the reality was far worse.

Trouble plagued her like a curse.

Between Paris, Niles, the flagging Desert Moon, and this lawless town, he had his hands full.

Life was complicated, but damned interesting.

Moving closer, he noticed she'd fallen asleep while scribbling words and musical notes across a sheet of paper. To her right rose a short stack of similar looking papers, displaying groups of lines, notes, and lyrics. Her treasured sheet music. He felt oddly heartened knowing she'd been bringing something to life while he'd been dealing with death. It brought a strange sense of balance and hope to this unchecked region.

Respecting her privacy, he fought the urge to read her scrawled lyrics, doused the lamp, and lifted her into his arms. Damn, she was tiny. A petite, silky-haired minx with more sand than the desert. Feisty, enthusiastic . . . stubborn. Although she'd changed into one of his dry shirts, she still wore her damp trousers. Did she *want* to catch pneumonia? He pressed his lips to her forehead, relaxing when he felt no fever.

Wrapping her arms about his neck, she sighed and snuggled closer. "Are you all right?" she asked in a groggy voice. Before he could answer, she sneezed.

She'd survived heat exhaustion only to succumb to a chill, and she was worried about *him*? Enduring an increasingly familiar skip in his pulse, he pressed her head against his shoulder and carried her into the bedroom. "I'm fine, kid. Go back to sleep."

Amazingly, she did. Relief blew through him like a cool breeze on a hot day. Yes, he wanted to come clean about the marriage—Lord knows he'd tried a half a dozen times—and, yes, he wanted to make love to her until neither of them could stand. But he didn't want to take her until she'd fully recovered from her ailments. He wanted her wide awake and in good health because it was going to be one hell of a ride. He'd promised her amazing. He planned on unforgettable.

Laying her on the mattress, he reached up under the oversized shirt and gently peeled off her trousers, revealing a set of cotton drawers. He'd undressed his fair share of women. Hell, he'd relieved this one of an alluring corset just last night. So why in the thunder did it unnerve him to strip Paris out of her man's clothing? His fingers actually trembled as he untied the waistband of her drawers and rolled the damp fabric over her slender hips.

It occurred to him that this wasn't just any woman.

This was his *wife*.

Swallowing hard, he ignored the throbbing in his pants when his callused palms slid over her silky thighs. *Don't think about her smooth skin, her clean, flowery scent. Don't think about her lying beneath you, naked and writhing.*

Yeah, sure.

Muttering curses, he shed his clothes and set his gun on the nightstand before joining her under the covers. Rolling to his side, he breathed in her familiar scent of lilacs while studying the gentle curves of her face. Full lips, small, wide nose, impossibly long lashes . . . Moonlight filtered through thin curtains, highlighting the freckles sprinkled across her sunburned cheeks. Those freckles did him in. Most women considered the golden flecks unfashionable, choosing to camouflage them with powder. Not Paris. Her concerns differed from any female he'd ever encountered, and that included domestic interests.

Speaking of domestic, what was he going to do with a cook who admittedly didn't know her way around the kitchen? He'd offered her the job in an attempt to honor Mason's word while hoping to deter her from working at the Desert Moon *period*. She'd called his bluff. He didn't know whether to be impressed or suspicious.

One thing was for sure and for certain, she intrigued him.

He longed to pull her close, to hold her in his arms and soak in her innate vibrancy, but he didn't dare. Though he'd purposely refrained from relieving her of his shirt, he'd thoroughly exposed her bottom half. A man only had so much restraint. Unfortunately, whether awake or asleep, Paris seemed compelled to test his limits. Mumbling something about gimmicks and matinees, she rolled into his arms, and snuggled her bare bottom against his groin.

Gritting his teeth against the sweet torture, he tightened his arm about her waist, bidding her still. When she settled, he kissed the nape of her neck and willed himself to sleep.

Hours later, he finally drifted into a restless slumber, his dreams riddled with snatches of the past. His ma. His pa. Mason, Celia, and Niles. The best and worst of times. And all in the name of love.

* * *

Paris woke at the crack of dawn. A breeze fluttered the muslin curtains of a partially opened window, carrying the scent of newly washed earth. A slash of sunlight warmed her cheeks. She sighed. The first day of her new life. A beautiful, *productive* day. She'd slept like the dead. She felt refreshed. Energized.

She felt something poking her in the backside.

She smelled sandalwood soap and jerked fully awake, shocked that she was in bed with Josh, her bare butt nestled against his . . . Oh, no. Not again. She didn't remember retiring. Didn't remember him crawling in beside her. How was it that she kept waking in this man's bed with no memory of the preceding night? "What's wrong with me?"

She felt him smile against her neck, his voice husky with sleep. "Do you want a list?"

Her breath quickened as his muscled arms flexed and tightened around her bare middle. Skin on skin. Her shirt was bunched up around her waist, and his hand, heaven help her, was splayed over her ribcage, his thumb brushing the underside of her breast.

She squeezed her thighs together to suppress the tingling between her legs.

"How are you feeling?"

Wanton. "Better." She sneezed.

He groaned. "Go back to sleep."

How could he think of sleeping at a time like this! So what if she had a teensy cold? They were naked . . . in bed . . . *together*. She felt so small, so feminine, spooned against his large, sinewy form and yet they fit together perfectly. Words like "destiny" and "forever" danced through her mind in the form of a melodic waltz. Her heart pounded in three-quarter time, slow, loud thuds as his breath warmed the back of her neck, awakening every molecule in her body. She'd never been so . . . aware. Strangely, she wasn't alarmed as much as curious.

His palm slid to the flat of her stomach, pulling her closer. "Stop squirming."

She wasn't squirming. She was feeling the music. Swaying her hips, ever so subtly, in three-quarter time. Not a conscious act, and apparently not so subtle. His splayed fingers singed her skin, kicking up her pulse and altering the waltz to a fandango. Merciful heavens, if he moved his hand lower he could touch her . . . there, and if she twisted just so she could touch his . . . he definitely fancied her. The knowledge made her smile. At least she wasn't alone in this confounding muddle.

I'm in love. She wondered how he'd react if she blurted that admission aloud.

He'd want to get hitched.

The music ceased and her stomach twisted. She'd never forget the way her parents fought. Or the way Athens grieved his wife's death. Whether you loved too little or too much, the outcome was always the same. Marriage equaled broken hearts and dreams. She refused to set herself up for either fall. No, she would have it all without risking anything. Like Victoria Kensington who traveled the circuit with her manager/lover, she would be unconventional.

She settled into the notion, summoning confidence and a bit of derring-do. Smiling, she rolled over and combed her fingers through Josh's rumpled hair while admiring the dark shadows and hard planes of his wickedly handsome face.

He lazily opened those hypnotic eyes, held her gaze for an intense moment before focusing on her mouth.

Her pulse raced. Wiggling against the evidence of his desire, she whispered, "I'm not sleepy."

"No?"

She swallowed hard, hoping he wasn't going to make this difficult. "Last night you said something about tiring me out."

He needed no further encouragement. Lightening

quick, he flipped her on her back and feasted on her lips.

She was vaguely aware of his fingers working her shirt higher and higher, until—*sakes alive*—flesh on flesh. Bare breasts to sinewy chest. She was on fire! Moaning, she kneaded the corded muscles of his arms and shoulders, her tongue tangling with his in a heated, sensual dance. She adored the feel of him, the weight of him. *The taste of him.* Her body tingled with icy-hot shivers when he shifted slightly, trailing his fingers down her cheek, her throat, across the swells of her sensitive breasts. He squeezed her puckered nipple, and she nearly shot off the bed. She grasped his hand, unnerved by the delicious assault on her senses.

He eased away, his hot gaze sparking with desire. "Do you want me to stop?"

She wanted him to go on forever. He inspired provocative thoughts and desires, poignant lyrics and euphonious melodies. He inspired passion. Not trusting herself to speak, she wove her fingers through his disheveled hair and yanked him down for another kiss.

He chuckled, a roguish sound that promised naughty pleasure. He nipped her lower lip, her chin, her *earlobe*. She groaned, shivering with delight as he planted whisper-soft kisses along her jaw, down her neck, between the valley of her breasts.

He closed his mouth around her nipple and sucked.

She gasped, shocked and aroused, the glorious

sensation mounting as he lavished attention on both breasts. She moaned and squirmed beneath him, the blood pounding in her ears like a timpani drum. The pounding intensified when his tongue blazed a hot path down her stomach to the hilt of her womanly mound.

She stiffened.

He lifted his head and scorched her face with a smoldering gaze. "Relax, honey."

Relax? He had to be kidding! Her cheeks blazed as he gently parted her legs. He kissed her soft folds then flicked his tongue over the center of her intimate ache. "Don't . . . "

"What?" Another flick.

"I can't—"

He anchored her hip with one hand, cupped her breast with the other then ravished her with his mouth.

"—breathe." She gave over to fabulously wicked sensation, her muscles tightening and quivering with every lap of his tongue. She dug her fingernails into his shoulders, unable to control the wild bucking of her out-of-control body. Sweat beaded her brow. Tribal music filled her ears, accentuated by the beating of her heart.

Her breath stalled. Her vision blurred. Certain she was going to die; she screamed his name as she reached some indescribable peak, and leapt. She was falling, floating. Drums gave way to chimes. Harps.

Heaven.

"So *that* was amazing," she whispered, when she at last found her voice.

"No," he said, sliding up and positioning himself on top of her. "That was a prelude."

She stared up into his eyes, her stomach coiling into a knot, anticipation heating her blood. How could it possibly get any better?

She heard distant pounding, a creak of a door. Footsteps.

Josh dropped his forehead to hers. "Remind me to put a lock on that front door before the end of the day." Muttering curses, he eased himself off the bed.

She caught a glimpse of his sculptured backside before he stepped into a pair of blue jeans and strapped on his holster. Her stomach tightened with desire. "You're leaving me?" she squeaked. "Now?"

He glanced at the bedroom door while shrugging into a clean white shirt. "Best I go out there before whoever's making noise comes in here." He leaned over her, retrieved his gun from the nightstand and banished her pout with a deep kiss. Easing away, he holstered the Colt and pinned her with a seductive gaze. "Tired?"

"Not a bit," she lied, her cheeks burning in memory of where his mouth had been just moments before.

He quirked an amused **eyebrow then** sauntered toward the door. "Guess I'll have to do better next time."

She bolted upright, clutching the blanket to her

chest. "When?" she asked, stifling a sneeze.

"When you're feeling one-hundred percent. Rest up, honey. You're going to need your energy." He winked, shutting the door behind him.

Paris fell back on the bed, her body tingling as though stung by a thousand bees. Sniffles be hanged. Unconventionality was going to be the death of her.

✳ ✳ ✳

His arousal throbbed within the confines of his jeans. Paris was killing him. Her uninhibited reaction to his oral play had kicked up his desire tenfold. Josh stalked into the sitting room, pumped to flatten the mysterious visitor who'd robbed him of his release.

Seth greeted him with a crooked smile. "Mornin'." Hat in lap, he lazed in a wing chair, his feet propped on a tapestry-covered footstool, crossed at the ankles.

"Make yourself at home," Josh quipped.

"Wouldn't be hard to do." His friend cast his green gaze about the large room. "Never would've pegged Mason as having a taste for the finer things in life. Up-holstered sofa and chairs, rosewood tables, roll top desk. Carpet, for chrissakes. Paris must be pleased. That's if she's of an amiable frame of mind." He looked at Josh. "How's she adjusting to married life?"

He tucked in his shirt, dragged his fingers through

his hair. "She doesn't know."

"If she likes it or not?"

"That we're hitched."

Seth uncrossed his ankles, planted his boots on the woven carpet and leaned forward. "How's that?"

"She doesn't remember the ceremony." Ignoring his friend's look of disbelief, he shrugged then motioned the man to follow him outside. "Let's head to the Moon for some coffee. Oscar's probably got a pot brewing by now."

"How can she not remember?" Seth asked, stepping onto the porch and shutting the door behind them.

"The whiskey. The fever."

"Why haven't you told her?"

"I've tried. Something keeps coming up."

Seth snorted. "I bet."

Josh ignored the lame inference and hurried toward the Desert Moon. A brisk walk and a strong cup of Arbuckle's would rid him of his tension. And put Paris out of earshot. "Heard anything more from her brothers?"

"They'll be in Florence in a matter of days. Haven't figured exactly how I'm going to break it to them that I tricked their little sister into marrying you without getting my ass kicked."

"If you mention the part about walking in on us in bed together, it won't be your ass at risk." Josh pushed through the backdoor of the opera house and followed his nose.

"You're not the least bit intimidated by the Garretts, are you?"

He looked over his shoulder at the man who'd policed the Mexican border with nerves of iron. "Neither are you."

Seth grinned. "No. Then again I'm not the one who stole away their baby sister."

"I didn't *steal* anything." She'd given her heart of her own free will. The marriage vows were another matter. If Seth hadn't instigated the proceedings, her brothers would have. By taking her into his home, his bed, he'd compromised the woman. Marriage was inevitable. Although knowing the way Paris's mind worked, she wouldn't see it that way. For sure and for certain she was going to kick up a fuss. The sooner he broke the news, the better. Maybe after breakfast . . .

"Mornin', gentlemen." Standing at the cast iron stove, Oscar greeted them with a smile and a pot of freshly brewed coffee. He nabbed three cups from the cupboard and placed them on the long, planked table. "Nice to see you again, Sheriff Wright."

"Coffee smells good," Seth said, pulling up a Windsor.

Oscar filled their cups to the brim. "Hope you like it strong."

"The stronger the better," Josh said, taking a seat next to his friend. He motioned to Oscar to join them.

"You here because of the shooting?" the barkeep asked Seth.

Seth frowned. "What shooting?"

"Cobb Sprite caught a belly full of lead last night after accusing someone of cheating at cards," Josh explained.

The stern-faced lawman eyed him over the rim of his cup. "I'm surprised you allow your patrons to carry."

"Didn't happen here. Happened at the Lucky Lady."

Seth narrowed his eyes. "Who pulled the trigger?"

"I know you'd welcome a reason to hang Niles, but it wasn't him. According to the men I interrogated he was backstage." He raised his eyebrows. "Otherwise engaged."

Getting the picture, Seth scowled. "Cobb survive?"

Josh shook his head. "Buried him last night."

"What'd you do with the shooter?"

"Couldn't identify him. There were only a few witnesses and they aren't talking. Claimed it was an accident."

"They're lyin'," Oscar chimed in.

Seth eyed Josh. "Protecting someone?"

He shook his head. "Scared of someone." He'd read it in their twitchy mannerisms. "Niles didn't help matters by pointing out I have no legal authority."

A slow grin spread across Seth's face. "That's what he thinks." He glanced at Oscar. "Get me a bible."

The barkeep scrambled from the room before Josh could stop him. "I'm a theater owner now."

"You're a lawman who owns a theater," Seth amended. "You think I made this trek just to deliver your supplies? I'm conducting an investigation of my own and I'm relatively certain your snake of a cousin is involved. I'm going to find out who burned down the original Lucky Lady and you're going to help me. I'm swearing you in." He winked. "You can thank me later."

Oscar burst back into the room sporting a bible and a look of alarm.

Josh rubbed the back of his neck. "What now?"

The somber man pointed out the window, indicating wispy plumes of smoke. "I'm not sure, but I think your house is on fire."

CHAPTER 15

Blast!" Paris fanned the white smoke billowing up from the frying pan. Another failed batch. Wrapping a cloth around the red-hot handle, she carried the pan to the log house's back door and tossed the crispy contents outdoors alongside similar looking disasters. A mangy brown dog trotted over, sniffed at the food and then trotted away.

"Not even good enough for a mutt." Sighing, she went back inside and clanged the frying pan on the stove. Never in a million years would Josh believe her cooking was *this* bad. She could hardly believe it herself. How many times had she watched Boston make his signature blueberry pancakes? Why hadn't she paid closer attention? Perhaps she'd used too many eggs or too little flour. Maybe the griddle was too hot. Or maybe she should have listened to her mama all those years ago when she'd insisted she spend at least as much time behind the stove as she did the piano.

If she'd learned anything after playing her scales day after day, practice makes perfect.

She mixed up another bowl of batter.

Ladling dollops into the frying pan, she decided that Josh's decision to hire her as a cook instead of a performer wasn't entirely disagreeable. After all, wasn't he really giving her what she wanted? Time to polish her act. To bolster her nerves before going on stage. Yes, things were definitely going as planned . . . in a roundabout way. She'd simply look at this culinary challenge as broadening her horizons. As it happened, food factored into one of the ideas she had for attracting patrons back to the Desert Moon. From what she'd observed, the Lucky Lady didn't even offer so much as pickles or peanuts.

Spatula in hand, she contemplated the crazy things a person did for love. Wait until she told Emily that she actually cooked for a man. She got all teary-eyed just thinking about it. Although maybe it wasn't emotion choking her up so much as the smoke from the charred pancakes. She scraped at the blackened mess with a mumbled curse.

The back door burst open. She squealed and jerked

as three men rushed the room. A burnt pancake flew off of her spatula and hit a duster-clad dandy square in his broad chest.

"What's on fire?" Josh snapped.

Me, Paris thought, gaping at the man who'd stolen her heart. Though he'd tucked his tails into his loose-fitting jeans, the fastenings of his white shirt gaped open revealing bronzed skin and a smattering of dark hair. She shivered recalling those chest hairs tickling her bare breasts. The things he'd done to her in bed . . . Belatedly she remembered his question. "Breakfast," she choked out between coughs.

Oscar Pike rubbed a hand over his curly black hair making it stand on end. "Seein' there ain't no emergency, I best git back. Left something on the stove myself." After a pained look at the smoking pan, he skedaddled.

Waving his hand in front of his face to disperse the haze, Josh glanced at the batter bowl then propped open the back door. "Smoke's thick enough to choke a horse. Just how many pancakes have you burned?"

She shrugged sheepishly, hoping he didn't note the dozen or so she'd tossed outside. "A few."

Chuckling, the handsome stranger brushed charred crumbs from his black vest and loosened the knot of his ebony tie. "You know what they say, Josh. Practice makes perfect."

"My thoughts exactly," Paris said, duly reminded

that they weren't alone. Tidying her braid, she studied the man who stood even taller than Josh. He cut an impressive sight dressed in black from hat to boots with the exception of a crisp white shirt. He swept off his hat to fan away the smoke, revealing a head of cropped blond hair. When he smiled, she relaxed. His dimples and sparkling emerald eyes reminded her of Athens. "You must be Seth."

His amused expression transformed into a mask of disbelief. "This is sure as certain a first."

"I beg your pardon?"

Josh laughed, while pushing open the window above the washbasin. "Seth generally makes a memorable impression on the fairer sex. He's not used to being forgotten."

Paris blushed to the roots of her hair and wiped her hands on the apron she knotted around her waist. "I'm sorry. It's just that . . . that night . . . I was . . . "

"Delirious," Seth finished. He shook his head, cast a sideways glance at Josh. "You gonna tell her?"

"Tell me what?" She glanced back and forth between men. Goodness they made an imposing pair.

"Seth brought your carpetbag," Josh said, shooting his friend a menacing look. "It's outside in a buckboard along with some housing supplies. We'll tote them in after breakfast."

Green Eyes hooted while taking a seat at the kitchen table. "The longer you put it off—"

"Stow it." Josh sidled up to Paris. His attention slid from the batter-encrusted bowl to the burnt remnants in the skillet. "Need some help?"

She glanced over her shoulder at Seth. A cloudy vision of him holding a shotgun sprang to mind. Trepidation skittered down her spine, or maybe Josh was simply rattling her senses with his close proximity. He pressed his hand to the small of her back, an affectionate gesture that sparked images of this morning. She suddenly felt as hot as the griddle. *Don't think about his hands . . . his mouth . . .* She handed him a pot of coffee and shooed him toward the table. "No, thank you." She cringed at the squeak in her voice. "Like your friend said, practice makes perfect and I need to be perfect by dinnertime."

She ladled fresh batter into the pan, watching out of the corner of her eye as Josh snatched two mugs from the cupboard and took a seat. His unshaven jaw and rumpled hair reminded her that he'd been roused out of bed in the midst of their love play. She sighed, causing him to look her way. He quirked a grin as if reading her mind. Embarrassed, she concentrated on her cooking. Merciful heaven, could he be any more handsome?

"I'm thinking we should postpone your official start," he said.

She spun around, eyes wide. "Why? Because of a few scorched pancakes?" She hated feeling so inept. If he'd only give her a chance. "First I can't sing. Now I can't cook."

"Official start of what," Seth asked.

Josh calmly filled the mugs then set the kettle on a folded towel. "Mason promised her a job."

"As a performer," Paris pointed out.

"Not specifically."

"It was implied." She stomped her foot. "Oh, I wish I would have brought M.B's initial telegram."

Josh angled his head. "But you didn't."

Seth cleared his throat, reached for his coffee. "So you hired her to . . ."

"Cook for the Desert Moon," she snapped, turning back to flip her pancakes. Bubbly batter meant time to flip, right? "And now he's back-peddling, which hardly seems fair since I told him three days ago!"

"Told him what?"

"That I can't cook!"

"At all?" Seth asked, clearly shocked.

Temper sparking, she flipped another pancake so as not to chuck her spatula at their visitor's head. "Is there a law somewhere that says just because you're born female, you're an innate seamstress and cook?"

"It has nothing to do with your abilities," Josh said. "If business is anything like last night—"

"It won't be," she assured him. "Red won't be able to compete with what I have to offer."

She heard a choking sound, turned, and saw Josh scowling at his mug. "Too strong?" she asked.

"Red Adams?" Seth sipped his coffee and grimaced.

Josh narrowed his eyes. "You're not prancing around on stage."

She harrumphed. "And you say *I* have a one track mind."

"Tucker always did have a good eye for entertainment," Seth said, heaping sugar into his coffee. "I take it Red's attracting a crowd."

"Standing room only," Paris said. "But I'll fix that."

"Dammit, Paris."

"How?" Seth asked, pushing the sugar bowl toward his grim-faced friend.

Confident she'd concocted a brilliant plan, she turned her attention back to the stove. "We're going to offer patrons home cooked meals."

"But you don't cook," Seth said.

"I'll admit I'm just learning, but how hard could it be to throw together some kind of stew?" She distributed six golden brown pancakes between two lovely china plates. Mason, she'd noticed, appreciated fine art and furnishings. He'd decorated his log house as stylishly as the Desert Moon, and in a fashion that appealed to her own taste. "Besides, the miners won't be able to resist. The first meal is free-of-charge."

"Free-of-charge," Josh repeated, staring at the plates

she set in front of them.

"A calculated risk," Paris explained, wringing her hands. Why weren't they digging in? True, Seth's serving consisted of five silver-dollar pancakes while Josh's singular monstrosity took up the entire plate, but size wasn't everything. At least they weren't burnt. She nodded to their food. "So, what do you think?"

Seth sampled his fare, stopping mid-chew to reach for the molasses. "Free is good."

She screwed up her face. "You hate them."

"Nope. Just like lots of molasses."

Josh swallowed a fork full, smiled.

Her mama's preaching came to mind. *If you can't say anything nice, don't say anything at all*. Exasperated, she nabbed the syrup out of Seth's hand and passed it to Josh. "All right. A free meal *plus* a substantial reduction on libations for the first hour."

Seth raised a suspect brow. "Isn't the idea for Josh to *make* money?"

"He will," she said. "First we have to lure back patrons. I think I'll have a talk with that pianist over at the Lucky Lady."

Josh jabbed the air with his fork. "You stay away from the Lucky Lady."

"Stay away from Niles," Green Eyes said with a fierce scowl.

"But—"

"No buts," Josh said.

The quiet demand brooked no argument. A sick feeling fluttered in her stomach. Had she underestimated the animosity churning between Josh and his cousin? Clearly Niles resented him for inheriting the Desert Moon. She'd pegged Fancy Pants as shallow and petty, and was relatively certain he aimed on running Josh out of business. Not that she'd let that happen. But was there something more nefarious at play? And how did Seth figure in?

Before she could ask, Tom Noggins wobbled over the threshold, rubbing the side of his head. He nodded at Paris, winced. "Mornin', Mrs. Grant."

Mrs. Grant? Had he been drinking? He certainly appeared shaky on his feet. Although to be fair, he had watched Josh carry her off last night, and now she was standing in his kitchen cooking. Drunk or sober, naturally, the man would assume. She straightened her shoulders, telling herself she had no reason to be embarrassed. This was all part of being unconventional. "Actually," she said, clearing her throat, "I'm not—"

"What happened, Tom?" Brow creased in concern, Josh gestured the man over and into a third chair.

He perched his bony frame on the edge of the seat, his weathered face wrinkled in disbelief. "I was robbed."

"Robbed?" Paris exclaimed.

"Actually," Tom said, looking guiltily at Josh. "You

were robbed."

Josh dipped his chin, silently entreating the man to explain.

Paris crumpled into the fourth and last chair. How could Josh be so calm? He'd been robbed! Violated! "Did they break into the Desert Moon?"

"No, no," the livery owner said. "Nothing like that. I was cleaning out the stables like I do every morning and—"

"Oh, no," Paris groaned, feeling heartsick for Josh. "They stole Buckshot."

"Your horse is safe and sound," Tom assured him. "But you can kiss that fancy saddle of yours goodbye."

Even though saddles cost a fortune, Josh retained a calm expression. She suspected he'd rather lose ten saddles to one Buckshot. From what she'd seen he was awfully fond of that horse. She also sensed he didn't want to add to the livery owner's distress. Pale and clammy, the old man looked ready to pass out.

That's when she noticed the goose egg swelling at his temple. Her mouth fell open in dismay. "Did the thief hit you, Mr. Noggins? Why didn't you say something?" She jumped up and hurried to the washbasin. Outraged that someone would attack an elderly, pencil-thin man, she soaked a rag with cool water and snagged an extra coffee mug, wanting to offer comfort.

"That's going to be one hell of a bump," Josh noted

before she applied the wet cloth.

"I feel so dad-blamed stupid," Tom said, pouring a cup of coffee.

"How many were there?" Seth asked.

"Just one. I caught him sneaking out of the tack room. He was big as a bull and smelled as strong as a sheepherder's socks."

Paris wrinkled her nose. "From what I witnessed last night at the Lucky Lady, that could be about anyone."

Seth braced his elbows on his knees, leaned forward. "Can you be more specific, Tom?"

He swiped a gnarled hand over his clammy face. "He hovered in the shadows. Hard to say. Oh, wait. He had a beard."

Josh scratched his stubbled chin. "That describes three-quarters of the men in these parts."

Tom shook his head in disgust. "Chance is goin' to hell in a hand basket." He bolstered himself with a gulp of coffee and grimaced. "Who made this?"

Paris blushed. "I did."

"Oh." He looked up at her and smiled.

Seth cleared his throat. "Well, at least we know it wasn't personal. With all the saddles stored in the tack room—"

"Oh, it was personal," Tom said, setting aside the mug. "Just before he buffaloed me, he said, *Sheriff owes me, and this is only the beginning.*"

Big, smelly, and bearded. Paris's stomach turned as an image of an odious bully came to mind. "Do you think . . . could it be Mr. Riley?" Josh had punched him twice, not to mention she'd done her share of damage.

"Burgess Riley?" Seth asked.

"He was on the stage to Florence," Josh said.

Seth shook his head. "I met the stage. One man disembarked. A flighty salesmen by the name of Hinklemyer. Tried to sell me a sewing machine. Can you imagine?"

Paris wasn't surprised. Probably recited his sales pitch to Mr. Riley too. She could imagine the pea-brained bully stealing a relief horse just to escape Mr. Hinklemyer. Although it didn't explain what he was doing in Chance, it confirmed the possibility. Well, heck. "That cinches it, I guess."

Josh took her hand and pulled her down on his lap. "Cinches what?"

If their two guests thought the action improper, they didn't show it. They merely raised their eyebrows waiting for her to answer. Josh squeezed her waist, signaling her to get on with it.

Fighting a bout of nerves, she nabbed her hair and wove loose strands back into her long braid. "I thought I saw Mr. Riley last night."

"Where?" asked Josh.

She winced. "The Lucky Lady."

"Why didn't you tell me?"

"I was afraid you'd want to investigate."

"So?"

She laid her ribbon on the table, loosened her braid and started over. "The last time I asked you to interfere, you almost got shot. I was afraid . . . I didn't want you to get hurt."

Seth coughed.

Josh smiled. "Slim chance of that."

She abandoned her disheveled braid, and caressed his cheek, her heart pounding with fret. "But what if he caught you unaware?"

Eyes brimming with tenderness, he covered her hand with his own then kissed her palm.

Seth laughed. "Josh was raised with a gun in one hand and a milk bottle in the other. I've yet to see a man get the drop on him."

Paris failed to see the humor. "You don't know Burgess Riley."

"Every lawman north of Phoenix knows Burgess," Seth said. He looked at Josh. "You two butt heads recently?"

"I ridded him of a few teeth."

"Must be more to it than that," Tom said.

Josh glanced at Paris. "There is."

Her stomach pitched. "Maybe we should let the law handle this."

Seth rose. "Good idea." He cast an enigmatic look at Josh. "Good thing I swore you in. Seems a criminal element has infiltrated Chance." He tugged on his hat and hitched back his duster to adjust his holster. That's when she spied the badge.

She blinked at Josh. "Your friend's a sheriff."

"County Sheriff," he clarified, rising and setting Paris on her feet.

Seth ushered Tom to the door then tipped his hat on the way out. "Thank you for breakfast."

Josh brushed his lips across her cheek, spoke close to her ear. "I don't know how long I'll be out. Do me a favor, honey, stick close to Oscar today."

Her thoughts spun with the fury of a cyclone. Seth was a lawman? Is that why she couldn't dispel the image of him toting a shotgun? What if he knew her brothers? Why had he sworn in Josh? Didn't he know about his uncle's dream? Had Josh taken one look at the flagging opera house and given up on his new life?

Agitated, she unwittingly dragged her fingers through her hair causing what was left of her braid to unravel. "But I have things to do."

He caught up her long locks and started weaving. "Ever since I've known you, you've been trying to finagle time with a piano. Spend the afternoon at the Moon, get a few songs out of your head."

She had every intention of doing just that, but that was only the tip of the iceberg. She couldn't help but feel that his uncle's and her papa's dreams were somehow entwined. Somehow, someway, she aimed to make them both come true. She couldn't do that with her butt glued to a cushy stool. It occurred to her then how easy it had been to take refuge behind the piano. Rather than participating in life, she'd merely observed.

Life experience inspires passionate prose.

Emily, she decided, was a genius.

"I'm serious, Paris." He snagged the ribbon off of the table, tied off her braid, and gave it a tug. "Don't wander off."

She glanced down at the tight weave, his thoughtful handiwork causing her heart to swell. "I do know how to defend myself," she reminded him with a grin.

He stroked his jaw, no doubt recalling the first night they met. "Be that as it may . . . "

"Oh, all right," she grumbled, hoping to appease him. "I'll stick close to Oscar."

He leaned forward, grazed his mouth across hers in a whisper-soft thank you. The hypnotic sounds of a heavenly choir reverberated in her ears, leaving her dazed and dreamy-eyed when he eased away.

He scrunched his brow. "You haven't sniffled or sneezed lately."

She stood on her tiptoes and returned the gentle kiss, aching for much, much more. "I'm feeling one-hundred percent."

A slow smile spread over his handsome face. "We'll

pick this up tonight," he promised with a wink.

Seduced into a stupor, she gushed, "I have something to tell you."

"I have something to tell you, too, but it'll have to wait. I need to get over to the livery before the trail turns cold." He gave her a quick, unsatisfying peck then hurried to catch up with Seth.

Weak-kneed she crumpled into a chair. Lord have mercy, she'd almost declared her love. Did he aim on making the same confession? If he loved her then maybe they *could* live together in harmony. Just like Victoria Kensington and her paramour. No marital ties. No promise of disaster.

Her life suddenly resembled one of Emily's romantic stories. A satisfying, heart-tripping adventure. She'd traveled hundreds of miles to lasso the moon. To perform her original compositions. To learn, to grow, to succeed.

Falling in love hadn't been part of the plan. Yet she was learning and growing in ways she'd never imagined. By experiencing life, she was bettering her art. Lyrically, her newest compositions possessed depth, something, according to the music publishers, her former submissions had lacked. She intended to try them out on the public. As soon as she completed them. As soon as she worked up a sufficient act. As soon as she could convince Josh that it was safe to allow her on stage. Yes, that was the solution. She needed to create a safe working environment within the Desert Moon.

She'd make sure to keep that in mind while winning back Josh's clientele. The mere notion of making his business a success catapulted her spirits. Her body tingled with the thrill of the challenge.

Home-cooked meals, discounted drinks . . . if only they had a *gimmick*.

Like a random bolt of lightning, inspiration struck fast and fierce. Instead of shying away, she surprised herself by embracing the crazy notion.

Giddy with confidence, Paris doused the fire in the stove and scrambled out the back door in search of her carpetbag.

Miracle of miracles, she no longer felt like a freak.

CHAPTER 16

It was sundown by the time the lawmen returned to Chance. After exhausting all leads at the livery, Josh had borrowed a saddle from Tom. Soon after, he and Seth had ridden out to interview every prospector and rancher in the region. Their badges and some harmless arm-twisting loosened a few tongues and by mid-day they had reason to believe that the robbery and Sprite shooting might be related. They'd never known Burgess to murder a man, but they'd known him to cheat at cards, and when riled, known him to draw quicker than you could spit and say howdy.

Stories were conflicting at best. Most claimed they hadn't witnessed the actual shooting. The few that had still called it an accident. Everyone agreed the offender wasn't one of their own and that they didn't want any trouble. Two men braved a description that pretty much pegged Burgess. No one knew where he was staying or if he was even still in town.

"I say we pay a visit to the Lucky Lady," Seth said, as they sauntered up the sole, deserted street of town. "It'll give me an excuse to badger your snake of a cousin."

Josh recoiled just thinking about the venomous man. "He didn't seem the least bit disturbed by Mason's death. My old man hurt me to the quick but I still grieved his passing."

"That's because you have a heart."

"And Niles doesn't?"

"Are you forgetting some of those stories you told me? The man drowned a sack full of kittens, for chrissake."

Josh flinched at the memory. "He was just a boy then."

"Yeah, well, imagine what he's capable of now."

He stopped in his tracks, his stomach tied up in a passel of knots.

"What's wrong?"

"Last night. Niles was wearing a pinkie ring crudely fashioned out of a gold nugget."

Seth braced his hands on his hips. "So?"

"Where do you think he got the nugget?"

"Hell, he could've won it in a game of poker. You know how these prospectors are. Half the time they don't even bother exchanging ore for cash."

Josh shook his head, sick at the direction his mind was taking. "He wore it like a trophy. Flashed it around like he wanted me to notice."

Seth stood akimbo. "You think Mason revealed the location of his find?"

Josh nearly choked on his words. "I think he'd die first." Mason had been tracking a notorious stage robber through the Superstitions when he'd happened upon the skeletal remains of a pack burro and a portion of a disintegrated packsaddle. The saddlebag contained gold concentrate. Fanning out, he found the remains of five other burros—five more saddlebags filled with gold. He'd stumbled upon a legendary fortune. Thinking it was a gift from above he'd left half behind for the next deserving soul. Niles was far from deserving.

"Mason kept the first nugget from his find in his pocket," Josh said. "Called it his lucky charm. When I inspected his belongings, the nugget was missing. Didn't think much of it at the time, figuring either he lost it or maybe left it in another pair of trousers. But now . . . "

Seth shifted his weight, glanced at the saloon. "Much as I'd like to jump on your train of thought, according to sources your cousin was in Phoenix the night of the accident."

"Double check your sources." Josh marched toward the Lucky Lady, a hundred scenarios flashing through his mind, all of them ugly. He near about knocked the door from the hinges breaching the threshold. The place was empty aside from two barkeepers, four lounging doves, and a troupe of rehearsing actors. Josh eyeballed a barkeep. "Where's Niles."

"Same as everyone else," he said, polishing a row of glasses. "The Desert Moon."

They were out the door and up the street in two minutes flat.

They topped the steps to the opera house just as Oscar pushed through the doors. The bear of a man looked as nervous as a prostitute in church. "Where in tarnation have you been?"

Josh tried to sidestep him. "Where's Paris?"

Oscar gripped his shoulder, anchored him to his spot. "In the kitchen. She's fine. Loony, but fine."

"What about Niles?"

"Sittin' at a corner table. Don't worry. Told him I'd boot him out if he so much as looked crossed-eyed at your woman."

Josh shrugged off the barkeep's hand. "If everything's fine, why don't you want me to go in."

Oscar jammed his hands through his wiry hair, making him look like a crazed sheep. "I just wanted you to know that I was not a willing participant in your wife's harebrained, half-baked scheme."

Josh clapped a hand to the back of his neck and rubbed.

Seth mimicked the action.

The barkeep folded his beefy arms over his chest, and lowered his voice to a frustrated growl. "She wanted to visit every mining camp in the vicinity. Wanted to extend a personal invitation to dinner. And get this, she told 'em their meal would be free-of-charge!"

"Her coffee's belly wash," Seth said. "And her flapjacks tasted like—"

"I know what they tasted like," Josh said. It was all he could do not to bust through the doors and shake the living daylights out of her for taking such an asinine risk. "Go on, Oscar."

"I asked her what she aimed on accomplishing with that noodle-brained offer. Here we're already losin' money and she wants to give stuff away? What kind of sense does that make?"

"I'm sure it makes perfect sense to Paris," Josh said. The thought of her visiting desolate places, fraternizing with lonely men, set his teeth on edge. At least she'd kept her promise by sticking close to Oscar, or rather, having him stick close to her.

Seth plucked a cheroot from his vest pocket and lit up. "You must have hit those camps after we'd come and gone."

"Yeah, well, we only managed three—Miss Paris is a might timid rider—still, you know how word spreads. Now, here's where it gets peculiar."

Like the situation wasn't peculiar enough.

"She introduced herself to every man on site, making a point to reveal a little about herself, but mostly she got the men to talk about their own personal lives. They was pleased as punch jawin' with a woman as pretty as your missus."

"I'll bet." Josh cringed at his jealous tone. "So what you're telling me is that we've got a house full of men expecting a free meal. An edible home-cooked meal."

"You're doomed," Seth said.

"Let's get this over with." Josh pushed through the doors. He expected ten, fifteen bodies. He was greeted with at least thirty, including Niles. He acknowledged the man's cocky wave with a curt nod. He itched like hell to question him about that gold nugget, but now wasn't the time. Reining in his emotions, he headed for the bar.

"Evenin', Sheriff," several men chimed.

"Evenin'," Josh and Seth answered.

"They bathed," his friend said, pointing out the difference between these men and the ones they'd interviewed scant hours before.

"And groomed," Josh added. Their hair, though still greasy, had been combed and all of them, each and every one, had a napkin placed on their laps. He turned to Oscar.

"There was a catch to your lady's free food offer.

The men had to clean up or clear out. They ain't had an honest-to-gosh home-cooked meal in who knows how long, and I suspect they ain't never been served by someone as pretty as this gal, so they slicked up."

"But she can't cook," Seth said as they bellied up to the bar.

"They don't know that. Yet." Oscar rounded the bar. "Oh, and another thing." Reaching down, he produced a .45 and a Winchester. "She made 'em check their guns. I got pert near forty pieces under here."

Despite his edgy mood, Josh smiled. "That's my girl." He scanned the room. "Why are they so quiet?"

"They're waiting for the next rhyme."

Seth swiped off his hat and set it on the bar. "She's reciting poetry?"

"Not exactly."

"What exactly?" Josh asked.

"Everyone's impressed." Oscar poured them a whiskey. "Myself included. She's in the kitchen. She should be out any second."

On cue, she floated into the room as cheerful and bright as the radiant summer sun.

Seth's mouth curved into a slow, appreciative smile. "She's wearing a dress."

Tongue-tied, Josh ogled the lemon-yellow confection. Lace-trimmed neckline. Fitted bodice. Full skirts. Stylish, yet simple. The gown must've been rolled up in her carpetbag. He swallowed the lump in his throat and tried not to drool. He'd never seen her in a dress. The transformation from tomboy to sophisticated woman was unsettling. She looked feminine, fragile, and too damned appealing to be circulating with these yahoos. She'd twisted her hair into a loose knot, a wasted effort since several tendrils had escaped, the wispy strands cascading down her back. Then again, when had her silky hair ever cooperated? He gawked in wonder as she flitted about the room, distributing baskets of bread to the moony-eyed miners.

He froze when they locked gazes, her sweet smile damn near knocking him off balance. His heart slammed against his chest, threatening to burst through his ribs, clean through his skin. He'd been away from her all day. He'd *missed* her. "I'll be damned."

"We're ready for the next ditty," someone shouted.

Several voices rang out in agreement.

She flinched, tore her gaze from Josh's. "I thought I did everyone."

Seth choked.

Josh downed his whiskey in one fiery swallow, hoping the miners had the good sense not to jump on that suggestive statement, otherwise he'd have to break some noses.

"Over here," someone called. "You ain't done Big Amos Rind!"

All eyes shifted to the back of the room. "Do Amos Rind! Do Amos Rind!" they chanted.

What the hell was she supposed to do to that two-hundred-and-fifty-some pound grizzly? Josh clenched his jaw and tapped his glass to the bar, demanding another shot.

Oscar hurriedly complied.

A hush fell over the room as she circled the table like a hawk surveying her prey. She looked Big Amos up and down, side to side. He did the same to her though his eyes had far less distance to travel.

She smiled at him.

He smiled back . . . sort of.

She whispered into his ear.

He whispered something back.

The crowd stirred, banging fists to table, chanting, "Di-tty! Di-tty!"

Paris raised her hand, signaling for quiet as she took a seat at the piano. She smoothed her skirts, cleared her throat, and flashed Josh a "forgive me" smile that he didn't quite understand. Her fingers danced over the keys, she opened her mouth and sang, and damnation, he got the point.

"Never, oh, never if even I could. Never I would. Never I would. Poke fun at someone so misunderstood. Never I would. Never I would.

"Look past the girth. Look deep inside. His heart is as big

as his stomach is wide. Never, oh, ever, will you ever find . . . a truer companion than Big Amos Rind."

She sang. In his opera house. Against his wishes. She *sang*.

Blatant defiance. Why wasn't he surprised?

"Gotta admit, she's got one helluva voice," Seth said, amusement lacing his tone.

If the crowd felt the same, they didn't show it. They simply stared at Big Amos Rind, waiting for his reaction. Apparently, the man's sense of humor was in question. But then he clapped and guffawed and the patrons erupted into boisterous applause.

Paris stood, curtsied, and then wove through the crowded tables toward Josh.

She looked so damned fetching in that gown, so feminine and petite, he fully expected one of the men to reach out and yank her down onto his lap—in which case he'd have to pound the daylights out of the bastard. But they merely stared up at her in reverent awe.

Seth laughed under his breath. "You've got it bad, my friend."

As much as he wanted to argue the observation, he couldn't. Annoyed, he shifted his stance and tempered his expression, but he couldn't tear his eyes away from Paris. His wife, the someday mother of his children, had just charmed a roomful of hellraisers. His heart hammered against his ribs when she threw herself into his arms.

"I know," she exclaimed breathlessly. "They're not the compositions I pour my heart and sweat into, but they come so easily. And here, at least, they seem to bring joy."

His anger evaporated as she melted against him, her heart on her sleeve. The ditties that had condemned her as a musical freak in her hometown pegged her as a special talent in Chance. What the hell was he supposed to do with that?

"If only Papa and Mason were here to see this," she whispered into his ear. Before he could rope a thought, she was out of his arms and on her way back to the kitchen. "You're just in time," she called over her shoulder. "Dinner's ready."

"Yippee," Seth grumbled.

Oscar leaned over the bar, whispering, "Don't worry. I set us aside something for later."

His mind jumping tracks, Josh eyed Niles, hoping for Mason's sake that his suspicions proved wrong. "Maybe it won't be that bad."

Seth snorted. "Famous last words."

The next half an hour crawled by slower than a snail on crutches. Paris served what she pronounced as her "special stew". It was special all right. Especially bad.

Josh had watched in stunned wonder as the men audibly gulped their first forkful. Barky Bob spit a potato clean over Tom's shoulder then lunged for his beer. He downed the brew lickety-split. In kind, all of the men drained their glasses dust dry. And like Josh, they were sweating profusely. His wife had gone a tad overboard on the spices.

Niles slipped out after his first nibble. If it hadn't have been for Big Amos Rind's intervention, the whole boodle would've run hacking from the opera house. "Ain't never tasted nothin' like it, Mrs. Grant," he'd barked out between coughs. "Surely do appreciate your efforts." Then he'd forked in another mouthful, daring the rest of patrons to follow suit. Forcing meek smiles, they complied. They also consumed a lot of liquor.

"Even if they don't set a foot back in this place," Seth said in a scratchy voice, "I think you sold enough booze to hold you over until you hire a new cook." He dabbed a folded bandana to his brow. "Please tell me you're going to hire another cook."

"I can't fire my own wife."

"She doesn't even *know* she's your wife."

Oh, yeah. That discussion loomed over his head like an ax. Between his troubles with Burgess and Niles he'd almost forgotten. He gulped down a glass of beer in one long swallow then sleeved sweat from his creased brow. "Maybe if I give her a few cooking lessons."

Seth rolled watery eyes. "There aren't enough lessons in the world."

Paris approached at that precise moment, looking wrung out and somewhat harried. "Excuse me, Josh, but I'm wondering if you could set these men straight."

"What's the problem?"

She batted wayward strands out of her flushed face then perched her fists on her hips.

He tried to focus on her concerns rather than the fact that she was so blasted pretty.

"They're under the misconception that we're married. I have tried to tell them differently, but one says he heard it from the other who heard it from someone who should know." Her voice strained louder and the room grew quiet, all eyes turning her way. "I just . . . I don't know where they got this ridiculous notion, and it's really most wearing to argue." She clasped her hand over her throat. "Between trying to set them straight and singing all those ditties, I think I strained something. My throat's on fire."

"Maybe it's the spices," Seth drawled.

Josh kicked him. He didn't need any help making a bad situation worse.

She flung her arms wide, her voice a strangled plea. "Please, tell these men that we are *not* married."

Thirty-some pairs of eyes shifted to him. Thirty-some I'm-desperate-for-a-pretty-woman eyes. He faced her full on, braced himself for a slap, a punch, hell, maybe even a knee. "Can't do that, honey."

"Why not?"

"I'd be lying."

She absorbed his words and staggered back a step, shaking her head, no, as if that would negate the realization.

Seth hefted a shotgun from over the bar, letting it swing at his side. "Do you really hear angels sing when Josh kisses you?"

She closed her eyes, groaned. "I do." After a moment, she fixed her sights on him and he knew, from expression alone, she'd remembered a good portion of the night. At least the shotgun wedding part. Without a word she turned on her heel and disappeared out the back door.

Seth tossed the shotgun to Oscar, elbowed Josh. "That wasn't so bad."

Josh dragged his hand through his hair. "I'm not so sure."

Just then two painted cats sashayed through the front door. "Lucky Lady's offering three shots of our best whiskey for the price of one, thirty minute's prior to Red's first show." They wiggled their fannies and winked. "That's just about now!"

The room emptied in a heartbeat.

Oscar sighed. "Glad Miss Paris wasn't here to see that."

Seth eyed Josh, then pushed aside his plate and motioned to the barkeep. "Let's get some fresh air."

Josh took a deep breath and headed for the log house.

* * *

SPLAT!

She nailed him with an egg, smack in the forehead, the moment he crossed the threshold of the log house's kitchen.

He stumbled back from the shock, swiped away the goo before it trickled in his eyes. "I know you're upset . . ."

SPLAT!

A second egg, square in his chest. She was more than upset. She was furious. She tried to curse him to the devil, but the words wouldn't come.

Pinning her with a look that he probably used when dealing with delusional bandits, he swiped away yolk and broken shells. "Let's talk about this like two rational—"

She heaved another egg.

He ducked.

SPLAT!

He eyed the assaulted wall. Eyed her. "—adults." Clenching his jaw, he rushed forward, just as she grabbed two more eggs. His momentum sent them crashing against the back door, crushing the eggs between their bodies.

She shoved him back, gawked at the yolk staining her bodice. Her eyes burned with tears. "You ruined everything!" she shouted, wiping her hands on her skirts.

"Oh, for the love of . . ." he shoved his hand through his hair, slicking it back with sticky egg white. "Don't cry, honey. I'm sure your gown isn't ruined."

"I'm not talking about my gown! I'm talking about us!" She stood frozen, stunned. She'd had it all planned. She couldn't have asked for a better turn out for dinner, or a better reception to her ditties. Later tonight, she'd intended to discuss their unconventional relationship. "Everything was perfect!"

He moved forward, took her into his arms. "It's still perfect."

"How can you say that?" She struggled, punched him in the shoulder. "We're *married*. We're stuck together." She hit him again. "*Forever.*"

He tightened his hold. "Is that so bad?"

She held herself rigid. "You knew how I felt about marriage, and even so you *tricked* me." She'd choke before confessing that she actually looked forward to sleeping in his arms every night for the rest of her life.

He rested his chin on her head, stroked his palm up and down her back. "I admit, I took advantage. But sweetheart, your reputation was compromised."

"How am I going to break this to my brothers?"

"Trust me, they'll approve."

Envisioning Green Eyes and his shotgun, she pushed back and glared. "I hope you don't expect me to believe Seth forced you to wed, not after you practically ordered me to marry you."

He smiled down at her, and darn it all, her heart skipped. "No, but *he* thinks he forced the issue. He's big on doing the right thing."

"But it's *not* the right thing. Marriage equals—"

"—two people trying their best to make each other happy." He sobered, his tone brimming with earnest conviction. "I can make you happy, Paris."

She wanted to believe that. But . . . "What about my dream?"

"You mean your pa's dream."

"And your dream?"

"You mean Mason's dream."

Her head spun. "I can't argue just now. I can't think."

"You don't have to think." He placed his palm over her heart. "Feel."

Her heart pounded beneath his touch, her knees weakened, and she swore the earth shifted slightly under her feet. New ground, she thought, hearing the sound of a distant harp. Higher ground.

He framed her face with his strong hands and brushed his lips across her mouth. "Do you really hear angels sing when I kiss you?"

"You know I do," she grumbled, refusing to be seduced.

He kissed her again, longer, deeper. "Do you love me?"

She melted against him, cursing her traitorous body.

Maybe she couldn't control her physical response to him, but she could sure as heck mind her words. "As if I could love a double-crossing, arrogant, dip-doodled mule."

He laughed softly, clasped her hand and squeezed. "Hitch your star to the Desert Moon. Destiny. Fate. Call it what you will. We were meant to be, Paris."

She studied their entwined fingers, overwhelmed by the affection in his possessive grasp. The wealth of sincerity glittering in his warm brown eyes tempered the last of her anger. "I think so too." Though something didn't feel quite right. Maybe it was because she'd been out of her mind with fever and drink and tricked to wed at gunpoint. Or maybe it was because he hadn't said anything about loving her back. She knew without a doubt that he cared about her, worried about her. Desire definitely figured in. But what about love?

She was afraid to ask.

"What were you doing, anyway?" he asked, gesturing to the mess she'd made on the table.

"Baking a cake." It was either that or break every piece of china in the cupboard. She'd had to do something with her pent-up rage. "Tomorrow's Barky Bob's birthday, and since he doesn't have any family here . . . " she shrugged.

"It was a nice thought."

"But?"

He scratched his forehead, rubbed the back of his neck.

She crossed her arms over her middle. "What?"

"Your cooking leaves a little to be desired, darlin'."

"A little?"

"A lot."

"I don't understand. Everyone seemed to like my stew."

"They were being polite. Your ditties, however, they loved."

It pleased her that he'd noticed. "You're not mad at me for singing, are you? I wasn't really performing. I wasn't on stage. I certainly didn't *prance*."

He laughed. "No, but you flitted."

She scrunched her brow. "I *never* flit."

"It was damned cute. You're cute." He smoothed her hair out of her face, his gaze softening. "I take that back. You're beautiful."

She flushed. No man had ever called her beautiful, and even if one had, she couldn't imagine the compliment sounding so sincere. Maybe he was right. Maybe marriage didn't have to equal broken hearts and dreams. How could something that felt so right, be wrong?

Rattled by his intense gaze, she noted the absurd. "You have egg in your hair."

He grinned. "You have flour on your cheeks."

She didn't doubt it. She'd mixed the ingredients in a fit of anger. A liberal amount of flour and baking powder had ended up on her skirt.

"And sugar lips."

"I don't—"

He leaned in, nipped her bottom lip and suckled. "Never tasted anything sweeter," he said, lifting her into his arms.

She sagged against him, distracted by an unexpected bridge to her love song.

Lose your heart, you may risk your dream. But are dreams really what they seem?

She'd have to give those cryptic lyrics due thought. That's if she ever regained her senses.

"You know," he said, as he carried her into the bedroom. "There are benefits to being hitched. *Amazing* benefits."

Her body tingled in anticipation. "You're just trying to make up for the fact that you took advantage of a feverish woman."

He laid her on the bed, tugged off her shoes. "Is it working?"

"I'll let you know." She sighed when his fingers made quick work of her buttons. "Seems you're always undressing me."

He parted her bodice, smiled. "Can't blame a man for wanting a glimpse of heaven." He lowered his head, skimmed his lips down her neck, over the soft hollow of her throat, and lavished attention on both breasts.

She moaned as a blissful heat spread throughout her limbs and time blurred.

Before she knew it he'd stripped her bare. Moonlight blazed through the open window, flooding the room in ethereal light, leaving nothing to the imagination. "Maybe I'm unconventional after all," she murmured, dazed by his passionate kisses.

He smiled, smoothing his palm over her flat belly. "What do you mean?"

Her skin prickled as his hand skated lower. "I'm naked."

"Gloriously naked."

"And I'm not embarrassed."

Her blunt admission caused his eyes to spark with unabashed passion. She reveled in the knowledge that she could arouse him with mere words. "You've got no call," he said. "Everything's proper between man and wife."

She squirmed as he teased her slick folds, stroked her sensitive nub. His touch was sensual, magical. "Everything?" she whispered, catching a glimpse of the stars.

"And anything." He took her higher . . . higher . . .

He suckled her earlobe, breached her channel with his finger . . . and the heavens exploded.

"Beautiful," Josh said.

Body tingling, she lazed open her eyes. Why was he looking at her with such wonder? *He* was the one who took *her* to new and exciting places. Inspired to reciprocate, she tugged at his shirt. "Take off your clothes." She wanted to see him, feel him. She wanted to show him the stars.

"Music to my ears," he said with a smile in his voice. He pushed off of the bed, shucked his boots and shirt, and reached for the buttons on his jeans.

She scrambled to her knees. "Wait. Let me." With trembling hands, she slowly slid his jeans down over his hips. His John Thomas sprang free and she openly stared. Intrigued, she wrapped her fingers around his shaft, wondering how something could feel so soft and yet so hard? She moved her hand back and forth, exploring the texture, stopping only when he closed his hand over hers and groaned. Glancing up, she marveled at his intense expression, his jaw clenched tight as though he were in pain. She knew all about exquisite aches. She thought about the way he'd pleasured her with his mouth. "Anything's proper?"

He managed a slow nod.

Curious, she leaned forward, brushed her lips over the tip—so soft—flicked her tongue over the ridge.

He sucked in a harsh breath. "You're killing me." In one fluid movement, he eased away, kicked off his jeans, and gently pushed her back on the bed.

"You didn't like it?"

He laughed, a husky, ornery sound that melted her bones. "Oh, I liked it, honey. But just now, my mind's on a different kind of pleasure." He wedged his knee between hers, urged her to spread her legs.

Although she welcomed the weight of him—all those breathtaking muscles flush against her soft skin—she stiffened when the tip of his shaft grazed her folds. Curiosity gave way to anxiety. "I know the way of things," she croaked, splaying her palms against his chest. "This isn't going to work."

Bracing his weight on his forearms, he smiled down at her, his gaze tender. "Why not?"

"You're too big," she said bluntly. She'd seen him, *touched* him. She couldn't imagine how in the world it would fit. The very idea made her light-headed.

"Thank you for the compliment. But, trust me, it'll work." He shifted and smoothed his hand over her furrowed brow. "You do trust me, don't you?"

The last week flashed before her eyes and she knew, without a doubt, that she could trust him with her life. Maybe even with her heart. "Remember," she said, forcing a shaky smile. "You promised me amazing."

He kissed her deeply, obliterating any lingering doubts.

She embraced the moment, reveled in the feel of his mouth and hands. She allowed nature to take its course. Soon her body was pliant and pulsing with need. She pleaded for release, begged.

Josh prolonged her agony, his sinewy body poised and quaking above her. "Since you know the way of things, you know there'll be pain before pleasure, right, honey?"

Throat clogged with conflicting emotions, she nodded then, unable to withstand the anticipation, grabbed his wondrous backside and pulled him deep inside. The intrusion was swift and painful. She blinked back tears and prayed for pleasure.

"I *was* going to take it slow," he said, his voice a strained rasp.

"Quick is usually less painful," she whispered. "Usually."

"A wildcat through and through." He kissed away a renegade tear, dropped his forehead to hers, and remained still for what seemed an eternity.

"I'm still waiting for amazing," she said, adjusting to the feel of him. It didn't hurt that bad, but it didn't feel that good either.

Then he began to move. Slowly at first, in and out, in and out, a strange friction that shocked her senses, making her tingle in a very good way. Then faster. Harder. She curled her fingers into his shoulders, holding on for dear life as he took her on an indescribable adventure. How had she ever thought him too big?

"More," she whispered, urging him deeper. Her mind swirled with vivid colors until a rainbow of sensations arced through her bucking body.

"Look at me," he beckoned in a foreign tone.

She met his heated gaze, registered the desire, the affection . . . the confusion. Maybe he didn't love her, but he felt something darn close. Tears pooled in her eyes as she experienced a grand epiphany. She no longer feared marriage. Loving him was worth the risk.

He thrust deep inside her, taking her beyond the stars. "Speak your heart, wife."

Melting under the intensity of those beguiling eyes, she bared her soul. "I love you, Josh."

He rasped her name and together they soared.

CHAPTER 17

Her husband was a cad.

What kind of man ignored his wife the day after they'd shared such an intensely intimate experience?

Last night, after they'd both recovered from her first time, she'd expressed interest in a second time. Practice makes perfect, she'd teased, but he'd told her it was too soon. She'd be too tender. Tomorrow, he'd promised, and then he'd wrapped her in his arms and they'd fallen asleep spooning.

Waking up alone had been a disappointment—she didn't feel *all* that tender—but then she'd brightened thinking he might be in the kitchen. Making her breakfast would be a very romantic gesture. She'd hurriedly washed, pulled on trousers and a shirt only to suffer more disappointment. He wasn't in the kitchen. He wasn't anywhere in the house.

Maybe he'd gone to pick her flowers.

She'd spent the next hour sitting out back admiring the Superstition Mountains, another hour tidying the house, rearranging furniture, trying to absorb the fact that this was now her home. Still no Josh. Concerned, she'd walked over to the Desert Moon. Maybe he was handling business.

He was. But not opera house business. According to Oscar, he and Seth, along with the help of a few other conscientious men, were building a jailhouse. "Civilization," he'd said, "is coming to Chance."

Fine. She understood the importance of law and order. There'd been a shooting and a robbery in the space of twenty-four hours. Something had to be done. But at least he could have left her a note. She was trying very hard to adjust to this notion of marriage. He'd sworn he could make her happy, and though he'd made her delirious last night in bed, this morning was another matter entirely.

Her anxiety mounted by the minute.

She knew she wasn't very good company and yet Oscar kindly invited her to join him for lunch. Now they sat, just the two of them, at the long puncheon table that took up the greater part of the Moon's kitchen. Paris obsessed and picked at her food. Oscar pored over paperwork in between bites.

"I could visit him at the building site," she said.

Engrossed in his ledger, Oscar nibbled the end of his pencil then scribbled a set of numbers. "You could."

"What if he gave me the cold shoulder in front of everyone?"

"Why would he do that?"

She shrugged, not that he noticed because his nose was buried in the thick ledger. Not that she'd confide in him anyway. Her fears were too personal. What if Josh was having second thoughts? What if her lovemaking was as bad as her cooking? Maybe that's why he'd taken off. Maybe he couldn't say anything nice so . . . "Blast!"

Oscar looked up from his paperwork. "Too strong?"

Paris blinked at her coffee. "Oh. No. I was just . . . " She set down the mug and folded her hands in her lap. "Actually, your coffee is delicious." *Unlike mine*. "And I very much enjoyed the biscuits and gravy. How would you feel about giving me some pointers on cooking?"

He raised his bushy eyebrows. "You think you need pointers?"

"Did you taste my stew?"

His lips twitched. "I could give you some tips. Mostly, I think you need to get a handle on your measurements. There's a big difference between a pinch and a fistful."

She was certain she had more to learn than that, but

was touched by his diplomacy. Oscar Pike was exceedingly polite, and a very hard worker. Josh was fortunate to have him. "Maybe in an hour or so? When you're finished with your bookkeeping?"

"Deal."

"I'd like to bake a cake for Barky Bob. Today's his birthday."

"I had no idea."

"I thought we could celebrate tonight at dinner. He's feeling pretty low seeing that his wife isn't around."

He shook his head in wonder. "You've been in town two days and you know more about these men then I do."

"It wasn't hard. I merely expressed a genuine interest. Maybe if you engaged the customers in personal conversation."

"Trust me. Men don't share their feelings with other men." His fleshy mouth drooped into a mystified frown. "Who knew Big Amos Rind was touchy about his size? Last time I tease him about it that's for sure."

It warmed her heart knowing that one of her ditties might have made a positive difference in someone's life. When she'd asked Big Amos what he wished for most, he'd whispered, "Friends." Apparently, his massive build and quiet nature kept most folks at bay. They thought he was mean, or stupid. He wasn't sure which. His admission had inspired her to give a musical lesson. She knew what it felt like to be misunderstood, an outsider.

A *freak*.

Only she didn't feel like a freak in Chance. Maybe that's because the residents were just like her, a little quirky. She very much looked forward to knowing them better.

"I realize my stew left a little to be desired, but do you think if we offer another free meal, the men will come back tonight?"

"Free?" He glanced at the numbers in the ledger, winced.

"Think of it as a party. A birthday party."

He grinned. "They'd come back regardless. They like your ditties. They like you."

She swallowed an emotional lump, still flattered and amazed that the men had enthusiastically encouraged her songs. Knowing that something she'd created, something that came so naturally, could bring such joy filled her with indescribable satisfaction. She recalled the way she'd felt the first time she'd heard Julio the Juggler sing his rhymes. She'd thought him clever and funny, and imagined herself accompanying him on the piano. Or maybe creating a few whimsical rhymes of her own. But Papa had made it clear that he expected much, much more.

Just as he'd expected more out of Mama.

Only Mama didn't care about stardom.

And neither did Paris.

For the first time in her life she felt more Elizabeth Garrett's daughter than Daddy's little girl. Like Mama, she'd fallen in love. Like Mama, she preferred family over fame.

The morning after the hot springs, Josh had mentioned something about making babies and her insides had turned all warm and squishy. She'd always loved being part of a big family. She adored her nephew and niece, and had often dreamed about having a similar brood plus four.

She wondered how Josh would feel about having three sons and three daughters, and somehow knew he'd embrace each and every one. The only thing bigger than his infuriating bossy streak was his heart. She also knew that, unlike her own father, he would never favor one child over another. It suddenly occurred to her how much attention Papa had given her in comparison to his sons. Sadly, it was probably because they'd shown no interest in the performing arts. How difficult it must have been for Mama to witness such blatant favoritism.

But regardless of her sudden empathy with the woman, she couldn't entirely shake her adoration of the man who had lit up her life like a Christmas tree. A sharp pang of guilt stabbed at her stomach as she imagined Papa looking down on her from the heavens, somber eyes glittering with disappointment.

Oscar tapped his pencil on the table and cleared his

throat. "Are you all right? You look a little pale."

She rose from the table, music roaring in her ears. "I just realized," she said, drifting toward the piano and a brand new life. "I'm going to have to break a promise."

❋ ❋ ❋

"You do anything around here aside from spouting flowery introductions and consorting with Miss Adams?" Josh studied his slicked-up, sweet-smelling cousin with blatant disgust. He and Seth had stopped by the Lucky Lady five hours ago hoping to interrogate the man only to learn from a loose-lipped fiddle player that Mr. Burke and Miss Adams rarely stirred before noon.

It was one forty five.

Niles took a seat across from the two lawmen, stretched out his long legs and crossed them at the ankle. Dressed in a brown striped satin sack coat, paisley waistcoat, and loose-fitting trousers, he looked polished and pompous, traits apparently appreciated by the saucy Miss Adams. "Seeing that you're a newlywed, I'm surprised you're not lingering in the sheets yourself." He cocked an eyebrow at Josh, a taunting sneer playing at his lips. "Trouble in paradise?"

The muscle in Josh's left cheek twitched, other than that he managed to keep himself in check. He and Seth had discussed the possibility that Niles might go so far as to use Paris against him in whatever game he was playing. In order to protect her, he needed to downplay his feelings. According to Seth, it was plain to everyone but the daft that Josh was head over heels. Looking back, he realized he'd fallen in love with Paris the first night they'd met, the moment she'd socked him in the jaw. He'd spent a week and a half in denial. He figured he would've resisted the notion even longer if they hadn't made love.

She'd overwhelmed him last night. Her courage. Her passion. She'd bared her soul and in return he'd silently pledged his heart. Something he'd sworn he would never do.

Well, hell. It's not as if his life was going as expected anyway. He had Mason to thank for that. If he were here he'd apologize for cursing that stipulation and grab up the man in a damned hug.

He'd woken up at the crack of dawn, taken one look at his pain-in-the-neck wife sleeping peacefully in his arms, and had known for sure and for certain he wanted this new life. Spending the entire day in bed, making love until they lapsed into exhaustion was almighty tempting, but he couldn't relax knowing she couldn't so much as visit the town's tented mercantile unprotected. Consumed with an urgent need to tame the likes of Burgess and Niles, he'd rolled out of bed and tracked down Seth. He wanted this mess done and over. He wanted to fill his home with love, laughter, and children. Passionate, creative, pain-in-the-backside children.

Unfortunately, Burgess remained elusive and Niles had been "indisposed." Needing to do something constructive, he'd snagged a hammer and taken his frustration out on a pile of lumber, the only result a newly erected jailhouse.

Wound tighter than a coiled rattler he leaned forward, one forearm on the table, the other on his thigh, his hand a breath away from his Colt. "Seeing that there's no love lost between us, why don't we get to the heart of the matter?"

Niles smoothed his hands over his lapels. "Sounds intriguing."

"What are you doing here?"

"Running you out of business," the man answered bluntly. "If your wife keeps serving up meals like last night, it won't take long." He poked his tongue in the side of his cheek. "That why you're up and at it so early, Josh. She as lousy in the bedroom as she is in the kitchen?"

Seth slammed a hand to Josh's shoulder, rooting him to his chair. "Since we're putting our cards on the table, Burke. I'm here to tell you that I've got call to believe you instigated the fire that demolished the original Lucky Lady."

Niles laughed. "You think I burned down Tucker's dance hall just so I could talk him into setting up business with me in Chance?"

Seth flashed a mirthless smile. "Pretty much."

"As determined as I am to ruin my dear cousin," Niles drawled, sliding Josh a loathsome glare, "even I wouldn't go so far as setting an occupied building on fire."

Josh glared back, his blood boiling with contempt. If it weren't for Seth he would have already broken the bastard's nose. "Maybe you hired someone."

"Like Burgess Riley." Never one to mince words, Seth laid it on the line. "Last year Josh locked him up for a spell after setting fire to the livery in Yuma. Word has it he's been seen here in Chance. In fact, some say he's the one who shot Cobb Sprite."

"Which is why you were so quick to cover for him," Josh said. "Wouldn't do you much good if your henchman landed in the hoosegow, would it?"

"I'm afraid I haven't a clue as to whom you gentlemen are referring. As far as Arnold Tucker goes, I was simply in the right place at the right time. He was strapped for cash and a venue. I had cash, thanks to dear old Dad, but was strapped for entertainment and expertise. There you have it." He yawned. "Don't you two have better things to do with your time other than badger an innocent man?"

Thinking back on all the despicable things Niles had done as a youth, Josh sneered. "There's not an innocent bone in your body."

"Funny," his cousin replied, idly twisting the gold pinkie ring. "Mason said that very same thing the last time we spoke."

Josh clenched his fist as he watched Niles toy with that damned ring. "Which was?"

The man shrugged. "I'm sure he told you all about it. The way he tracked me down after I ran away from home? Wouldn't call it a happy reunion, though tears were involved. I might've come home, if he'd uttered a kind word," Niles said, bitterness lacing his tone. "Seems he reserved all of his praise and affection for you. Your only downfall, he once told me, was that you'd vowed never to fall in love. Never to marry. He said he couldn't let that happen as it would sorely disappoint your ma and pa."

Josh's gut twisted as the gleam in Niles's eyes grew feral.

"Mason always was a man of his word." He pushed out of his chair and slithered toward the bar. "To think I would have had it all if you hadn't convinced that little gal to marry you within the allotted time frame." He tossed back a shot of brandy and conjured a slow, evil smile. "You did tell her about the will, didn't you? I'd hate to think Red might slip and say something out of turn. Did I mention she went to speak to Paris about writing her a song?"

"Strangers passing in the night, by chance their lips did meet. Though they shared a moment's fire, the kiss was incomplete.

"Fate conspired to lend a hand, desire became their curse. Both would fight against the fall, whose heart would be lost first?

"Destiny does as destiny deems. No forsaking. No in between. Forever in love. Forever you'll be. For destiny does as destiny deems."

Hunched over the piano, Paris let her anthem to Josh, now fully comprised of verse, chorus, and bridge, flow from heart to mind to fingers. *Destiny.* To think he had inspired such fierce musings. *We were meant to be, Paris.* She clung to the hope that he did indeed love her, and was simply too stubborn to admit it. Maybe in time . . . She trembled with emotion as she launched into the second verse, her voice reverberating throughout the deserted opera house.

"Lovers sleeping in the night their hearts and hands entwined. One has given up the fight, lost body, soul, and mind.

"One holds on to fear and doubt, won't say the words aloud. Both afraid of what could be forever and for now."

"Destiny does as destiny deems. No forsaking. No in between. Forever in love. Forever you'll be. For destiny does as destiny deems."

The music swelled.

"Lose your heart, you may risk your dream. But are dreams always what they seem?"

The last chord hung in the air as her fingers stilled, her mind working double time analyzing the meaning of that four-bar bridge. Josh's subtle probing and insinuations about passion and dreams wormed into her thoughts. She thunked the heel of her hand to her forehead as realization struck with the force of a head on train. No wonder her brothers had pitched a fit when she'd tried to explain about her childhood promise. The words they had shouted, the ones she'd so effectively blocked out, now rang loud and clear.

William Garrett didn't want fame and fortune for his wife *or* his daughter. He wanted it for himself. That's why he'd spent so much time at the theater, and according to London, so much time with the featured starlets. She cringed, realizing she had been so enamored with the charismatic man that she'd been blind to his true nature. She'd also been insensitive to her mama and brothers' feelings.

"Niles was right. You do have a beautiful voice."

Startled, Paris bolted to her feet. The stool tipped over, landing with a teeth-jarring thud. She inwardly cursed her clumsiness, praying for the earth to open up and swallow her whole as she locked gazes with the "Darling of Denver". Of all people!

Hazel eyes twinkling, Red Adams reached down

and righted the piano stool. "Forgive the intrusion. I came over to discuss a business proposition and was so intrigued by your music that I purposely failed to announce my presence sooner." Calm as you please, she cocked a hip against the Weber Upright and folded her arms under her well-endowed bosom. If she so much as coughed, surely the fleshy orbs would spill over the gown's plunging neckline. "That ballad's a real heart-string-tugger. Never heard it before. Did you write it?"

Paris's cheeks blazed. Tongue-tied, she managed a nod.

"Heard you were a talented songwriter."

"From who?" she squeaked.

"The thirty or so men you serenaded last night."

"Oh." She swallowed a giddy yelp. Someone, lots of someones, had bragged about her songwriting abilities! Pride surged through her veins.

The woman's painted ruby lips curved upward. "You're a dad-blamed triple threat."

"Excuse me?"

"Singer. Pianist. Songwriter." She gave Paris the once over. "I bet you're real pretty when you're gussied up." She clucked her tongue. "Shame to let all that talent go to waste."

Paris shifted her weight, uncomfortable with the accolades and the way Red was sizing her up. "I, well, I . . ."

"Arnold Tucker, the man who initially hired me to sing at the Lucky Lady, is due back tonight. He's bringing along an East Coast talent seeker." She winked. "Arnold's a peach of a man. Anyway, apparently this talent seeker's looking for new blood for a musical opera that's opening in New York City this coming spring."

"He'd be crazy not to hire you," Paris said, and she meant it. Beautiful, charismatic, and talented, Red Adams could outshine the brightest East Coast stars.

"That's sweet of you," she said with a tight smile. "Be that as it may, I really want to make an impression. I thought maybe you could write me a special song. Something humorous and catchy. They say you're good at that."

Her head reeled. "I don't know. I . . . "

"I'd be willing to pay."

"You would?"

"What's more you should come over tonight and sing a song yourself."

Paris took an unconscious step back. Was she nuts? Sing at the Lucky Lady? On that stage? In front of those wolf-whistling, gun-shooting rowdies?

"According to Arnold, this Mr. Maloy is scouting for a whole cast. Bet he could use a triple threat."

Paris dabbed her sleeve to her perspiring brow. "I couldn't possibly."

"Why so squeamish? Didn't anyone ever tell you to

reach for the stars?"

She massaged a heavy ache in her chest. "I just . . . I don't think I'm meant for the stage."

"I suppose your husband put that notion in your head." Red snorted. "Typical of a man. He got what he wanted . . . "

She thought about how Josh had made himself scarce after a night of lovemaking. How many times had she heard Athens lecture Rome about being more interested in the chase than the woman? She reined in her runaway thoughts, certain there had to be another reason for this morning's disappearing act. Still, her head pounded with dread. "What do you mean?"

Red pushed off of the piano, perched her hands on generous hips. "Don't tell me he wasn't up front with you?"

She forced the words past the lump in her throat. "Up front with me about what?"

Red pursed her painted lips, plucked a folded paper from her cleavage, and handed it to Paris. "And here Niles thought he was the last to know."

"Josh is an extremely honest man," she whispered, the paper burning a hole in her palm. *Except for tricking me into marriage.* Presently, she remembered how he'd passed up reputable accommodations to spend the night alone at the hot springs. She thought about the inappropriate way he'd touched her, and how quickly he'd proposed, no, *insisted* on marriage.

She'd refused. *"I have a dream to fulfill."*

"So do I," he'd replied, *"Maybe we can help each other out."*

Her hands trembled as she unfolded the paper and skimmed the official looking document. Tears filled her eyes as she zeroed in on the circled stipulation.

No wonder he'd never mentioned love.

Love had nothing to do with it.

Dizzy with a cyclone of emotions, she gripped the piano so as not to crumple.

Just then Josh pushed through the opera house door, Seth trailing behind, their expressions grim. Red faded into the background. Everything seemed to be fading from Paris's view, including her new life. She could scarcely breathe. Betrayed by her papa and husband in the very same hour.

She pushed off the upright, swiped away angry tears, and thrust out a palm as he neared. "Don't." If he touched her, if he pulled her into his arms, he'd scramble her thoughts further. If only she'd been thinking straight from the very beginning this wouldn't have happened. She'd known all along that he was dangerous to her future. Maybe Papa's dream wasn't her ideal, but neither was being shackled to a dishonest, manipulative sweet-talker. Unlike her mama, she refused to spend the rest of her life with a man who'd married for ulterior motives.

The ache in her chest nearly brought her to her knees. She realized then that she was still clutching that damned will to her heart. "I was right all along," she whispered, her throat constricted with misery. She thrust the crumpled document into his hands. She'd actually envisioned helping him oversee the Desert Moon, writing her ditties, and living happily-ever-after, inspired and in love. "Marriage does equal broken hearts and dreams."

She tried to walk away, from Josh and her shattered dream, but he nabbed her wrist. "It's not like you think, Paris."

Bitter disappointment rose in her throat like bile, her voice a strangled croak. "No? By your own admission you loved Mason like a father. It's obvious you despise your cousin. I'm thinking you'd do anything to honor your uncle's last wishes. Anything to keep his pride and joy out of Niles's possession. What if I hadn't happened along? Or what if I hadn't come down with that fever? I'm thinking you would have coerced or charmed some other woman into becoming your wife." His silence crushed the last of her composure. "It's exactly how I think." Heartbroken, she wrenched away and stalked for the back door.

"Where are you going?" he asked in a deadly quiet voice.

She didn't look back. "New York."

CHAPTER 18

"You're either an ass or completely inept with that woman."

Josh stood rooted to his spot, his heart hammering against his ribs. "Guilty on both counts."

Seth huffed a disgusted breath. "You realize that you botched it when you didn't counter her attack by telling her, *no, I would not have married another woman.*"

Josh stared down at his uncle's will. "I botched it long before that."

Grunting, his friend grabbed the wrinkled document out of his hand and focused on the circled stipulation. "You could have clued me in."

"Thought about it."

"Before or after you lost your mind? Dammit, Josh,

tell me that you didn't marry that girl solely to meet Mason's demands. Because if you did—"

"I didn't."

"Then why didn't you say so?"

"Because I wasn't sure."

"You just said—"

"I never gave it due thought. I set my sights on Paris and that was that. She asked me what I would have done if she hadn't happened along, and by God, I don't know." Seth looked like he wanted to strangle him and the way he felt he almost welcomed the try. "I don't know what I would have done if we'd never met. I can't imagine life without her."

"Why didn't you say something like that when she was in the room?" Seth threw up his hands. "Does she have any idea how you feel? Women like to hear the words. *The* words."

Josh swiped off his hat and palmed his brow. His head ached damn near as bad as his chest.

"I take that as a *no*." Seth folded his arms over his chest. "You missed a hell of an opportunity to fess up, my friend."

"She wouldn't have believed me. Not just now." He moved to the piano and fingered the document, the sole copy of Mason's will. "Someone swiped this out of the lawyer's office."

"Yeah. Niles. If nothing else maybe I can nail the

bastard for breaking and entering."

Josh shook his head. "He just came by this, otherwise he would have used the information against me sooner. Seeing he's been in town for at least the past four days . . ."

"Burgess."

"He could make it from here to Florence and back in twenty-four hours. That's why we couldn't find him yesterday. He wasn't in Chance."

"But why would Niles suspect the will contained anything other than he was told?"

"Who the hell knows how his mind works? All that's certain is that he and Burgess are both out to hurt me, and the best way to do that is through Paris."

Seth grimaced. "What do you think she meant by that New York crack?"

Josh didn't consider it a crack so much as a threat, and given her present state of mind he worried she'd follow through. "Not sure. But obviously, Red's involved."

"I'll be back shortly with the answer. When it comes to the fairer sex, *I'm* not inept." Seth tugged down the brim of his hat and headed for the front door. "In the meantime, if I were you I'd track down Paris and grovel. Works like a charm on most women."

Josh pocketed the will and forced his feet in the direction his wife had taken. Unfortunately, Seth's plan was flawed. His wife wasn't like *most women*.

* * *

Paris stood on the back veranda of the log house staring out at the wondrous landscape. Saguaros stood tall and green against the dark and mysterious Superstitions. Mesquite trees appeared almost graceful in contrast to the sharp ridges and vertical cliffs of the mountain's face.

A coyote howled. A vulture circled. A ground squirrel scurried nearby.

A man once said everything in the Superstitions bites, stings, pricks, or eats meat.

She guessed that included her husband. He'd proven as hurtful as one of those Gila Monsters he'd described, *damn him*. Tears clouded her vision, distorting the picturesque view. She didn't want to leave this place. She didn't want to leave *him*, and yet how in the world could she stay?

New York City. When he'd asked her where she was going, why hadn't she said *home*? Because home is where the heart is, she could hear Emily saying, and your heart is with Josh. Except he'd betrayed her. Utterly. He'd married her because of that stupid will! She could almost forgive him. People do crazy things trying to please a loved one. She should know.

If only he loved her.

Tears streamed unchecked as she massaged the

fierce ache in her chest. On second thought, maybe she'd be better off thousands of miles away. With an entire country between them, maybe he'd be easier to forget. Of course, it meant auditioning for Mr. Maloy, betraying Josh, and performing on his competitor's stage.

As if she wasn't miserable enough, guilt and stage fright swooped in for the kill. She leaned over the wooden railing and retched.

✳ ✳ ✳

He searched the town high and low.

Seth caught up to him, and after relaying the specifics of one Percival Maloy's talent search, suggested that Josh check back at the Desert Moon while he searched the perimeter for Burgess. "Ten to one she's sitting at that piano practicing her audition piece."

He found her in the opera house's kitchen stirring a bowl of batter. Clapping a hand to the back of his neck, he counted to ten and allowed his heart to settle back into place before speaking. "What are you doing?"

"Baking a cake."

He cast a wary glance at the bowl of eggs. "I can see that."

"Then why did you ask?"

Her voice was eerily calm, her posture relaxed, her gestures controlled. The hairs on the back of his neck prickled. Oscar stood to her right, glaring. Apparently she'd found a confidant. Josh angled his head toward the door. "Do you mind?"

Oscar scowled. "You bet I do."

Suppressing the urge to physically toss the man from the room, he turned his attention to Paris. "We need to talk."

"You don't have to explain." She poured the batter into a circular pan, refusing to make eye contact. "I understand."

"That so?"

"Oscar told me how Mason practically raised you. How you idolized him, so much so that you followed in his footsteps and became a lawman. He said Mason had a heart as big as Mexico." She slid the pan into the stove and wiped her hands on the seat of her trousers. "Going to great lengths to please a man you worship is a subject with which I am well acquainted."

His gut twisted as he latched hold of what was left of his tortilla-thin patience. "I know all about that East Coast talent seeker, Paris." Never mind that damned will. He hadn't lost his sense of self by marrying her. He'd gained a whole new perspective on life. Near as he could tell she still viewed the world through the impressionable eyes of an eight-year-old. "Is this really what you want? Aren't you tired of trying to live up to your daddy's expectations? For the love of God, grow up!"

"Don't yell at her," Oscar snapped.

"I'm not yelling!" But the rattling china cup on the table said different.

Paris turned slowly, hands on hips, her expression placid as a nun's. "Since you hired me as your cook, I feel obligated to serve dinner to whatever miners show up this evening. I also intend to celebrate Barky Bob's birthday. Naturally, what I do in my off hours is none of your concern. But since you'll find out anyway, afterward I'm going over to the Lucky Lady to audition for Mr. Maloy."

Her demure tone set his teeth on edge and he had to force himself to not rush forward and shake some passion into her. He wished to hell she'd rant or cry, wing an egg at him or, better yet, throw a punch.

Instead, she followed Oscar's lead and started clearing the table. "Consider this my official notice." She glanced at him then, her eyes sparking with defiance. "I quit."

❋ ❋ ❋

"Did you hear that applause?" Red flounced off the Lucky Lady stage into the cramped, dimly lit wing and gave Paris an affectionate rap on the shoulder. "The boys were right, honey, you're a damn good songwriter."

Paris forced a weak smile. "Thank you." She should

be doing cartwheels. Hearing Red sing one of her songs had been an unprecedented treat. The crowd's boisterous reaction to *Don't Kick Me When I'm Down* should've had her squealing with delight. Instead, she'd paced backstage willing herself not to throw up. She felt positively faint. It didn't help that Red had cinched her into a rib-crushing corset and too-tight costume. She glanced down at the gaudy blue satin gown, at her exposed ankles and cleavage, and cringed. "I can't do this."

Fancy Pants stood stage left, bellowing a flowery introduction. Thankfully, she'd been spared his company thus far, though every now and then he'd glance into the wings to give her what he probably thought was a reassuring wink. Instead, the gesture gave her the willies.

Red tugged her aside as the acting troupe rushed past to make their entrance. The crowd immediately heckled their Shakespearean efforts. "Listen here, kid. You'd be a fool not to capitalize on this opportunity. Maloy is your ticket clear of these ignorant yahoos."

Except Paris didn't consider the men of Chance "ignorant yahoos." Despite her questionable cooking, more than forty men had shown up for dinner. Fifteen more than the previous night. They'd cleaned up and checked their guns at the door, no questions asked. She'd heard plenty of "please" and "thank yous," and a healthy dose of pleasant conversation. And if she wasn't mistaken, as much as she'd tried to hide it, a good many had been sensitive to her solemn mood. Their enthusiastic response to her ditties had been a tad overzealous. But they'd seemed intent to cheer her up, especially Barky Bob who'd choked up when she'd presented him with his birthday cake. No, indeed, she couldn't think of one ignorant yahoo in all of Chance.

Except maybe for Josh.

That dip-doodled Romeo had disappointed her at every turn. She'd given him more than one opportunity to redeem himself today. *If only he'd professed his love.*

It had taken every ounce of her concentration to affect a casual persona. She'd turned herself inside out, disconnected with her emotions in order to present the image of a mature, worldly woman. When she thought about the restraint she'd exhibited when he'd walked into the opera house kitchen, the mind marveled. She'd ached to launch herself at the heartbreaker, to pummel him with her fists and curse him to Hades and back, but she'd remained detached. Reasonable. Calm.

Red was wrong. She wasn't a triple threat. Her creative tendencies had launched her into an even higher hemisphere that included consummate actress.

If only he'd begged her not to go.

"I told the pianist you'd open with *Buffalo Gals*," the woman said. "Prime the audience with something familiar, get them on your side, then impress Mr. Maloy with that song, *Destiny*. Since you didn't bring the sheet music you'll have to sing accapella. The musicians have decent ears. Just tell them the key and maybe they'll noodle something behind you." Red snapped her fingers in front of Paris's face. "Are you with me, kid?"

Just now, she wasn't even sure if her heart was beating. The crowd's heckling had digressed into deafening boos. She peered around Red just in time to see a royally-attired actor duck an empty bottle. "I can't sing *Destiny*. It's . . . personal."

"Exactly why it'll bring down the house."

Paris pressed her palm to her clammy brow. Would it bring down Josh too? She'd been too hurt and proud to tell him what was in her heart. Too angry to listen to his side of the story. What if he wrestled with his own personal demons? Could she soothe the beast within with song?

She knew without looking that he was out there amongst the rowdies. He was, by nature, a protector, and even though they were at odds, he wouldn't leave her to the wolves. Though he'd kept his distance throughout dinner, he'd hovered behind the Desert Moon's bar keeping an eye on the clientele, looking mad enough to eat the Devil with his horns on. His anger baffled her. *He'd* betrayed *her*.

"*It's not like you think, Paris.*"

What was she missing?

"You're almost on."

"What?"

Red gestured toward the stage. "They cut to the final act. *The Twelfth Night* in twelve-minutes." She snickered. "That has to be a record."

Panic ravaged her stomach. "I'm going to be sick."

"Nonsense. You've just got a case of nerves." Red hiked her gown to her thigh, revealing a small silver flask held in place by a lacy black garter. She slapped the flask in Paris's hand. "Drink this."

"What is it?"

"Courage."

* * *

"I hope these roughnecks like Paris better than those poor actors," Seth shouted over the jeers of the disgruntled audience. "I can't believe you're going to allow her to set foot on that stage. Just because Tucker swore Maloy's legit—"

"I'm not going to stand in her way." Josh's heart shriveled with each passing minute. He'd been so sure she had no real interest in being a musical star. So sure she'd spoken in anger, and that if allowed the space and time to cool off, she'd hear him out and back down from this audition. Yet she'd remained aloof throughout the day and night. No tears. No reservations. Either he couldn't compete with the footlights of a New York stage or she wanted to get as far away from him as possible. Both options cut to the bone. "If this is what she wants—"

"You really *are* an ass." Seth started to elaborate, but someone chucked a bottle at Orsinio's head, causing Viola to shriek and skip to a line in Act V. A boot sailed through the air and clocked Curio in the stomach.

Cursing, Josh and Seth pushed through the crowd and grabbed the offenders by the scruffs of their neck. They'd busted up two fights and tossed six drunks out on their ears in the last fifteen minutes alone. Half the county had turned out for Percival Maloy's talent search, a small faction as sociable as an ulcerated back tooth.

Josh was almost to the door when he heard Niles's announcement. "Welcome to the stage a diamond in the rough, a star on the rise . . . " He paused for dramatic effect as the band segued into *Buffalo Gals*.

Josh heaved the troublemaker outside and slowly turned.

Niles nailed him with a gloating smile then swept his arm wide. "Let's hear it for Paris!"

Shock rooted him to his spot as his wife sashayed on stage. Only she wasn't sashaying so much as weaving. What the hell? When she reached center stage and faced front, his stomach dropped to the puncheon floor. Someone, presumably Red, had twisted her hair into a loose top knot, painted her sweet face and trussed her up in a revealing costume. His mouth went dry as his gaze slid from her cherry-red lips to the milky white breasts that nearly spilled over her plunging neckline. Then he made the mistake of glancing down at her legs. Fishnet stockings? What exactly was she auditioning *for*?

Hoots and whistles quickly gave way to heckles.

"This ain't a funeral, honey, look alive!"

"Show us some knee."

"Don't just stand there, lady. Sing!"

The band was on their second time through *Buffalo Gals*, and Paris had yet to open her mouth. Looking glassy-eyed and none too steady on her feet, she cast a tremulous smile at Big Amos Rind who sat in the front row. Josh looked stage right and saw Niles sipping from a flask. He toasted Josh and laughed.

Ah, hell.

Josh caught Seth's eye, and they both started pushing their way toward the stage from opposite ends. Unfortunately, their progress was slowed by a mob of agitated drunks.

"Get the hook," someone shouted.

"Freak!"

She flinched at that, dammit. Josh wished he were close enough to wring the neck of the insensitive critic. Instead, he willed Paris to look at him, and when she did the fear and insecurity burning in her eyes branded his heart. Drunk or sober, she was scared to death. "Di-tty! Di-tty!" he chanted, nudging Oscar, "Di-tty! Di-tty!"

who whistled at Big Amos, "Di-tty! Di-tty!" who banged his fist on the table. At least forty others followed suit causing the perplexed musicians to fall silent.

All eyes were on her, but she only had eyes for Josh. He experienced an almighty, knee-buckling rush of joy when her sweet voice rang out, the message crystal clear.

"Destiny does as destiny deems. No forsaking. No in between. Forever in love. Forever we'll be. For destiny does as destiny deems."

For a moment no one spoke. No one moved. Then someone yelled, "That's it? I want my money's worth!"

"Me too!" another man shouted. "Kick up your heels, sister!"

No danger of that, Josh thought as he pushed forward, since her feet seemed glued to the stage. At least she was smiling.

Oscar banged his fist on a table. "Leave her alone!"

"Gladly! Get off the stage, lady!"

Barky Bob stood on a chair. "Creativity is an art, you no-account skunks!"

"Art stinks, and so does she!"

Big Amos Rind stood up and cold-cocked the loudmouth.

All hell broke loose.

Seth flattened a half-dozen men before someone smashed a bottle over his head and *really* ticked him off.

Josh ducked a roundhouse, punched one drunk,

and threw another over his shoulder. He looked up just in time to see Burgess Riley pushing through the green velvet backdrop. A sea of flying fists and chairs stood in between Josh and the stage. He jumped up and launched himself from table to table, fury giving him wings as Burgess made a grab for Paris.

She threw a punch and missed. With a roar, the hooligan snatched her up and over his shoulder.

Josh's foot touched down on the stage just as three Herculean men stormed in from the wings, black dusters billowing at their ankles, hardware holstered for a quick draw. Stetsons pulled low, he couldn't make out the shadowed upper-half of their faces, but he could feel the heat of their rage from eight feet away. The clean-shaven, fair-haired man kicked out, simultaneously slamming his heel into Burgess's knee while plucking up Paris. The one sporting a moustache and a dark brown ponytail buffaloed the troublemaker from behind.

The third—a broad-shouldered, square-jawed giant boasting a week's growth of dark whiskers—spied Josh's badge and frowned. "Get her out of here," he told the other two.

Josh stalked past the stern-faced man intent on getting to Paris.

"Sheriff Grant?"

"Who wants to know?"

A hand clamped down on his shoulder and whirled

him around. "Your brother-in-law."

The force of the man's blow sent Josh flying.

* * *

"I know you're upset."

"You mean furious." Rome hefted Paris higher in his arms and fought his way through the wide-eyed acting troupe, his eye on the backstage door.

"Hey, you look like . . . "

"They're shorter than I thought."

"Can I have your autograph?"

"That dime novel business is getting out of hand," Boston complained.

Paris choked on emotion, unsure whether to laugh or cry. Her life was as chaotic as the cast's capsulated rendition of Twelfth Night. Desperate for a happy ending, she skipped back to Act I. "I can explain, Rome. You see there was this advertisement—"

"We know about the advertisement."

"We also know about the will," Boston said.

"But how—"

"It's what we do," Rome snapped.

What a fool she'd been to think that she could hornswaggle two of Wells Fargo's best. She wasn't surprised that they'd tracked her, only that they'd tracked her so fast and learned so much. Mercy, they were mad! Strike that. *Furious.* "Where's Athens?" If she ever needed her even-keeled, diplomatic middle brother, it was now.

"Home with the kids." Boston shook his head. "Lost another nanny."

"That's the third one in seven months!"

"Six months," Rome grumbled.

Sensing their mounting agitation, she spit out another concern before they started lecturing. "How's Emily?"

"Ticked we wouldn't bring her along. I wanted to shake the stuffing out of her when she confessed her part in this." Rome gave her a squeeze. "Do you have any idea of the hell you put us through?"

Poor Emily! Just when she thought things couldn't get worse, London and Josh crashed into the wings, obliterating the prop table. She kicked her legs and socked Rome in the shoulder. "Put me down!"

"No."

"But London will kill him!"

"Good."

She struggled to gain her freedom, but the highly trained agent merely tightened his hold and whisked her outside. Usually she was better at tangling with her brothers—as kids they'd wrestled like raccoons—but apparently the mind-numbing bout of stage fright had compromised her reflexes. She'd even missed that big-as-a-barn target, Burgess Riley. Her brothers, on the other hand, never missed. Worried that Josh had met his match, she cast a pleading glance over Rome's shoulder.

"Don't look at me, squirt." Boston kicked shut the back door, muffling the sounds of the raging brawl. "If London doesn't beat the hell out of the Sheriff, I will."

On cue, the two men crashed through the door, knocking it from its hinges, plowing into the younger Wells Fargo agent.

Paris squinted in the moonlight, wincing as the three men rolled in the dirt, pummeling each other in a heated mismatch.

Boston rammed a fist into Josh's gut. "That's for compromising my sister."

Josh grabbed his leg and flipped him over, planting a knee in his chest. "She wouldn't be here at all if you'd been more sensitive to feelings, you bastard."

"We had her best interest at heart," Boston wheezed. "More than I can say for you, you sonuvabitch."

Paris cringed when London gripped Josh's shoulder and yanked him to his feet. Maybe if they knew it was legal . . . "We're married!"

"We know!" they all shouted.

Rome glanced from her bared cleavage to her fishnets, and cursed. "What kind of man allows his wife to dress like a trollop?"

She blushed and tugged up the neckline. "The gown was Red's idea."

"I don't give a damn whose idea it was." He dropped

her to her feet and whipped off his duster. "Put this on."

Josh let out a loud grunt.

She slapped away Rome's coat and tried to dodge his hulking frame. "Two against one isn't fair!"

"Stay out of this," Josh yelled, clipping London's chin with a fierce upper cut.

London retaliated, but Josh ducked, causing him to catch Boston with a roundhouse. The youngest Garrett brother landed in a water trough with a splash and a blasphemous oath.

Forcing her arms into the sleeves of his duster, Rome ordered her to stay put then turned to join the fight.

Josh was dead for sure.

Panicking, she lunged forward, snagged one of Rome's guns and fired.

Her golden-haired brother gawked down at the nicked toe of his boot. "What the hell, Paris? You almost shot me in the foot!"

Shocked by her own behavior, she staggered back, jerking the .45 out of his reach when he made a grab. "I was aiming for the cactus."

"Are you blind?"

"Booze blind, maybe," Josh wheezed.

Paris looked at her husband who stood hunched over, his hands braced on his knees. Rumpled and bloodied, he looked only slightly worse than her brothers. London dabbed his sleeve to his cut, swollen lip, while

Boston climbed out of the trough, shaking off like a wet hound. They all glared in her direction. Although she wasn't fond of the sudden attention, she was thrilled that she'd waylaid the beating. "I'm as sober as a monk," she assured them. She'd taken one sip out of Red's flask, gagged, and reconsidered. She didn't want false courage. She figured that if she were meant to be a musical actress, if she possessed one iota of honest desire, surely she'd overcome her nerves. She'd reached for the stars only to be paralyzed with stage fright.

Salvation had come by way of an encouraging request.

Mason wasn't the only one with a heart as big as Mexico. Her brown-eyed savior had looked into her soul, urging her to do what came naturally.

What came naturally was loving Joshua Grant. She didn't plan on doing it from hundreds of miles away. Even six feet was too far. Shoving past Rome and London, she closed the distance and placed her palm over his pounding heart. "I don't want to go to New York City."

"That's good," London said, coming up behind her. "Because you're going home with us."

Josh tucked her tousled hair behind her ears. "Over my dead body."

"Easily arranged," Rome said, nudging them apart.

Boston cracked his knuckles.

An acrid smell blew in on the night breeze, diverting their attention to the opposite end of town. Josh ducked his head in the Lucky Lady and shouted for help. Paris pocketed the gun and raced toward the sickening glow.

She nearly choked on the stench of dreams going up in smoke.

CHAPTER 19

Josh's blood boiled as he sprinted toward the burning veranda, three-quarters of the surrounding population on his heels. Since Burgess was incapacitated, Niles had to be at fault. He hadn't seen the bastard since the outbreak of the bar fight. Pushing his despicable cousin out of his mind, he ordered Paris to stop throwing sand on the fire and to make way for the men.

The same rowdies who'd been busting up the Lucky Lady formed a bucket brigade in a united effort to save the Desert Moon.

Oscar, Barky Bob, Tom, and Big Amos Rind shouted at the men to move faster. London Garrett assumed control, issuing directives and achieving miraculous results in record time. Rome and Boston worked alongside

Josh and Seth and no matter how many times they all ordered Paris away from the flames, she continued to show up with buckets of water.

"If you don't stay back by the rain barrel, squirt, so help me . . . " Boston shook his fist under her nose.

She slapped it away and trotted to the back of the line, tripping twice on the overly long hem of Rome's duster.

"I swear she's more sassy than ever." Rome cast an accusatory glance at Josh.

"Passionate," Josh corrected. He wouldn't want her any other way. Though he was relieved she had no interest in New York City, he would have helped her pack her bags if becoming a star was her heart's desire. Then he would have packed his own bags and bought a ticket east. He'd start from the beginning and court her proper like if that's what it took to prove his love. He finally understood the extent of his pa's despair when his own wife had left this earth. True love was all consuming, a fire that burned brighter, hotter with each passing day. How cold the world must have seemed when her light had been doused. How dark and unbearable.

He shook off the morbid notion, tossed an empty bucket to Seth, and snagged a spare ax. Hacking at the burning wood, he imagined Niles lurking in the shadows, getting his kicks by watching him destroy Mason's dream with his own two hands. The hairs on the back of his neck stood on end as he thought about another unscrupulous bastard. "Where's Burgess?"

"The jailhouse. Not that he's going anywhere." Seth cocked a thumb at Rome. "Golden boy busted his leg."

"He had his hands on my sister." Rome slammed the back of his hand into Josh's shoulder. "Speaking of which—"

"Burgess's suffering gave me some leverage," Seth interrupted. "Medical attention in return for a confession."

"What did you learn?" Josh asked, ignoring the aggressive Garrett.

"He admitted to stealing your saddle, and harassing Paris. Personal gripe. Admitted to shooting Cobb Sprite. Lost his temper. Took a bit, but he finally admitted to stealing that will for your cousin. As I suspected, the fires were set by Niles."

"Speaking of that will, or more to the point that stipulation . . . " Rome swung his own ax into a burning slat of wood then yanked it clear of the veranda. "You tricked my sister into marriage for your own selfish gain. Give me one good reason why I shouldn't kill you, Grant."

"I'd have to hang you," Seth cut in, waving away the thickening smoke.

"I'd like to see you try," Boston said, coughing as he breathed in a lung full of ash.

"Focus!" London bellowed over the heads of several

other men.

Josh focused on Paris who'd approached the opposite end of the veranda. Toting two heavy buckets, she lost her balance and teetered too close to the flames. The hem of her brother's coat caught fire. "God*dammit*." He bolted across the grounds, stomped out the flames, hauled her up and carted her across the street. "So help me, if I have to tie you to this hitching post, I will!"

She punched him in the chest, jolting his pulse back to life. "I'm trying to help, you obstinate baboon!"

"Fine." He nabbed an abandoned piece of twine and roped her wrists to the rail. "You can help by staying out of trouble."

He was halfway back to the Moon when she screamed, "Wait'll I get my hands on you, Joshua Grant!"

"Looking forward to it!" He grinned. No matter what happened to the Desert Moon, he'd still have his pain-in-the-neck wife. Mason, and fate, had made him a wealthy man.

Rome glanced over at Paris, who wiggled while biting at the twine. "You hitched my sister to a rail," he noted in a gruff tone.

"You got a problem with that?"

"Actually . . . no." He tossed Josh an ax, and together they attacked the ebbing fire. "You don't give a tinker's damn about being a theater owner, do you? You're trying to salvage this place for her."

"I'd snuff out the sun if I thought it would make her happy."

Boston groaned.

Rome sighed. "I hate it when I misjudge a man. Means I'm slipping."

Fifteen sweltering backbreaking minutes later the fire was doused, the wraparound veranda and the stained-glass pane were history, the front wall charred, but still intact. Josh thanked the exhausted men and invited them back in a couple of days—drinks on the house.

Oscar entered the Desert Moon via the back door to inspect the smoke damage. Seth left to check on Burgess.

By the time Josh and the Garretts crossed to the hitching post, Paris was gone.

London swiped a sleeve across his sweating face, streaking dirt across his singed cheeks. "Who taught you how to tie a knot, Grant?"

Josh fingered the twine, a sick feeling in his gut. "She didn't wiggle free."

"Someone cut her loose," Rome said, inspecting the fray.

"So why didn't she rejoin the brigade?" Boston rasped, his voice hoarse from the smoke.

Josh jerked the Colt from his holster, checked the chamber.

Noting his sense of urgency, the brothers nodded at

each other then readied their own hardware. They had their reservations about his role as a brother-in-law, but they obviously respected his instincts as a lawman. It was a start.

Rome produced a half eagle coin, rolling it over his knuckles like a seasoned gambler.

Josh's stomach twitched. "What's that?"

"My lucky charm. Never travel without it." He slid the five-dollar goldpiece back into his pocket then adjusted his shoulder holster. "So, who are we tracking?"

Josh fought the urge to roar, gut instinct confirming his worst suspicion. "A murdering bastard."

✳ ✳ ✳

She was dying.

Her head throbbed mercilessly causing her stomach to roll with nausea. White light exploded behind her eyelids as someone yanked her into a sitting position.

"Rise and shine, little girl."

Paris swallowed the bitter bile rising in her parched throat and opened her eyes with painstaking effort. Sunlight filtered in through crude windows and decrepit, slatted walls. Dust particles danced on the blinding rays. She must have been unconscious for hours. She laid her palm to the side of her head and winced. No wonder. Her temple pulsed with a bump the size of an egg. Bleary-eyed, she scowled at the man stooping in front of her. "You hit me."

Niles Burke smoothed a hand down the lapels of his striped jacket. "Would you have come willingly? No? Well, there you have it."

She remembered him cutting her loose. She'd even thanked him. Then she'd darted for the bucket brigade only to be snatched into the shadows. After that, she was clueless. Even now she found it hard to focus. "Where's Josh?"

"He should be here any minute. Tracking will be easier now that it's daylight."

"I don't understand. Where are we?"

"Near the hat-shaped peak dubbed *Sombrero*. The Peralta's lost mine is around here somewhere so those pack mules can't be too far off."

Oscar had told her about Miguel Peralta's legendary gold mine. Convinced the Mexican miners were desecrating their Thunder God's home, the Apaches had annihilated the interlopers in 1848. Pack mules loaded with extracted gold had wandered deep into mountains where they'd later died. According to Oscar, Mason had happened upon a few of the skeletal remains. Or so he thought. Peralta gold or not, he'd stumbled upon a fortune. Some of which he'd left to Josh.

Flooded with dread, Paris folded her arms over her queasy stomach. "I don't know anything about the location of the mine or those other mules."

Niles shrugged. "Maybe not, but Josh does."

"What makes you think that?"

"Just before he died, Mason told me he'd willed me a substantial amount of money. He'd left the bulk of the fortune to a *deserving* soul."

Spooked by the fiendish glint in his eyes, she scooted away until her back hit the wall. "You had something to do with Mason's death."

He rose and spread his hands wide in casual disdain. "If he'd simply given up the location of his find, I would have ridden off ahead of him, and he would have continued on to the Desert Moon. Instead, he lectured me on my loose morals and extravagant lifestyle. *Why can't you be more like Josh?* Do you know how many times I heard that in my life?" His pretty-boy features distorted in anger. "I lost my temper, broke his neck. It just . . . happened."

She sucked in a horrified breath. "You murdered your own father?"

"If he *was* my father. My mother, a one-time dove, was pregnant when they married. There was a one in five chance that he was the father. Enough for an honorable man like Mason Burke. Seeing that I didn't inherit that trait . . . " He clucked his tongue. "I'm thinking he was wrong."

"But he claimed you." She blinked up at the man,

sickened by his cynicism. "After the killing, directly after, you must have felt some sort of remorse."

"Afterward, I rifled his pockets hoping to find a map. All I found was a lone gold nugget. I tossed him back in his wagon and spooked the team, knowing the buckboard would eventually flip. I'd just lost my shirt in a poker tournament. I needed a windfall then. Not later." He polished his pinkie ring on his shirtsleeve. "Ironically, I couldn't part with the nugget."

No wonder Josh despised this man. He was wicked. Furious and exasperated, her swollen temples throbbed. Fisting her hands in her lap, she glared up at the demon, while saying a silent prayer for poor Mason Burke.

Hands on hips, Niles towered over her, eyeing her exposed cleavage. His lips curved into a lecherous grin.

Disgusted, she buttoned Rome's duster to her chin. He laughed then, a hollow cackle that stoked her anxiety. She didn't understand this man. Did he truly think Josh knew where those other pack mules were? Did he think to use her as a bargaining tool? He was to be severely disappointed. She knew from Oscar that Mason's "deserving soul" was a person to be decided by fate. "What if you're wrong? What if Josh can't lead you to those other mules?"

"Then I'll shoot him. Actually, I'll do that regardless. Initially, I thought it would be enough to ruin him. Run him out of business. Sabotage his marriage. If only

you'd proven more interested in fame than in my cousin."
He snorted in contempt. "*Destiny*. I nearly gagged when
you sang that sentimental drivel. I'll be damned if there'll
be a happy ending for Josh." He eased back his jacket,
brushed his fingers over the butt of the pistol wedged in
a fancy shoulder holster. "I know now that the only way
I can get on with my life is by taking his."

Tamping down her panic, she curled her fingernails
so tightly into her palms that she winced. "Seth will
hunt you down."

"Not likely since he'll think it was Burgess's doing."

"Burgess is locked up back in Chance."

He smiled and pointed to the far corner of the shack.
Propped against the wall, bound and unconscious, one
leg splinted, was Burgess Riley. Somehow Niles had
busted him out of jail.

She willed her pulse steady, assuring herself that his
plan was absurd and doomed to failure. Seth was not a
man easily fooled. Josh would be here any second.

And so would her brothers.

It occurred to her that Niles didn't know about her
brothers. Upon their arrival, he'd be sorely outnumbered. Still, what if he got off one good shot?

She remembered then that she wasn't entirely helpless. All she had to do was reach in her pocket, grab
Rome's gun and . . . Niles reached down and grabbed
her wrist. Incensed, she tried to jerk free. "What do

you want?"

He hauled her up into his arms and licked his lips. "Everything that belongs to Josh."

The door slammed open at the same time she jerked up her knee. Hard.

"Bitch!" Niles stumbled back, his face contorted in pain.

She fumbled for her hidden peacemaker as his hand darted for his holster. The sound of multiple guns cocking caused him to whirl around, one hand cradling his injured privates, the other wielding his pistol. Paris nearly fainted with relief at the sight of Josh hulking in the doorway, her brothers looming outside the open windows, guns drawn and aimed.

"Go on, Fancy Man," Rome taunted. "Take your shot. Nothing would make me happier."

"Who are you?" Niles raged.

Boston smiled. "Your worst nightmare."

"Wrong. That would be me."

Paris glanced at her husband, her breath catching at the fierce look on his ash-streaked face. If looks could kill, Niles would be cashing in his chips. "How long were you out there?" she croaked.

"Long enough to hear a confession." His gaze flicked to hers, eyes brimming with concern. "Are you all right, honey?"

She managed a nod.

With a crazed howl, Niles whirled around.

Someone shot the gun out of his hand.

Josh blew over the threshold and grabbed him by his throat. He slammed him against the wall, tightening his grip until the man's face turned blue. "I should break your neck. Tit for tat."

"I want him alive," Seth called from the threshold. London shoved past him.

"This is for manhandling my wife." Josh rammed his fist into his cousin's face. "And it's only the start."

Stone-faced, her oldest brother tried to drag her from the premises. Fearing Josh would make good on his threat, she broke away, rushed across the shack, and placed a calming hand on his shoulder. "Don't," she said softly.

Her husband's body quaked with rage and, as Niles continued to twitch and wheeze for air, she worried that her plea had fallen on deaf ears. He finally loosened his hold.

When he stepped away, Rome shot the gasping man in the knee. "That's for touching my sister." Niles crumpled to the ground with an agonized howl.

"Dammit, Garrett!" Seth bellowed.

"He's alive," Rome said, glaring through the window at the bleeding man. "You're lucky I didn't shoot you in the balls."

Niles grabbed his shattered knee and roared.

Burgess awakened, shifted, and let out a tortured groan.

Josh swept Paris up into his arms and whisked her outside, leaving Seth and her brothers to attend the outlaws.

She snuggled her face into his neck, breathing in the scent of smoke, sweat, and goodness. "I'm glad you didn't kill Niles," she said, hugging him tight. "Even though he deserves to die. I wouldn't want that on your conscience."

He kissed her forehead then set her on her feet, smoothing away her hair to examine her bump. "Trust me, honey. My conscience would not have suffered." He gently nabbed her chin, brushed his lips over hers and then deepened the kiss, rendering her boneless. Holding her steady, he eased back and locked gazes, his voice hoarse with emotion. "Let's get one thing straight. You're not going anywhere with your brothers. The opera house needs you. *I* need you. You didn't just lasso the moon, you lassoed my heart."

Her knees fairly buckled at his earnest admission and the worried look in his beautiful eyes. She pressed her hand over his heart, trying to soothe its erratic beating. "I figured out what you meant when you said it wasn't like I thought. You would have tricked me into marrying you regardless of that will," she said with a smile.

"I can't fathom why that makes you happy, squirt," Boston grunted as he breezed past them and into the shack.

Josh grinned down at her. "Because she knows it means I'm in love."

Seth strode by, dragging along Niles. "For chrissake, say the words, Josh."

He dropped his forehead to hers. "I love you, Paris."

His tender words wrapped around her heart, filling her with hope and joy. "Marriage equals two people trying their best to make each other happy." She looped her arms around his neck, tugging him closer, aching to become one. "How do you feel about three sons and three daughters?"

He tightened his arms around her waist, nuzzled her ear. "Delirious."

London stalked past with Burgess slung over his shoulder. "This isn't over, Grant."

"Damn right." He placed a hand over her belly and smiled down at Paris, his eyes sparkling with affection. "It's only the beginning."

Chapter One

"Declined."

"Excuse me?" Afia blinked at the quasi-Euro sales associate, a black-rimmed spectacled, chic-suited man who three minutes before had been all smiles and pleasantries.

"Your privileges have been revoked, Ms. St. John."

The woman standing behind her in line snickered. Afia blushed. Exclusive shops such as Bernard's treated their patrons like royalty. So why did she suddenly feel like the rabble? "There must be some mistake."

The associate retained a deadpan expression. "Perhaps you'd like to try another card."

Her business manger, Henry Glick (a financial wizard according to her mother), had asked her to make all of her purchases on one specific credit card until further notice. Something to do with interest rates and consolidation. So seven months ago she'd handed over the bulk of her cards to Mr. Glick, except for the American Express that she'd tucked away for emergencies. As her dignity was at stake just now, she considered this a genuine crisis. Fishing her Gucci wallet out of her matching handbag, Afia handed the sales associate her backup card. He slid her platinum plastic through the gizmo next to the cash register, starting the process all over again, leaving her to ponder the mystery of her "declined" Visa. Obviously, the card was defective. As soon as she got home she'd call Mr. Glick and have him order her a replacement.

The clerk glanced up, with one haughty eyebrow raised, and a trace of a smirk playing at his glossed lips.

Afia's stomach clenched. *Stop looking at me like that. I haven't done anything wrong.* Funny how many times she'd wanted to scream that sentiment in her cursed life. But as always she kept her feelings inside. Calm. Dignified.

The associate sidled over to the phone and placed a call.

Afia tucked silky strands of poker-straight hair behind her diamond-studded ears and willed her pulse steady. *I haven't done anything wrong.*

Casting her a sidelong glance, the associate mumbled a cryptic "uh-huh" and "I see," and then hung up. He returned and passed Afia her American Express. "Declined."

Bernard's four other patrons—plump-lipped, tight-skinned women who looked as though they frequented the same plastic surgeon—conversed in hushed tones. Afia hated being the center of gossip. Mortified, she leaned over the counter and crooked a finger at—she glanced at his nametag—"Douglas. There must be something wrong with your credit card device."

"Our Zon is functioning properly. I'm afraid it's your credit that's in question. Perhaps you'd like to write a check."

"I don't have my checkbook." Mr. Glick oversaw her bank account and paid her bills. She'd been relying on cash and her Visa for months. She'd yet to have a problem. Until now. "Please try again." Panic fluttered in her chest as she re-offered Douglas her Glick-approved Visa. Those strapless, wedge-heeled Chanels sat on the counter waiting to be bagged. The perfect mates to the silk shantung dress she'd

2

just purchased at Saks.

Two minutes later, Douglas re-shelved the wedge-heeled Chanels. On the verge of hyperventilating, Afia fled Bernard's. The shoe fiasco had dashed the last of her tremulous composure as she navigated the bustling city sidewalk. She'd survived two high profile weddings and three funerals in seven years. Not to mention the unflattering media surrounding her bizarre personal dramas. Being labeled "The Black Widow" by an unfeeling gossip columnist had been the cruelest blow. Anyone who knew her, knew the insinuation was absurd. Still, her second husband's sudden death had earned her a fair share of suspicious double takes. Her small circle of friends had dwindled to one. She'd managed to cope and found shopping a temporary cure-all for her ever-increasing bouts of depression. But surely, surely she hadn't shopped herself into the poorhouse. Each of her husbands had left her a fortune.

Her mind racing with one horrible possibility, she quickened her spike-heeled steps and avoided walking under a workman's ladder only to step on a crack in the pavement. Out of habit she clutched her left wrist and stroked the charm bracelet her dad had given her to counteract ill luck. That's when she felt it. The gap. She quickly fingered the charms, ticking them off in her mind—horseshoe, wishbone, four-leaf clover—stumbling twice in her haste to make it to the car. The third time she went down. Face down on the crowded sidewalks of Fifth Avenue.

Rudy came to her rescue. The muscle-bound chauffeur whisked her up and carried her to his double-parked limousine. "Animal," he said of a snickering passerby and then opened the door and helped her into the back seat. ✳

3